An Artist in Her Own Right

Ann Marti Friedman

Published by Accent Press Ltd 2018

Octavo House
West Bute Street
Cardiff
CF10 5LJ

www.accentpress.co.uk

ISBN 9781786157065
eISBN 9781786154118

Cover image based on a painting by Antoine-Jean Gros.

In loving memory

Mary Sebastian

Marilyn Stokstad

Chapter 1

Paris and Toulouse

July-September 1840

Paris July 1840

They are bringing back the body of Bonaparte, a name I had hoped not to hear again in this house. For months Paris has buzzed with news of nothing else, and I am sick of it. The former emperor will be exhumed from his ignominious grave in St Helena and brought "home" – albeit to Paris, not Corsica. A splendid catafalque has been ordered for the funeral cortège, a funeral mass commissioned from Hector Berlioz, fulsome speeches written, invitation lists drawn up.

The artists, too, want to play their part in this fanfare. Was not Bonaparte a generous patron of the arts? My late husband, Antoine-Jean Gros, spent twenty years depicting his accomplishments. Horace Vernet, who makes a virtual industry of scenes glorifying Bonaparte, calls a meeting. Though I have little patience with this nonsense, it is good to get out of the house. When I arrive at his studio, I have several minutes' pleasant conversation with Antoine's contemporaries, while one of Vernet's pupils hands round cups of tea. But when I tell him my name, Augustine

Dufresne, I see him struggle to place me. Though I, too, am an artist and exhibited paintings at three Salons, those art exhibitions at the Louvre that were the ultimate mark of prestige for an artist, these were probably before he was born. There is an awkward silence. Finally someone explains, "She is Baroness Gros."

I inwardly cringe, knowing what will come next.

"Oh, Baroness Gros!" breathes the young man reverently. "Your husband painted *Jaffa*!" His voice rises in his excitement, conversations stop, heads turn in our direction.

Again, I think, clicking down my teacup in disgust. I loathe being introduced like that, known only for my husband's famous picture of Bonaparte visiting the French soldiers' plague hospital at Jaffa during the Egyptian campaign. That painting brought Antoine so much joy in 1804 and so much grief in the years that followed. He was never able to escape from the shadow of its fame or its subject matter. Nor have I. It has followed us like – well – like the plague. I suddenly decide I must leave Paris, lest I be faced with still more of this. Where could I go to be well away?

My dissatisfied mood persists as I return home to the apartment in the rue des Saints Pères and walk through the rooms in the gathering dusk. I had been so delighted to decorate it in the modern fashion as a new bride in 1809, but now it seems more like a museum of Empire taste – so much mahogany, so many Egyptian heads, eagles, sylphs, and griffins. There is even a carpet strewn with N's and bees, made for Bonaparte while he was emperor but discarded by his successors. Once, too, these rooms had voices in them.

"Bonsoir, chèèèrrre Maman! Ça va?" *Antoine loved to draw out that word, rolling the r. I heard two kisses, as boisterous as his greeting, planted on her withered cheeks.*

"Bonsoir, mon fils. I hope you are hungry – I asked Cook to make boeuf bourguignon, your favorite."

"Merci, Maman – but you know such rich dishes don't agree with Augustine."

"That one has been painting all day. She should poke her nose out of her room and attend to the menus herself!"

I emerge from my studio. *"No need to shout, Maman Madeleine. I'm here now."*

"Bonsoir, Augustine." A quieter greeting for me, with more decorous kisses. "Maman says you've been keeping busy."

Keeping busy. In the Gros household I was not Augustine Dufresne, artist, practicing my art, but Madame Gros, wife, keeping busy.

No use fuming about the past. I shut the door on that memory.

I go to the bedroom and sit on the bed Antoine and I shared. Too restless to sleep, I begin to sort through my clothes to decide what to pack. There are only a few things besides the half-dozen mourning dresses made for me as a new widow five years ago. They are shabby now, but I have grown indifferent to clothes. For whom should I dress?

Then, in the back of the armoire, I notice a crumpled bit of pink and reach to bring it out into the light. It is the red fabric rose that Antoine bought for me during our wedding trip to Toulouse. A vendor had a basket of them on her arm, and on a whim he purchased it and gave it to me, telling me that it and I should never fade but stay as fresh and blooming as we were at that moment. He could be charming, my Antoine. No, I think sadly, this flower and I have faded together, and I have been too long soured by life.

Toulouse. Why did I not think of it before? I will go to Toulouse. I will walk again in its streets of brick buildings; enjoy again the majesty of Saint-Sernin; be cheered by the singsong cadence of the native speech; walk along the river and canal, breathe the air that is both invigorating and relaxing.

I sleep very little that night, reliving memories of the city, making practical plans for the trip, mentally packing my trunk. My determination grows stronger the more I think about it. I will flee from the forthcoming funeral. I will relive the happiness and hopeful beginning of our married life before the bitterness set in.

When my maid Marie-Louise (named after Bonaparte's second empress) brings my morning coffee, I tell her of my plans. She is dismayed. "Leave Paris? Travel now? When all Paris is preparing for the Emperor's return?"

I reply tartly, "Oh, but the Emperor is traveling now – he has inspired me!"

The more I think of it, the more the idea grows on me. How long has it been since I did something on impulse? That in itself has the pleasure of novelty. Why should I not please myself?

Two days later I tell my sister Ange-Pauline my plans. She objects, "Antoine would have wanted to be here."

"I'm not so sure of it. He would have wanted to pay his respects, but seeing the actual casket and the proof of his hero's death, he'd have had another nervous breakdown. The last one was bad enough."

My comment brought a shrill note into the conversation that felt out of place. Ange replied softly, "I think it would have broken his heart all over again." We were both silent for a moment. "Tine, haven't you forgiven him yet?"

I am startled. She is right. Disdain of Antoine has become an engrained habit. I think again of the rose from our honeymoon and feel a fresh stab of regret. It is time I left bad memories behind.

Toulouse, September 1840

I stir in an unfamiliar bed in a comfortable hotel. How delicious to not need to get ready for another day of riding in a coach! The church on the corner chimes seven. Rays of sunlight are already making their way across the building across the street, softening its worn red brick to pink, earning the city its nickname of "la ville rose." The sounds of the street waking up below have become familiar and comforting. I am glad I decided to come here.

6

I made the right choice, breaking out of the routine of Paris. Breathing the warm air, rejoicing in the beauty of the place and the memories of our honeymoon, I feel liberated.

For a week I simply wander where my fancy takes me. The buildings and the light are enchanting. Why did I not remember this? I purchase a sketchbook and pencils so that I can capture the effects. It is a pleasure to have new subject matter.

Toulouse, three weeks later

The month does not end as well as it began. For ten days it has rained steadily, and I have had to remain indoors and distract myself with reading novels and the latest papers from Paris, but there is nothing in them that holds my interest for very long. I am pleased to note that Bonaparte's return, so prominent a farce upon their pages is, in Toulouse, no more than a distant rumbling.

At the next break in the weather I go back to the bookseller's. He assures me a local worthy's memoirs are of interest, but I find them very dull. And his treatment of his wife, as though she had no importance, no inner life of her own aside from him, makes me shut the book in disgust. I feel great sympathy for her. I, too, have been a

7

great man's wife. Monsieur Delestre has been very persistent in having me share Antoine's papers with him for the biography he is writing. Twenty-five years of Antoine's life were mine also, but my portion of the thick volume of his life will be an occasional fleeting mention. Privately, his biographers will say what a bad wife I was, how unhappy I made the great man. The causes of my own unhappiness will never be taken into account.

Why should I let an account of my days rest in the hands of these men? Why should I not write down my own story for the world to read and make its own judgment? I too have lived through tumultuous times for France, from the depths of the Revolution to the pinnacle of the Empire. I have seen the Bourbon kings regain the throne only to lose it again. I have met Napoleon and Joséphine. I have known the greatest painters of our time and am proud to be an artist myself. Surely I have things to say that are of interest not only to myself?

The next morning I return to the shop and purchase a ream of creamy white sheets smooth to the touch, watermarked laid paper to ease the flow of the pen over its surface and lend importance to the words it carries. I request quills, but the bookseller urges me to try instead the new steel nib pens from England favored by several customers. I select several pens, good black ink, a clever traveling case for ink and sander and pens, and a fine leather portfolio for carrying a quantity of sheets at a time.

"Allow me to present these as a gift, Madame –" and he holds out a pair of cotton sleeve protectors such as he wears, to keep my dress safe from wayward splashes and blots of ink.

"Thank you!" I exclaim, startled out of my usual formality, feeling as pleased as a little girl being given a birthday present. I haven't felt that way in years. He offers to have my purchases delivered to the hotel, but I am too impatient to wait for it.

I hug the parcel to myself as I hurry back to my room. I clear the table by the window, arrange my new purchases on it, and ring for a pot of tea. Momentarily I am daunted by the task before me, but the hot drink revives me. I smile. It is really very simple. I will begin at the beginning, 1789, the year of my birth, when the world as my parents had known it was swept away.

Chapter 2

Paris, 1789-1806

I grew up in the shadow of the guillotine. My mother was six months pregnant at the fall of the Bastille. She had felt the heat and closeness of the July day all the more keenly because of her condition. Rumors and unrest had been building for weeks, even in our neighborhood of the Bourse, at some remove from the old fortress. Throngs of people were out in the streets and along the river, seeking a breath of fresh air but finding only the smells of packed bodies and sweating horses. They had been slaking their thirst with wine but were made sullen by it instead of cheerful, and open to the urging of rabble-rousers. Now there were shouts, voices, and the angry murmur of crowds. Few people in Paris slept that night. My father and his friend Monsieur Robin, the notary in whose house we lived on the rue Neuve Saint-Augustin, went out to investigate, much to the consternation of Maman. She told me how she grew chill with fear despite the stifling heat, and how this fear seems to have transmitted itself to me: that was the first time she felt me kick. It was, she told me, the one good thing to come out of that evening.

The men stayed out for several hours. Papa had seen enough to frighten him. He would never give us any details, no matter how often we asked – things not fit for the ears of children, he said. He, too, stayed in after that. It seemed, at first, to be just another riot, perhaps powerful enough, for once, to get the sluggish government to act. By the date of my birth, 10 October, it was clear that it was something far more serious, though few predicted the bloodbath it would become, with so many people being guillotined in the Place de la Révolution.

The political situation did not diminish my parents' joy. Maman was thirty-seven, Papa even older, and they often told me how eagerly they had awaited their first child. I was named Augustine after Maman's mother, one of the few times my grandmother was proud of me. Papa purchased a fine cradle with a gauze canopy. A teething coral on a silver handle hung on its side. Visitors came bearing cornets of sugared almonds. I lay in the christening gown that had been Maman's, surrounded by several dolls which were then carefully put aside for when I was older. The cradle and gown were used two years later for my sister Ange-Pauline and three years after for my brother Baudouin-Henri. The cradle was then sold, and the gown and coral were put aside and later used by

Pauline's boy and girl. I wish I could have used them for a child of my own.

Papa, in particular, showed his delight in me. Rather than send me to a wet nurse in the wholesome countryside, as was the custom, he brought in a nurse so that I could remain as home. Papa worked as an *agent de change*, buying and selling bills on the exchange. Honoré de Balzac has depicted the profession in an unflattering way in his novel *César Birotteau*, but Papa was known to be scrupulously honest. Every evening, however weary he was from his day at the Bourse, he nonetheless had the energy to climb to the nursery in the attic to spend time with me. As careworn as he became in the years of turmoil, he always had time for a smile, a kiss, and a story for me.

Papa and Maman were very devout. As long as it was safe they went regularly to mass. When the Faith was outlawed, the family prayed in private behind closed doors, out of earshot of the servants. They had been with us a long time and would not have betrayed us, Papa carefully explained, but he did not want to give them anything they would need to lie about if questioned. I learned early to be worried and suspicious; in this way the Terror left its mark on me for life.

Maman was equally devout in her support of Louis XVI. Every night she prayed for the safety of the King and Queen, their son Louis and daughter Marie-Thérèse, and the King's sister Madame Elisabeth. After the King and Queen were sent to the guillotine and the young Louis XVII died in prison, she prayed for their souls. I named my three dolls Marie-Antoinette, Elisabeth, and Marie-Thérèse after the women of the royal family and played endless games helping them escape first from imprisonment in the Conciergerie and then from Paris. When Marie-Thérèse was released just before my sixth birthday, Maman gave a fervent prayer of thanksgiving for this sole survivor of the royal family. "I told you not to worry," I said to my doll. Years later I met the Princess when she had become the Duchesse d'Angoulême. Her bearing was far too formal to permit mention of my doll, but I told her about our family prayers. She remarked, with one of her rare smiles, that she wished half her supposed supporters at court could claim to have done the same.

They were fearful years. No one knew when his or her life might be forfeit. Papa was careful to follow all the outward signs of obedience to the new régime. He brought home red, white and blue cockades for all of us to wear on our coats. I protested at first, saying it was dishonest. "We

13

do what we must in order to survive," he told me quietly but firmly, "until times change and the country returns to its senses." Like many, he was a pragmatist in the face of disaster. Even baby Henri had a cockade that he was always putting in his mouth. My sister and I often had to wipe red, white and blue saliva off his chin, while he giggled happily at our disgusted faces.

One day, two soldiers paused to watch us, and I froze inwardly, wondering whether Henri had transgressed some ruling of the Tribunal. Surely they would not drag an infant to the guillotine?

"He eats the Tricolor," remarked one, amused. "Yes, he'll be a good son of the Revolution," replied his companion. They laughed and continued on their way, to my profound relief.

When I was old enough, I was sent to the local *lycée* for my education. The convent schools had closed, the nuns fled or in hiding, but the government believed in educating us all to be good citizens of the new Republic. I learned to read, to write in an elegant hand (no longer, I fear, much in evidence on these pages), to do mathematics well enough to enable me to keep household accounts, to play the pianoforte, and to draw. It was the drawing master at the school who first discovered my ability.

On the long days when Papa was at work and Maman was fretful and wanted to lie down and my friends were not free to play, I discovered the solace that drawing and painting could bring. I was wholly absorbed when I struggled to capture an image on paper. The hours flew by without my noticing, until an ache in my back and neck told me I had bent over the paper for too long. Sometimes I would be startled by my father's return or the maid's entry with a lamp in the gathering dusk. Maman was more worried that I would ruin my eyes and my posture than she was appreciative of my efforts, but then Papa showed them to Monsieur Denon.

Dominique Vivant-Denon had been Papa's friend since before he met Maman. In the years of which I write, Denon had the acumen to attach himself to the staff of the young general who was working such miracles in Italy. The name Bonaparte was on everyone's lips, and I remember the thrill we felt at being able to claim acquaintance with someone who actually knew him.

Denon went with Bonaparte to Egypt, too. When he returned after two years, he regaled us with tales of its wondrous ancient monuments, the ferocity of its people and crocodiles, the bravery of our warriors, and the acumen of the savants who studied the natural and human history of the land. We hung on every word, eagerly poring over his drawings. The scarab he brought us became five-year-old Henri's favorite toy, turned over and over in his hands and examined from every possible angle. Even when Denon became a figure of importance in the new régime of the Consulate as Director-General of all the museums in France, he had the time to concern himself with the artistic training of his friend's young daughter.

Only Grandmère Augustine was not pleased. "It's a waste of money," she declared flatly, surveying the contents of my portfolio and obviously mentally calculating the cost of the materials. "It might be something if she had a talent for faces. A portraitist can always find someone to pay for her work. But what good are landscapes, country scenes? Who will pay for that? Better to learn something that will catch you a husband, *ma fille*." Little did she suspect that one day it would.

I remember vividly the day Monsieur Denon took me to purchase supplies as a gift for my fourteenth birthday. I was very excited. I had never had him all to myself before, and I was just reaching that age when being alone with a man, even a family friend old enough to be my father, had a tinge of excitement. It was a crisp October day. I wore a white dress with a high waist, the neckline showing just a hint of my still modest bosom and the short puffed sleeves displaying my arms to advantage. With it I wore practical ankle boots and a coat of the deep yellow color called *tabac d'Espagne*, Spanish tobacco.

He was punctual to the minute, a habit he had learned as a young man working for Madame de Pompadour. Gravely he threaded my arm through his and all the way to the shop kept up a stream of lively conversation on the art world of the day – the vanity of Jacques-Louis David, the odd behavior of Anne-Louis Girodet, and the promise shown by Antoine-Jean Gros. That was the first time I heard the name I was myself to carry for so long. Gros was working on a scene from the Egyptian campaign that would astonish us all, he said. I asked him to tell me more about it, but just then we arrived at the shop.

It was a busy place. Shop assistants wearing color-splotched aprons to protect their clothes scurried back and forth filling orders. Several men were waiting their turn, but when we entered they immediately deferred to Denon. Serenely he moved us to the head of the queue. The artists came up to be presented to me, eager to meet the powerful man's new protégée. He made quite a show of picking out the right paper, leads, pencils, and sketchbooks. I was delighted with the virgin surface of the smooth paper and the authenticity of the pencil with its lead-holder, the same kind I had seen him and other artists use. At the same time I could feel the others' eyes on us. It started to make me feel uncomfortable. I could tell instinctively that his attentiveness was no longer principally for my benefit, but to show everyone there how gracious he was in his condescension. My cheeks grew warm, and he smiled slightly as if my shy discomfiture amused him. I was relieved that when he set up an account for me at the shop, he did so in a quiet voice none could overhear. As we left he made a great show of carrying my portfolio and pencil box, and he all but bowed as they all but applauded.

Once outside, however, he reverted to his usual self with a sigh of relief and proposed that we go to the Tuileries Gardens to draw. It was a mild October day but with a cool breeze that tugged at my bonnet ribbons and riffled the pages of the sketchbook. The towering trees of the regimented groves were just beginning to turn color; the mottled green, yellow and orange foliage was very pretty. Children ran back and forth around the tree trunks, laughing and calling to each other, while more sedate parents and nannies kept a fond eye on them. Others gathered around the large basin that marked the junction of the main *allées*.

"What should I draw?" I asked Denon, as we each took out sketchbooks and pencils.

He smiled approvingly. "An excellent question! Nature – or any scene before you – will provide a confusing wealth of detail and incident." He swept his arm wide to encompass the natural and man-made elements before us. "The artist's role is to distill the scene to its essentials, and organize them into a pleasing rhythm on the page or canvas. What aspect of the garden pleases you most?"

I looked about me again. It was difficult to decide. "The trees," I said finally. "The changing colors, the full foliage before the leaves start to fall, the way you notice from one viewpoint that they've been planted in regular rows, but when you look straight ahead at the trunks when the children are running among them, the trees seem to be in a completely random order."

He nodded, his eyes full of lively interest. "So – how would you like to depict the trees?"

I looked at the grove again, from the ground with its occasional eruption of thick roots to the tops far overhead. "The grove as a whole," I replied.

"Then you're sitting too close to this particular one to get the proper perspective on it – you need distance." He gestured to the grove on the far side of the central basin. "Take that one as your subject for today. Later, you can learn how to show large spaces from a bird's-eye perspective."

I nodded enthusiastically and made bold to ask, "What subject will you choose?"

"This sculpture will suffice for today." He inclined his head toward one of the large, elaborately carved marble vases that punctuated the *allées* at intervals, reminding visitors that however lush the elements of nature, it was the hand of man that was uppermost here.

We spent a companionable hour working side by side. Gradually the noises of the garden faded as I became absorbed in my task. When I later glanced at Denon, he was recording the details of the ornamental vase with the same scientific detachment as if it were an ancient Egyptian monument.

I was brought back to the present only when a cold damp nose pressed itself between my ankles. I gave a little chirrup of fright that dissolved into laughter as I bent to pet the silky-haired dachshund. Its owner called it back. Only then did I hear the crunch of feet on the gravel paths, the clop of horses' hooves and the rumbling of wheels on the Quai des Tuileries. I wiggled fingers that had become stiff holding the pencil for so long and shivered in the breeze that was now noticeably cooler. We put away our sketchbooks and crossed the new rue de Rivoli to finish the afternoon with hot chocolate and cakes in the garden at Galignani's English bookshop. I remember he cast several penetrating glances both at my work and my person, shrewdly assessing my talent and the pleasure I took in drawing. I seemed to pass his inspection, for when we returned home he recommended to my father that I be placed in the studio of Nicolas-Antoine Taunay, one of the leading painters of the day, for drawing and painting lessons.

When the Salon, the most important art exhibition of the year, opened in September 1804, I begged Papa to take me to see it. This would be the first Salon at which I could feel myself a member, however fledgling, of the company of artists. When he at last announced that the family would go the following Sunday, I was so excited.

On the day I dressed with care in that summer's new white frock trimmed with red ribbon rosebuds and a matching red sash, and Maman helped me put up my long brown hair in a new grown-up style. I blushed with pleasure to see my image in the mirror, and the heightened color suited me. My sister had a similar dress trimmed in pink but her figure had not yet begun to fill out and she wore her hair down: there could be no doubt, I thought, as to which of us was the young woman, which the mere girl. It was too warm for us to enjoy wearing our summer bonnets, but Maman insisted that she would not have our complexions spoiled by the sun.

From our home on the rue Neuve Saint-Augustin, we walked down the rue Richelieu to the Palais Royal, where we detoured to stroll through its extensive gardens, nodding to acquaintances as we went. A few steps after leaving the garden at its southern end, we crossed the rue de Rivoli and joined the crowds streaming into the Louvre. Admission was always free on Sundays so that all citizens could visit and imbibe the lessons of the works exhibited there, especially those extolling the deeds of First Consul Bonaparte. The museum's hallways and galleries were filled with the magnificent statues that he had brought back from Italy years before, and I was later to find out that Antoine had been responsible for selecting the pieces sent from Rome. I chattered all the way up the Grand Staircase, but Mama and Papa were both short of breath from the climb. (So would I be, if I attempted it today.) We doubled back through the galleries of the upper floor to reach the *Salon Carré*, the great square room where most of the paintings were hung. Because of its immense size, Gros's *Bonaparte visiting the plague-stricken soldiers at Jaffa*, the canvas Denon had told me about, was in one of the large adjacent galleries. It was there that the crowds were thickest, the air buzzing with excited voices. There was no way to view it up close without impolitely shoving our way through. Fortunately it was hung high enough that all could see it. Then Denon, who was standing in front of the painting, caught sight of us, and motioned us to approach. The crowd obligingly parted, and we stood before the painting.

Many words of praise have been and continue to be written about this work, and I am sure they will continue for generations to come. Both its name and its fame are now nauseatingly familiar to me. But nothing can describe the impact, on first seeing it, of its dazzling freshness, of its color and the glamour of its setting. We had heard about the Egyptian campaign from Denon and pored over his drawings, but here was a scene large enough for us to step into. It brought his tales of Egypt to life in all their heat and splendor, bravery and valor, sickness and squalor.

I stood awestruck, my words of explanation to my family driven from my head.

The painting was immense. The interior of the whole plague hospital was revealed before us. Bonaparte, then a general, now First Consul, and soon to be Emperor, had entered its gloomy depths to visit and encourage his men. Could he even cure them by sheer force of his personality? My eyes were immediately drawn to his brilliant figure that seemed to capture the sunlight. This image caught all our hearts. That the campaign had ultimately been a disaster could momentarily be forgotten. I was not alone in my wonder – all around me I heard "Ah"s of delight. Laurel wreaths, palm branches, and poems of praise were pinned to the frame of the painting.

Denon beamed at me and enthusiastically greeted my parents, sister and brother. "Well?" he asked me. "Is it not as good as I promised it would be?" I nodded and smiled, but could not speak, glancing quickly to his face and then back to the painting. I scanned the work, seeing yet more details – the brilliant green of the Arab doctor's robe, the man with the bandaged eyes groping his way along the columns, the almost comic figure of cautious Marshal Berthier covering his nose and mouth instead of bravely reaching out to the men.

Before I could examine it further, however, Denon gestured me to his side. He had been talking with a short, slight, plainly dressed man of no particular distinction, who seemed ill at ease in the jostling, murmuring crowd surging around us and leaned on an ebony cane to steady himself. "May I present Monsieur Gros?" Denon asked. "He has been suffering from rheumatism and this is the first time he has seen his painting in the Salon. Antoine, this is Mademoiselle Dufresne, a young lady in whose talent I have taken an interest."

This was Gros, the creator of that marvelous image? I managed somehow to say the proper words of greeting, but my eyes kept flicking back and forth in disbelief between the brilliant painting and the unprepossessing artist in his sober black suit. It was as though the one had sucked all the brilliance out of the other and taken it for its own. Fortunately, he did not seem to guess my thoughts. At least I could wholeheartedly express my admiration for the painting as a whole and for the figure of Napoleon in particular. At my praise, his face lit up and he drew his body a little straighter: I caught a glimpse of the inspired artist within the ordinary shell. Then Denon claimed his attention as another acquaintance approached. I turned to examine the painting again, but Maman and Papa were ready to move to another room.

My brother Henri was as reluctant to move on as I. Ten years old and just discovering his own artistic talents, he was impressed not only by the painting but also by the acclaim and admiration and accolades accorded the artist. He later told me that he resolved then and there to become a painter.

Although I was not able to see as much as I would have liked that day, I was able to return several times. I looked at the other paintings, of course, but it was *Jaffa* that drew me again and again.

Papa and Maman were hesitant about allowing me to go alone to the Salon, but they permitted me to go before and after my art lessons, if I went with a group of students. Several of us would set out with our drawing boards, paper, and pencils or chalk and walk to the works we were going to copy that day. Other art students did so as well, and it was a welcome chance to meet them. Women were always in the minority and sometimes we were simply ignored by the young men, but at other times they would talk to us, even indulge in mild flirtations. It seemed to me even then that the students of Jacques-Louis David, the most eminent painter of the age, held themselves apart, having absorbed their teacher's sense of superiority to the rest of the art world.

Only rarely did David himself deign to put in an appearance. One memorable day he stood in front of *Jaffa* while Gros and several others waited attentively for his pronouncement on the work. After examining the painting in some detail, he proclaimed, "One could do as well – but one could not do better." Antoine's face lost its anxious look and flushed with pleasure. David then turned to his students to exhort them: "Monsieur Gros was one of my students and you see the height to which he has risen. Work hard, develop your skills, and one day you too will be able to do as well as he has." At such high praise from his master, Antoine's face lighted up with devotion, looking almost boyish in its delight.

I treasured the rare occasions when I found myself the only one sketching before *Jaffa*. Then I could lose myself in the scene. Once, as I sketched, two veterans of the Egyptian campaign approached the painting and saluted the figure of the Emperor. It was touching in its way, echoing the gesture of the sailor in the picture. One of them had to salute with his left arm, his empty right sleeve pinned to his coat. The other had an eye patch. They grew animated as they talked, gesturing extravagantly and raising their voices. I was very quiet in my corner and they seemed to have forgotten I was there.

"It's the General! Not as he looked in Egypt, however, more like he looked yesterday."

"He was thinner in Egypt."

"Weren't we all – godawful food and the dysentery that wouldn't stop! Somehow the General never got sick – he had the luck of the devil."

"This Gros fellow paints a good picture, but you can tell he wasn't really there, can't you?"

"Who'd want to know the real truth? All that misery, and for what? We lost in the end."

"*He* didn't. *He* got home okay."

"Quiet, you idiot! You'll have the police on us." He glanced around nervously and belatedly noticed me. Before I could think of what to say to reassure them, they bowed apologetically and left the gallery. I tried to concentrate on the painting then, but they had spoiled it for me for that day.

The most memorable occasion was the day I copied the figure of the dying doctor in the lower right corner. His noble death in the course of duty never failed to touch my heart. To capture his blond good looks on paper was a challenge I was not certain I was equal to, but one day, as the end of the Salon drew near, I knew I had to try. Few people were in the galleries that morning, and I hoped there would be no one there to witness my frustration and failure. A young man in the blue and red uniform of the horse artillery stood looking intently at the very figure I had come to draw. I was annoyed at first – he blocked my view. As I set up my chair and drawing board I wished he would soon move on as most visitors did, but he continued to stand and stare. Suddenly I sneezed, the sound unnaturally loud in that echoing space. Startled, he turned around, and I was amazed to see tears shining on his cheeks. My heart warmed to this man who could be so affected by art. Embarrassed, he brushed away the tears with his hand. He could not help sniffling, and muttered with annoyance at finding himself without a handkerchief. I held out one of mine. He took it with a slight smile and I averted my gaze while he blew his nose and made a final dab at his eyes.

"He was my uncle," he said by way of apology, "my mother's favorite brother. She was so heartbroken when we heard of his death..." His voice trailed off.

And you were, too, I thought, *but you were trying to grow up and be a man, and refused to let yourself cry as much as you needed.*

"He was my favorite. I always wanted to be just like him, strong and brave and adventurous. I have no talent for medicine, but at least I could go into the army."

And break your mother's heart a second time. It was the rare young man of my generation who did not wish to be a soldier, however, and I knew better than to question his hopes. He must have found my silence encouraging, for he continued.

"I'm training for artillery – I'm good at math, for cannon trajectories – but what I really want to do is become a cuirassier so that I can serve in the cavalry under Marshal Murat."

On and on he went. It was a world far from mine of stockbrokers and art students. He was, I gathered, learning how best to kill as many of the enemy as possible while exposing the absolute minimum of his own men. That all of their mothers would weep as bitterly as his had done seemed not to occur to him. In the gallery, men were uncles to be mourned, but in the military classroom they were nameless and faceless forces to be deployed.

The young man had ceased to talk while I was musing; either he had no more things to say or perhaps he was waiting for a more encouraging reply from me. Then a clock in a nearby bell tower struck three, and he started, almost stiffening to attention. "I'm meeting my mother at three – I'm late!" The budding military officer fell away to reveal the boy caught out in some naughtiness. "I'm sorry, I must run, I – " He became aware that he was still holding my handkerchief, a sodden ball crushed in one hand – not his property, but in no state to return to me. I almost laughed out loud at his confusion and hastily scribbled my name and address on a scrap of drawing paper. "Augustine Dufresne," he read, and extended the hand not holding my handkerchief. "Charles. Charles Legrand."

He left the gallery. My eyes followed his retreating figure with its confident military stride – so tall and handsome a young man was not an everyday occurrence. With their blond good looks and their uniforms, it was easy to believe that he and the dying doctor could be uncle and nephew. I could not help letting out a small sigh of regret at his departure.

But further reverie on Charles Legrand was forestalled by the sound of a man laughing. It startled me, as I had thought Charles and I were alone in the gallery. The laughter was soft, but not pleasant, with a mocking note to it. I was painfully self-conscious, as one is at fifteen, and I thought he might be mocking my conversation with Charles or my drawing, although there was nothing on the paper yet. Perhaps he thought me not an artist at all but a poseur, someone who only pretended to sketch as a pretext for meeting young men? My cheeks burned, and I was gathering the courage to confront this interloper, when he spoke.

"His uncle, was it? That's a new one! Usually I'm every mother's son." He removed the hat he had been wearing low over his eyes, and faced me. There was something familiar about his face but I could not quite place it. He shook his blond locks impatiently to dishevel them. A vacant, unfocused look came over his face as he leaned his head to one side. I gasped. It was the dying doctor from the painting. He came out of the pose, and grinned.

"Jacques Dupré, artist's model, at your service." He gave a slight bow. "Yes, I sat for that figure, and very dull it was, two days of Monsieur Gros positioning me this way and that until he'd got the pose he wanted. That's a long time for someone who works as fast as our Monsieur Gros – and *so* serious! All my friendly overtures rebuffed in

32

stony silence. If Girodet had not stopped by from time to time, I should have died of boredom. *He*, at least, is not afraid to flirt. I was positively glad to be paid and let go, let me tell you. Little did I know he'd make me *immortal*." The mocking note was replaced by grudging respect. "I come here sometimes just to watch the crowd. Your young man is not the first to have cried for me. Usually it's mothers or grandmothers. Jules! Louis! Michel! You can see them longing to touch my cheek, kiss my brow." He sounded moved despite himself. "Fortunately it's hung too high for that, or my famous image would be gone by now."

"And what do they say when you tell them the truth?" My voice was hostile.

"I *never* do. That would be cruel, my dear. There's a fine line between mocking and hurting, and I try not to cross it. I didn't tell your friend, did I?"

"Then why tell me?"

"Oh, but you're an *artist*. You understand about models and painting and emotional impact. *You're* not taken in." The mocking was back again. He seemed to know how to take my good motives and twist them around to make me hate myself for them. He could see me inwardly squirming and enjoyed it.

"Shall I sketch you, then, instead of the painting?" My voice had an edge to it, showed him I was hurt, which made me even angrier. I picked up my pencil as if to begin.

"You don't want to sketch me, my dear. You want to sketch what Monsieur Gros has made of me. It's much better suited to your imagination and sentiments." He gave a deep bow with a sweep of his hat, like an old-fashioned gallant in a play, and left the room.

I sighed with relief. At last I could get down to work. I was looking forward to learning how Gros had created so moving a figure from such unpromising raw material. It took some effort to give my figure on canvas the same unfocused, moribund look as the doctor in Gros's painting; try as I would, he would seem to have Jacques Dupré's mocking smile. It took all my skill to erase the real man from my mind and regain the thrill I had felt on seeing his transformed image in Gros's canvas. Only then could I give the figure the expression that Gros had given him. It was a valuable lesson in how to prevent being overly swayed by imperfect reality, when there was a nobler goal to pursue.

As 1804 turned into 1805 and 1806, the focus of my life turned from my family to the studio. I went to Taunay's studio at the Louvre two mornings a week. It was exciting to be part of the world of the artists – of prizes to compete for; prestigious clients to win; and the big official commissions that only rarely went to someone new. Taunay was one of those favored few, and we all felt proud to be studying with him.

I learned to prepare a canvas: to construct a wooden frame so that it was light, yet strong enough to support the sometimes ponderous weight of the linen canvas; to unfold the stiff fabric and nail it tightly to the wood so that no trace of folds remained on its taut surface; and to prepare the surface to receive the paint. The raw canvas was primed with one layer, and then another, of lead white mixed with oil and turpentine. The primed canvas was then sized with a thin layer of rabbit skin glue, warmed in a little pot on the studio stove, mixed with gesso. Finally a layer of ground color was painted over the sizing. Only then were we allowed to begin to apply our oil paints. In the process, I learned patience and attention to detail – mix the materials in incorrect proportions, or apply one layer before the previous one had dried, and I would waste hours, sometimes days of work. In extreme cases, the canvas would need to be thrown away, wasting money as well. I wondered how long it had taken Gros, who, as I had been told, liked to work alone, to prepare his immense canvas for *Jaffa*.

The time waiting for our canvases to dry was not wasted, as we spent it learning how to grind and mix our pigments with the correct amounts of linseed or walnut or poppy oils, depending on each color's preference. Once mixed properly they were my friends; until then, they were like Grandmère Augustine and her cronies – fussy, demanding, obstinate, and determined to demonstrate I could never do things correctly.

Only when we had mastered the preparation of the canvas and the pigments could we begin to realize in paint the ideas we had worked out so meticulously with pencil and paper. It was not a process that encouraged carefree spontaneity, but I did not mind; it fit well, I thought, with my new sense of maturity as I grew from a girl into a young woman. I treasured the warm inner glow when the work was going well and I could lose myself in it.

When Maman complained that I had a dusting of pigment or a smudge of paint still on my hand, I would protest: "But, Maman, it shows I'm an artist!"

"You're a young lady of good family first and foremost, and you should look and behave like one."

When, despite my smock, a splatter of red paint stained my white dress, this garment was demoted to "that dress you wear to the studio." None of this mattered when Papa proudly framed one of my early paintings and hung it in our salon.

Taunay would grow exasperated at his female students' daintiness. "You are *artists*, or wishing to be. Do not be afraid of your paints!" He said this more than once. What marvelous advice it was for a young woman: do not be afraid but be bold and take risks and chances. As I grew older I discovered the restrictions that hampered a painter, even a man, of subject matter and rescinded commissions and pleasing the patron, or by one's own fears and timidity, as in Gros's case. Taunay, too, was aware of those, which is why he wanted to give us as much courage as possible while he could.

This was when I took to wearing bold jewel colors – red, gold, deep blue and green. No more the white dresses of my girlhood favored by my mother, meant to emphasize our purity but, it seemed to me, making us seem insipid as well. White was the color of a blank canvas: I resolved to paint mine boldly and live my life in color. Maman objected but Papa supported me.

My friends were envious when I told them about the studio, where most of the students were male. "All those young men," they sighed. I tried to talk about the paintings but they were as little interested as Grandmère had been. I sensed myself growing away from them.

Then I saw Charles Legrand again, and was one of them once more.

Chapter 3

Paris, 1806-1808

Tine. He called me Tine. It was a family nickname given me by Baby Henri when he couldn't pronounce Augustine. I was starting to outgrow it, but Charles said it with such affection, such a smile and a caress, that it became an endearment. "Augustine" was Grandmère, stern and critical; "Tine" was myself, a girl in love; "Mademoiselle Dufresne," hovering somewhere between the two, was the budding artist.

Charles had returned my handkerchief but never answered the letter I sent him. Sadly, I let go of the daydreams our meeting had inspired. It was a loss not only for my future possibilities but also for my current status among my girlfriends from the *lycée*. We would meet in each other's houses or in a café where our parents were known and the proprietor could be trusted to keep an eye on us. My painting studies made me different from the others, who stayed at home to learn how to run a household, in preparation for the marriages we all expected to make. I, too, received domestic instruction, but I did not listen to it as intently as did my friends. I had indulged in a few mild flirtations with other art students but had not yet had the kind of romance that was the stuff of novels, swooning in the arms of a devoted young man.

We all dreamed of young officer husbands: they looked so handsome in their uniforms, and the army was a quick route to advancement and riches. Charles's father, a career soldier who had achieved only modest promotions during the Ancien Régime, was promoted much more rapidly under Bonaparte, commanding key divisions at Austerlitz and other important battles. It was not surprising that Charles wished to follow in his footsteps. More than one friend's older sister had begun married life in a modest flat and later bought a country house. It was possible for us, too, we told each other fervently. The young men not already in the army talked of nothing but when they would be old enough to join. Charles's eager monologue on this subject was not the only one I heard in these years.

Of course, we girls did not have this to look forward to, just our usual lives made more difficult by their absence. Unfortunately, Bonaparte's penchant for war was swallowing up our generation.

My friend Lucie's sister Mireille lost her husband Paul. The day she heard the news, we were helping to prepare her trousseau. It was the week before Christmas. They had married on his last leave, and he had departed to join his regiment. Mireille's eyes sparkled with pride when she told us "my Paul" had taken part in the Battle of Austerlitz two weeks before, a great victory for France against the combined forces of our enemies. She was sure he would be promoted for his bravery! Mireille and Paul were to move to their own home upon his return. Linens embroidered with the couple's initials were spread around the room. A wedding gift of engraved silver napkin rings had just arrived and Mireille caressed the monogram as she expanded upon the dinner parties she would give for other officers and their wives, the faience plates she had now but would replace with porcelain when she was able, the table and chairs she would order from Bernard Molitor's fashionable shop near the Church of the Madeleine.

We did not hear the knock on the door. The maid came upstairs to say that two military gentlemen wished to speak to her. Mireille started, grew pale; the napkin in its ring clattered to the floor, and Lucie stooped to retrieve it. With an effort, Mireille made her face calm again. "Thank you, Lucie," she said as she went down to find out what they wanted. The rising fear I felt was mirrored in Lucie's face as our eyes met. Would he return like Reine's brother, with only one arm, or like Ninette's sister's fiancé, missing his right leg below the knee? In my mind's eye I saw Paul at the dinner party we had just imagined with one sleeve pinned to his shirt.

We had left the door ajar and we could hear an indistinct rumble of male voices below. Mireille's "No!" was all too clear. She began to scream; the maid shouted for Lucie; I hastily folded up the scattered linens and put them aside as Mireille was brought in. She had fainted; one of the officers carried her upstairs and laid her gently on the bed. Seeing her in his arms, I felt a thrill despite myself. "Was Paul badly wounded?" I asked him.

"He was killed," the officer said gruffly, clearly apprehensive lest I make a similar outburst.

"Where?" I asked inanely. As if it mattered.

"At Austerlitz. He died bravely, helping to bring about victory." That must have been a phrase he repeated over and over. It came out in a flat voice telling it by rote.

"Can I do something?" I asked Lucie.

"Find Mama and Papa and tell them to come home." She gave me directions to the friend they were visiting, so it became my sad duty to break the news to them.

I went to the private service held for Paul in their home. Mireille was inconsolable. She began correspondence with a school friend who had entered a convent in Belgium and eventually joined her there, taking the napkin rings as an offering for their treasury.

Lucie married the middle-aged sergeant who had broken the news; they have five children and are by all accounts a happy and devoted couple.

By the time I saw Charles Legrand again I had almost forgotten him in my growing interest in my painting studies. It was much more difficult to forget Jacques Dupré, for artists' models and their role in bringing to life the history scenes so prized by our professors, had become a constant presence in my life. No longer could I take them for granted and lose consciousness of their personality apart from the characters they portrayed. Taunay criticized me more than once for being too particular in my sketches of models instead of transcending them to state a higher truth.

Charles and I met again by chance early in 1806. A fellow painting student had a brother at artillery school, who one day brought Charles to the studio. He paid me the flattering compliment of recognizing me and remembering my name. I later learned that the other cadets had found the handkerchief and the paper with my name and address on it, and teased him unmercifully about "your

Mademoiselle Dufresne": he had had little chance to forget it.

Twice more Charles came with his friend to visit my colleague and said little more than "Bonjour" to me. I had resigned myself to his lack of interest when he appeared alone one day. "Edmond isn't here," I told him. "He didn't come to the studio today."

"I know. He and his brother are visiting their parents in Meudon. I came to see you." I startled and blushed, then recovered my composure to smile at him. "Are you free this afternoon? Would you like to go for a walk?"

I was, and I would. I was glad that I had worn a deep blue dress that day and my wine-red coat, colors that showed my complexion to advantage. It was a mild winter's day, the right weather to bring flattering roses to my cheeks when out walking with a handsome young officer. Charles had matured in the fifteen months since we had first met – no longer a gangling youth but a muscular one, his chest filled out, his voice deeper, with a new ease of bearing: no longer a cadet among his instructors but well on his way to becoming a man among men. He now wore the uniform of the cuirassier, white trousers with a blue coat.

We left the Louvre and turned west toward the Tuileries. By Napoleon's order, the space between the two palaces was being cleared of the houses, shops, and other buildings that had been there for centuries. The Louvre was connected to the Tuileries Palace by the Grande Galerie that ran parallel to the river, and it was reported that Napoleon planned construction that would connect the two palaces on the side facing the rue de Rivoli. Although paths had been mostly cleared through the rubble, we had to pick our way carefully. Considerately Charles did not break into his natural long-legged stride but kept pace with my short steps further constricted by my long straight skirt. Once clear of the palaces, we made our way to the Tuileries Garden. I had long envied the young women who strolled in the company of young officers. Finally, I was going to be one of them!

We said little at first. I could sense that he wanted to start a conversation but was unsure how to begin. For my part I could talk to young painters easily enough but was not sure what to say to a young lieutenant. Happily, I remembered that he had mentioned his mother at our first encounter. I inquired after her health. She was well, and happy to have him again in Paris. His father, too, was well, and had been decorated for his bravery at Austerlitz.

Charles should have liked to be there himself. Ironic, was it not, to prepare for action and never see the most glorious example of it? He chafed for the *gloire* of it. He had graduated from artillery school and was now receiving further training in Paris. He hoped to fulfill his dream of joining the cavalry division led by the dashing Joachim Murat. For the first time I truly understood the impulse of our young men to throw themselves into battle for their own sake. Charles had grown up in a military tradition, trained from the start to look forward to risking his life.

Suddenly he stopped, embarrassed. "I did not mean to go on like this. You're very easy to talk to." Indeed — being a good audience to the ambitions of men is drilled into women from birth. We walked a little further in companionable silence. "Edmond says your painting studies are going well. What do you like to paint?"

"Landscapes. The gardens." I gestured to the scene about me. "The Seine — I love to catch the light on the water."

"When I met you that day in the Louvre, you were copying my uncle's portrait — I *thought* it was my uncle — in Gros's painting. Do you want to paint portraits?"

"I wish I could, but I don't have the talent for faces one needs to be a success at it. I want to paint military scenes

46

but my parents would never permit me to attend large gatherings of soldiers on my own."

"I could take you there one day," he offered.

Thus chatting, he walked me home. In the weeks following, he would come to the studio to meet me on his free afternoons, and we would go walking. Our courtship was in those walks. Sometimes we would stroll east along the river to Notre Dame Cathedral or across the river to Panthéon, or through the Luxembourg Gardens to the Observatoire, not so much to see these monuments of the city as to be together for the day.

I met several of his friends. One who had known him at artillery school smiled and said, "Ah, *the* Mademoiselle Dufresne!"

Charles laughed. "Yes, she does exist, I did not invent her."

"But you didn't tell me how pretty she was either," the other replied, with an exaggerated wink at me. I did not blush at this; I was learning how to flirt.

For the first time I began to look at the military with a proprietary air. "My young man" belonged to the Grande Armée, and the army, as a consequence, now belonged to me. It became my subject matter as well. Taunay was impressed and praised my work: "You are thinking less like a girl and more like an artist."

Charles often took part in the cavalry exercises held on the Champ de Mars, the large parade ground in front of the former École Militaire, now used as a barracks, on Sunday afternoons. These served a dual purpose: to enable the young men and their horses to practice formation, and to keep public enthusiasm for the Emperor's campaigns at a fever pitch. They provided a heart-stirring display of the glory of war without any of its grim reality. Whole families attended this free entertainment, cheering wildly. Twice I saw the lone figure of Gros among them, observing intently the horsemen and the reactions of the crowd.

The exercises began promptly at two o'clock with a blast of trumpets. The horse artillery rode out first, serious and intent, positioning their (empty) rifles and taking aim as their mounts increased speed from a trot to a canter to a gallop. The hussars of the light cavalry followed. These officers were the most showily dressed, each with his elaborately braided jacket slung over one shoulder like a cape, and a tall black shako on his head. The colors of the jackets varied according to the men's regiments, and our eyes were drawn to the bright rainbow formed by the

48

group. They charged, swords drawn. Finally, the cuirassiers of the heavy cavalry rode out in full battle dress, each wearing his cuirasse – breast and back plates of burnished steel with brass fittings – and casque, a steel and brass helmet with a flowing horse tail and short red plume. They shone in the sunlight, dazzling our eyes. They stopped and, on a signal, withdrew their sabers in one fluid motion and held them aloft. With a mighty yell they galloped forward in a battle charge, their bodies moving in union with their horses, the horses' tails and helmet tails streaming, the ground shaking with the pounding of the horses' hooves. My own heart was thudding with excitement. I was so proud of Charles and how well he looked seated on his mount. I was sure he sat up straighter, moved with superior grace and strength. I stood clutching my closed sketchbook to my chest. How silly of me to think I could observe something so stirring and calmly sketch it. That was better done later in the studio, when I was no longer too caught up in the moment.

Seeing him afterward come down to earth, his armor and weapon put away, wearing his everyday uniform, my heart continued to beat fast with the excitement he had stirred in me. Encouraged by the example of the wives and sweethearts around me, I impulsively threw my arms about him and kissed him passionately. He responded in kind, enfolding me in a strong embrace. Chills went up and down my spine. I had read about these sensations in novels but this was the first time I had felt them to my core. Had he asked me to go to bed with him, I would happily have thrown caution to the winds. To my disappointment, he drew back and grinned broadly down at me. Confused, I dropped my eyes and looked at our feet. Before my tears could fall, however, he brought my chin up with his forefinger and bent to kiss me tenderly on the lips. He offered me his arm and escorted me home as decorously as he had always done.

When Charles and I went to the Palais Royal, it was I who played guide. The former home of the Orléans branch of the royal family, it was now a popular public garden surrounded by shops and cafés on the ground floor and apartments above. At that time, the Bourse was located there, and I had visited often with Papa as he went about his business of buying and selling shares. Being with him had always been a special treat – partaking of the excitement of the shouting buyers and sellers, the promise of money changing hands – afterward, being taken by Papa and his friends to Berthellemot's for ices, or to one of the cafés for hot chocolate, while they drank wine. It was there that we had celebrated Bonaparte's first victories in Italy. Charles and I would sometimes see Papa or one of his colleagues, and I would present Charles to them with the grave and becoming air of a young lady.

We did not often stop for refreshment at one of the cafés. His lieutenant's pay was not large and his gleaming new uniform had to be paid for out of that. On one memorable occasion he asked me to help him pick out a birthday gift for his mother, so that we had the pleasure of browsing the many shops together. At least, I enjoyed it; for Charles it was clearly tedium.

Another aspect of the Palais Royal was the many prostitutes who plied their trade there, strolling and catching the eye of any passing officer, then whisking him off to the rooms they kept upstairs. They would assess Charles saucily, note my presence in his company with a more critical eye, and shrug slightly as they determined he was not worth the effort. I accepted them as part of the landscape but looked at them with new understanding of sexual desire. I even smiled inwardly at causing them to turn away from a man they clearly found attractive. Charles, to my surprise, was disturbed less by their attention than by my calm acceptance of it. I teased him about it: surely their existence could come as no surprise to one in the army?

He blushed. "I have," he struggled for the right words to use in polite society, "known them." It's a man's right, his gaze said defiantly. "But you, Tine, who were brought up to be a young lady—"

I almost laughed out loud at his serious face as he explained this to me but stopped myself just in time. "They have been part of the Palais Royal as long as I have been coming here. It's too late for me to be shocked by them. I just ignore them." I shrugged as if to dismiss them.

Charles continued to look doubtful but thought the better of continuing the conversation. I could tell he was disappointed in me but did not know what I could do to make amends. By mutual consent we got up and left the café. It was our first disagreement.

Charles and I had first made each other's acquaintance in front of *Jaffa*. Sentiment dictated that we should go together to see Gros's *Battle of Aboukir* at the Salon held in the autumn of 1806. The fame of this scene of the Egyptian campaign, showing Murat leading the French cavalry in a charge against Turkish troops at the port of Aboukir, is almost as great as that of *Jaffa*. Murat had commissioned an even larger canvas, in which Napoleon, who had in fact led the French into battle, did not even appear. The painting's action centered instead on Murat, the noble hero on his startled white horse. Like *Jaffa*, it attracted a large crowd that buzzed with excitement, echoing the energy of the painted scene. Eagerly we took our place among them. I realized now why Gros had watched the cavalry displays so intently. Charles' eyes lit up at the sight of his hero and lingered lovingly on the horses. He scowled at Mustapha Pasha and looked smugly content at the terrified faces of the fleeing enemy troops. He gave a derisive laugh, however, at some parts of it. "It's a *battle*. Where is the blood? There's got to be more than that little drip coming from Mustapha's hand!"

His voice rose in indignation; heads were turned our way. "Hear, hear!" said an officer with a medal pinned to his coat. I did my best to explain.

"There's no blood, but look, the color red is everywhere, suggesting it. To show blood would make this a scene of carnage, not battle. It would be too specific. A painting of battle," I explained, paraphrasing what I had learned from Taunay, "elevates the scene. It's not just Murat and Mustapha but also good versus evil, the brave versus the cowardly, and the good and brave are winning.

The artist suggests a large messy battle but distills it to its essentials." Earnest and passionate in defense of the painter's art, I was finding an eloquence I had not known I possessed.

"But, Tine, what about the naked men – surely they're not essential to battle!"

"To battle itself? No. They belong to battle *painting*."

"Why add this and subtract that and elevate the next thing? Why not just show what really happened? Wouldn't that be simpler?"

"It would be illustrative, but not *art*."

The officer who had interjected the comment tapped Charles's arm and said knowingly, "Monsieur Gros wasn't at the battle, you know. He 'observed' it from the comfort of his Paris studio, using eyewitness reports. So when he thought of it, he thought like a painter. Artists!" Had we been outdoors, he would have spat.

"Were *you* there, sir?" asked Charles respectfully, standing to attention, a salute implied in his demeanor.

"No, at that time I was in Italy with our artist, escorting the baggage you see displayed around us here." He gave a dismissive wave in the direction of the Grand Staircase. "Guarding a boatload of old marble rubbish instead of facing an honest battle! I ask you. Still, I got my chance later on. And young Gros was all right. He took hardship like a man when it found us." His eyes had ceased to focus on Charles and looked inward at his memories.

Abruptly he came back to the present. "But if your young lady wants to talk about Art with you, lad, better indulge her. Your uniform looks too new to have seen battle yet. You'll find out about its realities soon enough." He clapped Charles on the shoulder, inclined his head to me, and limped swiftly away. Only when he moved did we notice that one trouser leg concealed a wooden limb whose echo on the wood floors could be heard even above the noise of the crowd.

We looked at each other, startled, unsure how to pick up the thread of the conversation. The dictates of Art seemed small indeed.

After France's great victories of 1805, thousands of youths like Charles were eager to share in Napoleon's glory. Charles wanted his father to be proud of him. Like the very young man he was, half his efforts were directed at impressing his elders. It was all a grand adventure. That he would come back safe, he never doubted.

After he had finished his training in Paris, he was sent not to Murat's division as he had hoped but to the

Netherlands troops of Napoleon's brother Louis, now king of that country. Charles was bitterly disappointed but I confess I was relieved to have him somewhere peaceful and relatively safe.

I threw myself into my painting with renewed fervor, working up my sketches of the cavalry exercises into two paintings. One centered on the charge of the cuirassiers, the exhilaration of their forward momentum, with the crowd only a blur in the background. The other focused instead on the reaction of the crowd to the colorful hussars. Both Denon and Taunay were pleased with these canvases. Denon helped Papa to hang them on the walls of our salon.

My parents liked Charles and trusted him – or we would not have been allowed so much time alone together – but they felt that it was ridiculous to pin my hopes on a soldier. They urged me to find someone who would remain safely in Paris. As if such a man would interest me! Much as I loved Papa, I wanted someone more adventurous than a stockbroker.

Charles returned to Paris just before Christmas in 1807. We spent Christmas together and exchanged miniature portraits as presents. He gave me decorous kisses under the mistletoe with our parents looking on and more ardent ones when we were alone.

The order to depart came early in 1808. He had at last received the assignment he longed for. He was to accompany Murat and Napoleon into Spain, where yet another Bonaparte brother was to become a king. Finally he would have the chance to take part in real battles, to take his place as a man amongst other men. I was happy for him but also fearful. The Spanish were known to be a fierce, proud people. Would they accept a foreign king and his troops as calmly as the Dutch?

I shed tears over it in private but put on a brave face for Charles. I did not want our few weeks together to be spoiled by my worries. Your sweetheart is a soldier, I admonished myself sternly. You too must learn to be mentally tough in the face of fear.

Charles purchased a new uniform and came to show it off to us. Maman and I were duly impressed. The shining breastplate, helmet, and saber were, like Charles himself, not yet scratched or dented. His leather boots were so new they creaked a little when he walked, and I teased him about it. I asked if he would need to spend a long time polishing his armor. No, he replied with complacent superiority, he had an orderly to see to it. His business was to fight, to serve his Marshal and his Emperor, to bring glory to France and to his family.

"If I get to Madrid, I'll bring you a fan and a mantilla," he promised, "and a pretty lace veil you can wear at our wed –" he bit off the last word. He never formally proposed to me but his intentions were clear. From that moment I considered us engaged. I sparkled too. I was young and pretty and he seemed to me the most glamorous creature on earth. I couldn't bear to be parted from him and said I wished I could follow him to Spain. Again I wanted to give myself to him; I was both ashamed of myself and proud of my daring. I thought, he is a man and a soldier and he will appreciate my gift. But he laughed and said I was not the sort of girl who followed the army. The women who did were working-class wives who supplemented their husbands' pay by doing laundry. Or they were women of the streets who became, as it were, women of the field. To follow him would be to lower myself to the level of those others. His face looked as it had when referring to the women of the Palais Royal.

Then I thought of something else. The army employed artists to travel with them; perhaps I— But the thought died unsaid. I was a girl, barely eighteen years old. To propose this idea would be to invite further ridicule. I was ready to cry with frustration. My role, it appeared, was to sit sedately at home, to wait for his return. Charles longed for adventure but did not want me to be part of it.

"Tine, don't be upset with me. This isn't a parade on the Champ de Mars. It's war. War is men's business. I want you here, where you'll be safe."

I shook off my disappointment then and rallied to smile bravely for the rest of his visit and tenderly kiss him farewell. I did not attend, sketchbook in hand, the next morning's exit from camp; I knew I would not be able to see the paper through my tears. Perhaps, I thought, Gros was right: some scenes are better left to the imagination.

I missed Charles fiercely in the weeks to come, imagining myself again in his arms. I treasured the brief notes he wrote from the field, visited his mother once a week, and dared to plan a wedding and a future. I dreamed of the home we would have and furnished it, in my imagination, with new pieces in a modern style. I would direct my own household, although we would not need more than two or three servants at the beginning. I paid attention now to Maman's lessons in household management, much to her relief. I gladly helped a friend prepare for her wedding, taking mental notes. In my diary, I practiced over and over, Madame Charles Legrand, Augustine Legrand; I designed monograms with C-A-L and began to embroider a set of napkins, to be followed by a tablecloth. I lived a dreamy half-life in the present, consumed with Charles's return and the proposal I knew was imminent. It was so real to me that it was difficult, sometimes, to realize it had only existed in my imagination.

He did not come back. Neither his breastplate nor his helmet nor his saber had saved him, nor had his father the general, his commander Murat, nor the Emperor. He had ridden out on patrol in Madrid as usual on 2 May 1808, been pulled from his horse, and knifed in the belly by someone who knew not him, Charles, as an individual at all, only that he wore the hated French uniform, and that killing him meant one less Frenchman in this world. The doctors could not save him. He was buried in a mass grave and all his glowing, impressive, ultimately useless armor had been put aside to be given to someone else. His parents received his meager personal effects – including my letters and miniature portrait – and a glowing, impressive, and ultimately useless letter from his colonel assuring them his death was not in vain.

Nor was it unavenged. Retaliatory action was taken on the following day. Suspected rebels were rounded up and shot on the third of May with an impersonal efficiency that matched Charles's killing. The Emperor and Charles's father had been satisfied, but they were accustomed to ordering men to their deaths. All I could feel was the emptiness of his absence from the world, my life, and the future I had imagined for both of us.

Charles's parents were very kind to me. Madame Legrand took off the gold ring she wore on her little finger and pressed it into my hand. "For you, my almost-daughter-in-law." She cried again after she said it, mourning all his years unlived, all her grandchildren unborn. I whispered, "*Merci, belle-maman*," and my own tears flowed. I have worn that ring on the little finger of my right hand from that day to this, even on my wedding day. I have it on now as I write.

I completed but one napkin with our initials. I used it to wrap his letters, his portrait, and the part of my heart that went with him, and stored them in my trunk with other girlhood keepsakes. For years at a time I forgot they were there, but I kept them always.

I had not the heart to pick up my pencils and paintbrushes. I did not go to Taunay's studio for weeks. Fellow students came to offer me their condolences and sit with me in sympathetic silence. I much preferred that to the reassurances of my parents and their friends. "You're young," they told me. "You will recover. It will hurt less. One day you will find someone else." It was all I could do not to scream at them. I did not want to recover. I did not wish to contemplate a future with someone else, as though Charles could be so easily replaced. I wanted to die, too.

I wondered if Charles's death pleased Maman and Papa in some obscure way, vindicating their belief that loving a soldier was unreliable at best. They never said so, but my suspicions caused me to keep at arm's length what genuine solace they might have given, and to further enclose myself in my grief.

Of course, Grandmère Augustine chose this moment to make one of her rare visits and tell me how unbecoming black was to one so young. "No need for you to wear widow's weeds," she said briskly. Maman made me put on a blue dress, but it no longer fit properly; I had lost weight. This gave Grandmère a new subject to harp on. Cakes and rich cream sauces were thrust in front of me until I felt like a Strasbourg goose, force fed to fatten me up. It was a relief to me when the hot weather drove her back to Besançon.

Oh, Charles! When I imagined our future, the Empire was at its apogee and we thought its success would go on forever. We could not imagine the humiliation, and political chaos that lay ahead, and the hard choices we would need to make. Would you, too, have grown as bitter and disillusioned as I? Perhaps, after all, it was better to go out in a blaze of youthful enthusiasm.

Chapter 4

Paris, 1808-1809

All too soon after Charles's death, I was again in mourning, this time for my beloved Papa. His final illness came upon him suddenly in the autumn. He was not so very old, perhaps sixty. The doctor said it was his heart. Maman, my brother and sister and I sat at Papa's bedside, hands quietly folded in our laps, too stunned at first to cry. When Maman began to sob and my brother and sister reached out to comfort her, I sat still. Papa had been the anchor of our world. Losing him, I feared, would bring chaos. I kept vigil the rest of that long day and dolorous evening, long after the others had gone to bed, until I fell asleep in the chair.

The front room of the house became a mourning chapel, hung with black velvet cloth embroidered with silver tears. Dressed in his best suit, Papa lay in the fine coffin Maman had ordered. Candles burned at its head and foot. Papa had been a popular man; we received a steady stream of visitors. Their kind words were a comfort, especially to Maman.

There was also some comfort in the forms and ceremonies of the funeral, my prayers and the priest's blessings. With two wrenching deaths coming so close together I was afraid that if I allowed myself to feel pain, I would be overwhelmed by it. I preferred to be numb, feeling and doing nothing at all. I stopped painting, drawing, reading, embroidering. I ate very little. Soon my face was thin and drawn, but I was indifferent to my appearance.

Denon had been away with the army when Papa died. When he returned, he came to the house to pay his respects. He opened his arms to give me a big hug, so that for a moment I felt as if I were again in my father's arms. My tears started to flow. He held me while I cried and produced a large white handkerchief so that I could blow my nose and dry my tears. Looking up to thank him, I realized that he was in his sixties, even older than Papa, and was gripped with a pang of fear that this protector, too, might be snatched from me.

He gave me a long assessing look and was not pleased by what he saw. He talked with Maman in a low voice; I heard only snatches of their conversation. He was relieved to hear that Papa had left an estate of over two hundred thousand francs, so that we were far from destitute. "But Tine concerns me. Has she been ill?"

Maman told him. He had not realized the depth of my attachment to Charles, but he had met him and was able to say kind things in a voice pitched just loud enough for me to overhear. I was grateful and gave a faint smile. "That's better," he said approvingly.

A month later, Denon returned to the house and announced that he had an important matter to discuss with Maman and me. We sat in the front room, which had been returned to its everyday function and appearance. Maman and I were dressed in black. I had put up my hair in the style that Charles liked best, with dark ringlets framing my face. I wore no ornaments or jewelry except for the gold ring Madame Legrand had given me. Every so often I would touch it and turn it round my finger for comfort and strength, the way another woman might touch a cross at her throat.

Denon had momentous news – he had found a candidate for my hand! Maman smiled. A prosperous man, an artist, one of the select few favored by the Emperor himself, and a particular favorite of the Empress! Maman relaxed and beamed more at every word. I kept my face neutral but inwardly grew wary. The artists favored by the Emperor were all, from my nineteen-year-old point of view, old men. I wished for a husband nearer my own age, as Charles would have been.

"Which one?" I asked in a resigned tone of voice.

"Antoine-Jean Gros, your favorite."

My favorite painter? Perhaps. My preferred bridegroom? "But he's so *old*!" I exclaimed, before I could stop myself.

Maman scowled. "There are very few men your age who are not soldiers. You know all too well the risks they run!"

"Maman!" I protested, shocked that she should say something so unfeeling, so soon after Charles's death. I bit back the bitter reply that rose to my lips.

"He is of an age and state of health that will prevent him from being conscripted into the army. He will be able to care for you for years to come," Denon replied in a soothing voice. "His artistic skills are highly valued by the Emperor and Empress."

I was reassured by this despite myself. Such stability seemed very attractive.

"I agree to receive a visit from Monsieur Gros, if it will make you both happy," I told them with a resigned sigh, making clear my reluctance. I averted my gaze to avoid watching them conspire to marry me off. Out of the corner of my eye I could see Maman nodding enthusiastically to make up for my indifference.

Before he departed, Denon came over to me and cupped my chin in his hand, raising my head gently so that I looked into his eyes. "Tine, I want only what is best for you and your family. With your Papa gone, you need a mature man to look out for all of you. Henri is too young – and anyway the sort that will always look out for himself," he added wryly. He smiled at me. "I think you will find Gros worth a closer acquaintance."

Far from being reassured, however, I felt ill. Maman and Denon were in such perfect agreement that the match was so eminently sensible that what *I* thought and wanted did not seem to matter at all. This marriage seemed to be settled before Monsieur Gros and I had properly met. I wanted to scream; but what good would it do? What alternatives were possible? I was not cut out for the religious life. I did not yet have the painting skills that would enable me to support myself as an artist. I was finally emerging from the numb emotional state with which I had coped with the deaths of Charles and Papa. I felt raw and vulnerable, like a sea creature without its protective shell. I wept that night, missing Papa, his love, and his power to intervene on my behalf. I did not go to my mother for comfort, knowing I would find little there. I thought of going to Madame Legrand, but I could not bring myself to tell her of another man in my life. I felt alone and afraid.

Gros wrote the next day, proposing to call upon us two days after that. Maman replied on our behalf.

For our meeting, Maman insisted that I wear something other than black. Deep mourning was not the most auspicious of costumes for meeting a prospective suitor. I chose a dress of simple white cotton that my sister had embroidered with white flowers – a blank canvas for the start of a new life – and small gold earrings. I refused to leave off my gold ring, over Maman's objections. She was in black, as was the custom for widows; one saw all too many of them as the Empire dragged on. Her black dress formed a backdrop against which, she assured me, I would shine all the more brightly.

As the hour of his visit approached, I sat nervously with Maman in the front room. When the maid announced Monsieur Gros, we stood to welcome him. Shyly I met his eyes for a moment but looked down again quickly as he greeted my mother.

I had seen Gros several times since first meeting him at the Salon of 1804, but always at a distance, never to talk with him. I had certainly never contemplated him in the role of lover and bridegroom. I scrutinized him now as carefully as manners would allow. He was short and slight, unlike my tall imposing Charles, and exactly twice my age. His brown hair was no longer curling over his collar but cut short and graying a little at the temples, not an unpleasant effect. He was scrupulously clean and dressed in his customary immaculate black suit and white shirt and cravat. Magpie colors, I thought, and could almost imagine the blue sheen that he would give off in the sunlight. For the first time in months, I felt an impulse to giggle. He wore proudly in his lapel the insignia of the *Légion d'honneur* that he had recently received from the Emperor's own hand. His unsmiling face looked very stern and I inwardly quailed at the prospect of "loving, honoring, and obeying" him. Although he no longer carried his ebony cane (his health, he said, had improved when he no longer needed to stand for hours on end in his damp, cold Versailles studio), he stood stiffly to attention, all too like a reluctant groom at the altar. I did not realize until afterward that the rheumatism he had contracted in painting *Jaffa* made some movements stiff and painful for him. For a moment neither of us spoke, as we regarded each other.

"Enchanted to meet you," I said, softly and nervously, falling back on formula. The ice was broken. At last he smiled, animation came to his face, and the stiff mask was gone. I realized in some surprise that he was as shy as I. I gave one of those nervous little laughs that one so often feels embarrassed about afterwards, but to my relief, he too laughed. His eyes began to sparkle and he acted more naturally. Warming to his role of suitor, he began to say witty things. I wish I could recall some now. Clearly, he was exerting himself to please me. He was a man who knew how to be charming in the presence of women, an invaluable quality in a portrait painter. I *was* charmed.

Moreover, he moved in high circles. He spoke of Joséphine, our Empress; of the Emperor's sister Caroline Murat; of the Duchesse d'Abrantès, wife of General Junot, the hero of the battle of Nazareth; of palaces and salons and ladies' dresses, fans and tiaras (he had an eye for fashion and for what would suit each woman best); of the splendors of the Tuileries, Napoleon's chosen palace; of the Elysée Palace, where the Murats lived; and of Joséphine's beloved Malmaison, with its grey and gold silk interiors and its gardens with hundreds of roses and rare flowers. He had seen them all. His paintings, he said modestly, hung in each one. The two hours flew by. We were entranced. When Maman invited him to visit again, I seconded her warmly.

Three days later he came bearing a large box of bonbons from Debauve, whose chocolate coins called *pistoles* were all the rage. On this visit he was introduced to my sister and brother. Ange at sixteen found the thought of any suitor exciting. Thirteen-year-old Henri, who wanted to be a painter and had been studying at Taunay's studio for several months, regarded Gros with open hero-worship.

Maman drew Gros's attention to the paintings on the wall of our salon. He looked over Henri's student work and said, in a non-committal voice, what every mother hopes to hear: "He shows promise." Maman beamed; she and Henri tactfully withdrew.

Gros looked at my two military scenes much more attentively, examining them minutely without saying anything. Why did he not smile? I grew nervous, fearing to have my work dismissed as Henri's had been.

Finally, he turned to me with a warm smile of approval, and I could let out the breath I hadn't realized I was holding. "You've done well, with lively action and good use of color. I like the brushwork here and here," he said, pointing out passages. "You haven't quite got the twist of this figure" – a woman casting an admiring glance over her shoulder at the hussars – "but I commend you for not being afraid to try things beyond your skills. That is how you will learn how to do them." He went on in this vein, warming to his role as teacher.

Encouraged by his praise, I told him, "These are the kinds of subjects I wish to paint. Not the grand battles you do so beautifully – I would not dream of attempting something so vast – but military scenes."

His smile faltered for a moment. "You have ambitions for a career as a painter." It came out as a statement rather than a question, but in a thoughtful voice, as if he were considering the idea for the first time.

It was my turn to be surprised. "Didn't Denon tell you? It was he who first encouraged me."

"Of course he told me of your studies. And your work is quite good. It's just that my mother gave up her painting when my sister and I were born, to devote herself to taking care of us and my father, so I assumed…" I must have looked as disappointed as I felt, because he quickly amended, "It appears I was hasty in my assumption."

I could breathe again.

Our courtship fell into a comfortable pattern. One evening a week he came to dinner; on another evening, he took me to a play or concert or opera. On Sunday afternoons we went out again, sometimes on our own, sometimes with my family. After two weeks we began to call each other by our first names and use the familiar *tu* instead of the formal *vous*. I had yet to meet his mother or sister, however, as they were visiting friends in the country.

We spent one memorable afternoon with Anne-Louis Girodet, his best friend since their days as David's students and a painter of immense talent and unconventional imagination. Their bond strengthened during their time in Italy, when Girodet nursed Gros back to health in Florence, and Gros did the same for him in Genoa. Girodet told me, warmly, how happy he was that Antoine would now have someone to look after him. "He needs more taking care of than he likes to admit," he said. (Fortunately Antoine was across the room and could not hear us.) Girodet's ungainly face with its heavy jaw and wild aureole of dark hair softened into an unexpected beauty as he gave his friend a fond glance. With a rare flash of insight, I knew that he loved Antoine, who did not reciprocate that love in the same way, and that Girodet had long ago come to terms with this, but not without regret. That he should nonetheless welcome me so warmly was another act of love on his part. On impulse I stood on tiptoe and kissed his cheek, startling but pleasing him. "I will," I promised, with tears in my eyes.

Reluctant as I had been to consider Antoine as a suitor, I found myself warming to his attentions. He knew how to charm and to please. He did not press physical attentions upon me, merely chaste kisses on both cheeks in greeting and parting. I was grateful that he did not expect more of me than that. But one day when I was by myself in the Tuileries, strolling in search of a likely sketching spot, I came across a blond hussar kissing his sweetheart with youthful exuberance, eliciting from her a response in kind. I do not think they even noticed me. All the pent-up desire that I had locked away after Charles died came rushing upon me. I ached to be held and kissed with such ardor. Had another young soldier approached me, I would willingly have thrown myself into his arms so that I could again feel desired. But every man in uniform seemed to have a sweetheart on his arm or be deep in conversation with a friend. It was as if I, too, had died and now returned no more substantial and visible than a ghost, to haunt the garden. Tears running down my face reassured me that I was among the living, but no one stopped to inquire what was wrong.

I could not go home in this state. I made my way to a nearby garden café and sat at a table in the corner. A pot of tea helped to steady me. I will be married, I thought. Antoine and I will share a bed. I tried to imagine making love to this chaste stranger who had never shown passion in his courtship, and I shivered.

Two days after this, Antoine stopped at our home in mid-morning to explain that he could not take me for our planned outing, as he needed to go to the Versailles studio where he produced his monumental works, to pick up a drawing that Denon wished to show to the Emperor.

"That's all right. I would enjoy seeing your studio!" I assured him. "Just let me change my shoes and fetch my shawl."

He looked startled. "I don't allow—" he began to say, until he reminded himself, with a visible effort, that I was the girl whom he was courting. He smiled and added, "But of course, you're a very special visitor. Wrap up warmly – it's a cold drafty place in any season."

I put on boots and long sleeves, and took a coat instead of a shawl. It was the first time I had been to Versailles. To my disappointment, we did not approach the imposing palace through the front gates but entered the grounds by a utilitarian side gate. Antoine's studio was in the Jeu de Paume, the old tennis court at a little distance from the palace, a plain box of a building from which any royal insignia had long since been stripped. Inside, it was an impressive space with a high ceiling and windows that flooded the interior with light. The scents of oil paints and turpentine were familiar ones, however, like being back at Taunay's studio in the Louvre, and I felt at home. But unlike the Louvre, with the noise of a teeming city making its way through even closed windows, here it was eerily silent.

While Antoine looked for the drawing he wanted, leafing through a portfolio here, a haphazard pile there, I examined the finished and half-finished paintings that hung on the walls or stood on easels. I smiled in recognition at small early versions of *Jaffa* and *Aboukir*. I was puzzling over a study for another battle scene I did not recognize, when Antoine came to stand beside me.

"The battle of Nazareth, a great victory for General Junot," he told me. "It was to have been even larger than

Aboukir. That is when I was given this space for a studio. But the commission was canceled because of politics." He gave a frown of disgust at that word but did not elaborate. "I re-used the canvas for *Jaffa*."

The sole large canvas in the studio was one with portraits of Napoleon and Francis II of Austria. The painting had evidently been unfinished for some time. "The *Meeting of the Two Emperors*," he explained, his eyes lighting up as they dwelt on Napoleon's face, "not one of my more inspiring Imperial commissions, not enough action to it. I had to put it aside when they asked me to paint *The Battle of Eylau*. I was about to take up work on it again when I got a new commission this spring." He took my hand and led me to a table with several sketches of the Emperor in a tent, receiving an apologetic group of men who stood hat in hand.

It was the first time I had had the opportunity to see how he developed his ideas from loose pen sketches to more careful studies, and I examined the series of drawings with great interest. "What is the subject?" I asked him. It could have represented any of a dozen cities or countries Napoleon had conquered.

"It's the surrender of Madrid," he replied. "I think I might need to put in a figure in native dress to make clear the location."

"Madrid," I repeated. I shut my eyes, trying not to let the tears fall, without success. I started to turn away so that he should not see me, when I felt his arms go around me and hold me tight. He kissed my hair several times and murmured endearments. He could be affectionate after all. I leaned against his coat, comforted. We stood like that for several minutes before I felt composed enough to draw back and wipe my eyes. I started to apologize but he shook his head.

"Denon told me about your friend who was killed there. I envy him: to have been loved so much is a precious gift indeed." He averted his eyes as he said it and his face was pained. He knew he was not my first choice.

I felt a stab of compassion for him, a funny little twist of the heart. I reached forward to take his hand. He turned to look at me then.

"That doesn't mean I can't learn to care for you, Antoine," I was surprised to hear myself say.

"I'm thirty-eight and it is high time I married. The lean years of my youth are behind me. Napoleon's Empire will continue for many years – many more commissions will

come. I can afford to support a wife and raise a family."
Was he seeking to persuade me – or himself?

I sneezed and he came out of his reverie. "You are cold
– let's go into the town for a hot drink." To my
disappointment, we did not venture into the palace or its
fabled gardens. I was not to see them until Louis-Philippe,
our current king, had made them a museum – and it was
my artist friend Josée I came with, not Antoine.

We had been keeping company for several weeks when
I received a note from Antoine inviting me to go with him
the next day to Malmaison, where Empress Joséphine was
to pose for a portrait. Would I like to meet her and see the
fabled residence of which he had spoken so often and so
warmly? I was not to worry about what to wear, as this
was not a formal presentation at court but a visit to her
home; any of my dresses would be suitable. He would hire
a fiacre and call for me at eight. He apologized for the
early hour, but the sitting needed to take place before her
busy daily schedule began. When it was done, we would
be free to explore her famous gardens.

Of course I wrote back that I would be delighted to
come. Malmaison! Joséphine!

Maman was in ecstasies, tempered only by regrets that there was not time to purchase a new dress for the occasion. I reminded her that I had bought two in the last month to wear for Antoine; they could hardly be called *old*.

"Tine, let your foolish old mother have her little excitements. A new outfit for you to meet the Empress is one of them." She spoke in a tone half-humorous, half-petulant. It struck me forcefully then, as it had not before, how much her dreams and hopes now centered on me.

"Of course, Maman." I kissed her, startling her. "Dream of me in a court dress all you like." I bade her good night; she was smiling as she turned to go to her room.

I wore a white dress with a high waist that Pauline, already skilled at embroidery, had decorated with floral designs in pale blue that gave the fine muslin a subtle richness. I was delighted to be able to show off Pauline's fine work. Over it I wore my new coat with a red plaid ribbon at the waist and rows of ruffles at the sleeves, neck and hem. My carefully curled brown hair framed my face under an equally ruffled bonnet with a red flower at one side. Pale blue shoes, with ribbons that laced over the instep and around the ankle, completed the outfit.

It was a crisp spring morning, a perfect day for the drive out to the pretty town of Rueil, where the Empress' house was located. It was only a few miles outside Paris but everything was fresh and green, the sounds and smells completely different.

Our fiacre was given immediate entry at the gate; Antoine addressed the sentry by name and inquired after his children. On the drive to the house he pointed things out with the ease of long familiarity. The cab drew up at the porte-cochere and a liveried footman handed us out and through the doorway. A woman met us there.

"Ah, you've arrived; she's been waiting for you." Although we were in good time, this was said with an air of reproof. Gros, to my surprise, seemed faintly amused by it. ("That's Mademoiselle Bonnelle for you," he told me later. "Joséphine is the center of her world and she regards all things only as they relate to her mistress – usually as they fall short in relation to her." I thought, by her superior air, she must be a lady-in-waiting of noble rank, but he explained that she was merely Joséphine's personal maid of long standing. It always amused him, he said, to hear her refer to her mistress and herself with the imperial "we.")

Mademoiselle Bonnelle took us to the Empress' dressing room. Through an open door I could see her bedchamber with its fabled swan bed. I had to remind myself not to gawk like a simpleton. Antoine presented me, and I gave my best curtsy, having practiced before my mirror that morning. I feared I might catch my heel or otherwise blunder at the crucial moment. Joséphine acknowledged me briefly and returned to the business at hand, dressing for her portrait. She had already put on a short-sleeved white dress trimmed with gold braid on the bodice and showed us the overskirt she would wear with it, made from a creamy white cashmere shawl with borders of large red and green leaves on each end. Its drawstring waist was threaded with long gold cords that hung down in front.

Now she needed to choose which one of the several dozen shawls she owned should go over her shoulder to form a train to the dress. Another maid had been busy for some time unfolding them in the dressing room so Gros could help her select one. The effect was of an oriental cloth merchant's shop. I found myself drawn into the decision-making, helping the maid unfold yet more. Being able to tell Maman, Pauline and my friends that I had handled the Empress' shawls made it well worth an hour of acting as her lady's maid. It was a pleasure to handle such beautiful soft material, far more luxurious than anything I could afford. I was flattered when Joséphine asked my opinion and immensely gratified when she chose, in the end, the red shawl that I had suggested. I said earnestly that it would not only complement the other components of the painting but was also a favorite color of Antoine's to paint. Afterward I blushed because of course Joséphine had known him and his work for years longer than I had. But she smiled and told him that my air of shy possessive pride was very bride-like and appealing. He arranged the red shawl over her left shoulder and agreed that its color went beautifully with the border of the skirt. He added a red sash to the dress. She did not wear any of her rubies for the portrait, although she was well known for her legendary jewels. A simple white lace veil covered her hair.

Antoine then set her pose and made his preliminary sketch. He worked quickly, as was his custom. The maid and I began to fold up the other shawls but Joséphine told us to wait. When the sketch was finished, she told me to pick one out as a gift from her, to thank me for my help.

"Oh, you don't need to do that – it was my pleasure!"

"To congratulate you on your engagement, then. Don't be shy – which one would you like?"

Antoine signaled me urgently to accept. Encouraged, I reached for one in pale yellow, but Joséphine shook her head. "No, not that, it will make you look sallow." She made me try on a dozen before she was satisfied with my choice, creamy white with smaller flowers on the embroidered border and red petals scattered throughout. Snuggling in its warm folds, I was speechless in my delight.

This was enough for Joséphine. "I wish half the ladies at court showed such genuine pleasure." Then, to Antoine, "I congratulate you on your choice of bride – may you be together always." To my surprise she gave a little sob on the "always." Gros reached out and put a sympathetic hand on her arm. She took it in hers and clasped it briefly for comfort, like an old friend. She smiled apologetically at me. "You must not think I am taking liberties with your fiancé, but he is one of the few I can rely upon these days to be unchanging in his affections."

Antoine explained as we strolled through the gardens to find the ideal background for the portrait. "The Emperor wants a son to inherit his empire and start a dynasty –

rumor has it that he wants to divorce her to marry the daughter of Francis of Austria."

"How *could* he?" I exclaimed, indignant. David's painting of the *Coronation*, with the imperial crown being conferred upon the Empress by the Emperor, had been the sensation of the Salon the previous autumn.

"Keep your voice down!" he cautioned, nervously looking around to see if anyone had overheard. Satisfied that no one had, he continued, in a voice quieter still, "He is the Emperor; he can do as he pleases." He was neither condoning nor excusing: it was a simple statement of fact. Then he smiled at me. "Don't worry, my dear, we lesser mortals wed for life."

We walked on. From time to time I stopped to smell the roses that were just beginning to blossom, agreeably surprised by the variety in their scents as well as their colors. Enough chill remained in the air to make me glad of the cashmere shawl. Made bold by it, I said, "The Empress congratulated you on your choice of wife but you haven't actually proposed to me yet."

"Oh – I thought Denon made clear – it has been understood since the beginning – I was only waiting until you had met my mother —"

"He did and it has, and I am looking forward to meeting her – but we are already being congratulated on our wedding, and you still haven't asked." A petulant note had crept into my voice. I didn't want it to spoil an otherwise splendid morning. "A woman still likes to be asked," I said with a smile and an arch look, to take away any sting in my words.

He turned to face me then and removed his hat, holding it over his heart. His other hand reached for mine. "My dear, I hope you will forgive a middle-aged man if he does not go down on arthritic knees on this rather muddy garden path – but my request is heartfelt nonetheless. Mademoiselle Dufresne – Augustine – will you marry me?"

"Monsieur Gros – Antoine – I will."

Maman and Pauline were thrilled that the engagement had been made official. Their admiration of Joséphine's shawl, too, was all that I could have wished for. The two events combined to make me feel transformed into a woman of fashion and prospects. Men raised their hats to me. Antoine's acquaintances complimented him on me. I could sense other women's envy. (I have the shawl still and am wearing it as I write, to ward off the chill and keep good memories close.)

I saw Joséphine several times more but never again on such intimate terms. Her divorce from the Emperor was decreed at about the time of our wedding in July 1809. After that, she largely retired from public life and saw only a few intimates, of which Gros was one. He usually visited her alone, as he had done before our marriage.

Soon after our visit to Malmaison, Antoine took me to meet his teacher David, whom he revered as a father figure. Much as I detested his politics – as a member of Parlement in 1793 he had voted for the execution of Louis XVI – I could not but respect him as the finest painter of our age. He said a few polite words to me that I found almost unintelligible because of his injured mouth, the result of an old fencing wound. He interrupted my reply to tell Antoine about a new idea he had for a painting with a classical subject. My compliments on the *Coronation* died in mid-sentence; I was left feeling a fool. I stole a look at Antoine to see how he had reacted to this rudeness. His face was shining, eager, drinking in the master's words. Both men seemed to have forgotten not only that I was there but that I, too, was an artist. I wished I could weigh in with an intelligent contribution, but the painting's subject was not one with which I was familiar. Perhaps it was one of those lesser-known self-sacrifice subjects from Roman history that were meant to stir grand emotions but always left me cold. All I could do was stand there and try to look interested while they talked over my head.

Antoine, who had been offering me his arm, had dropped it to be able to gesture more freely with both hands. Suddenly Antoine said my name, pulling me back to their conversation, wanting me to chime in that David's concept was superb. I had lost track of it but of course agreed with an enthusiasm that sounded false to my own ears. David, who could not be bothered with me for my own sake, was immensely gratified to lap up my words of praise. Only then did he congratulate Gros on his choice of bride.

I was seething by the time we finally left, but Antoine, still in high spirits, didn't notice. He went on to excitedly tell me another tale of the master, expecting me to enter into his mood.

"I was humiliated. I felt like a fool when he cut me off like that. I was trying to pay him a compliment!"

"Oh, but that's just David being David. You mustn't take it personally." This was the first but not the last time I had heard that explanation for someone's unpardonable behavior. It has always seemed to me no excuse at all. Gros said it fondly, even proudly, as though it set David apart from the ordinary race of mortals.

"And what of you, my fiancé? Was that just Antoine being Antoine?" I had come to the real subject of my dissatisfaction.

He stopped and turned to face me. "Augustine." His voice was low and unhappy. "You know it isn't." I said nothing. I looked down, not meeting his eyes. What he said was true, and I blamed Monsieur David rather than him for the incident, but I did not want to forgo my advantage. I was taking my revenge by testing my power.

In April, Antoine's mother at last returned from the countryside, and Maman and I were invited for a Sunday afternoon visit. For the first time I would see the home that would become mine. (It would not have been proper for me to be there alone with him in his mother's absence.) I decided to wear the dress in which I had met the Empress, with the shawl she had given me. Afterward I realized how appropriate this had been: his mother was a far more forbidding imperial presence.

Madame Gros was seated at the far end of the salon. Its furnishings were of good quality, but worn and shabby, the carpet threadbare in places. The paneling was in the Rococo style of sixty years before with a green and white color scheme that must have been sprightly when new but was now dingy and peeling in places. I was surprised – I had thought him prosperous enough to afford a better home than this, with newer things.

Madame Gros remained seated as Antoine introduced us. She smiled at Maman and shook her hand, then patted the sofa for me to sit beside her. "When I left at Easter, my son was a contented bachelor. I return to find him engaged to someone I have never even heard about, much less met. Come, let me see the charmer who has captured his heart." The words were said in a flat, humorless tone.

I sat, unsure how else to reply.

"How did you meet?" she asked me.

"Through Denon. He was an old friend of my father's."

"Taking time out from his many duties to play matchmaker. I suppose I should be thankful that it was a woman he saw fit to introduce to Antoine." She turned to her son. "What did he do, send a letter of commission promising the usual fee of twelve thousand francs?"

"Maman! He introduced us, that is all. As we grew to know each other—"

"You found each other irresistible. So much so that you would not think of telling me about her, trusting that when I met her, I would understand. So here I am. I have met her. Enlighten me."

Even Maman's determined smile faltered at such rudeness. Antoine said nothing, like a little boy scolded by Mama. I drew the folds of my shawl closer, comforted by their warmth and the thought of Joséphine's approval. I fought back tears.

Having made her point, Madame Gros relented. "Forgive an old woman's teasing." Teasing? "He should have been married long since. I am happy for him that he has found someone he likes." The words were warm and Maman and Antoine both relaxed, but there was an undercurrent to them that I could hear even if they could not: *don't ever delude yourself that you will replace me in his affections.*

It was a daunting prospect that gave me serious doubts about the match. It might not have been so bad had she lived with Gros's sister and her family, but Antoine expected us to live at home as he had always done.

Fortunately, I did not then realize that we were to live with his mother for the next twenty-two years.

I tried to discuss my fears with Maman, but she was no help. Having made up her mind for the match, she would hear no doubts, no second thoughts. Nothing would stand in the way of concluding my marriage to a wealthy, successful man at the peak of his career. It was the one thing that had cheered her since Papa's death, bringing congratulations from her friends instead of pity. To tell them that I had broken it off because I had taken fright at my future mother-in-law was unthinkable. Worse, it would call forth ridicule. "You'll work it out," she said firmly. "She seemed perfectly nice to *me*. You're imagining things."

Not for the first time, I missed Papa. Denon was away on campaign again. None of my friends faced the same situation. I felt very alone.

My mind went round and round the problem. *Perhaps she won't live very long*, I thought hopefully. Hastily I crossed myself and said a prayer of penance. I did not want to wish for her death – just her acceptance and perhaps one day her love.

I was hesitant to discuss it with Antoine, though he was now the one to whom I must learn to turn for help in all things. How could I tell him that I disliked his mother at first acquaintance? Young and inexperienced though I was, instinct told me not to divide his loyalties. It would be up to me to get along with his mother. But how?

To my relief Antoine himself brought up the subject at our next meeting. "I scolded Maman for her rudeness on Sunday. It was I with whom she was angry. She should not have been angry with you." Away from her presence, he sounded manly and determined, but I remembered how he had stood like a scolded little boy while her ire was heaped upon us. "She asked me to give you this with her apologies, and she hopes you will visit again soon so that she will have the chance to get to know you properly."

He handed me a small jeweler's box. I lifted the lid in anticipation but instead of gold or silver I found, nestled on velvet, a miniature portrait of Antoine, younger, his face thinner and his hair not yet tinged with grey. I didn't know what to say.

"It was painted when I returned from Italy eight years ago. She commissioned it from—" He named one of those who made their living from faces, reliable and talented but of no grand ambitions such as Antoine's and mine. "She asked if I had given you a portrait yet, and when I said I had not, she asked me to give you this one."

What an appropriate expression of a fond mother's love. His words were reassuring, but my doubts remained. My subsequent meetings with his mother were better, but we never felt any genuine warmth for each other. I was always wary of more barbs and slights.

The courtship moved inexorably forward. All too soon, on 10 June 1809, it was time for the families to meet with Monsieur Robin, our notary (Papa's friend, in whose house we still lived), to draw up the marriage contract. Antoine came with his mother; Maman and I came with Pauline and Henri. The latter, as the man of the family, would be a witness to the contract. Monsieur Robin, who had prepared it in advance after discussions with both parties, read it aloud. Antoine would bring assets worth over one hundred thousand francs to the marriage. Madame Gros gave him a proud smile. This was clear evidence of his success: three important government commissions completed in the last four years, two others now under contract, and a steady stream of portraits. The Empire was then at its zenith and we expected official favor to continue for years to come.

Robin then turned to the assets that I would bring to the marriage: one-quarter of my father's estate, approximately fifty thousand francs, only half that amount. My heart gave a leap of hope. Perhaps the wedding would not go through after all.

Then my mother spoke up. "I will give to Augustine my own portion of the estate, so that she will have one hundred thousand francs and be on an equal footing."

"Maman!" Three voices protested simultaneously.

Robin was properly concerned. "Are you sure about this, Madeleine? You are giving away one-third of your combined capital. You still have two children at home. When Pauline marries, she will take her portion with her. Henri will not be earning for several years."

"I still have money of my own that I brought into the marriage. Neither my children nor I will starve. If we have need of aid in the future, I know my daughter and future son-in-law will not leave me in need." Madame Gros nodded approvingly and emphatically. "They will see that we do not want."

I was not about to give in easily. "Maman, think about Pauline and Henri. It's not fair to them to give me all your share!" My brother and sister looked grateful. We were too well bred to engage in a family disagreement in front of strangers, but they could not have been pleased at Maman's abrupt decision. Perhaps she announced it in public without prior discussion precisely to forestall arguments.

"Tine, I have made up my mind. I am only doing what is best for you."

I glanced at Antoine and his mother, who remained silent during this exchange. Gros had been watching the scene with interest but looked away when he saw me observing him. Madame Gros, her eyes lowered, was busily doing mental math with the aid of her fingers, calculating how much additional income the extra capital would bring. Antoine nudged her to stop; her air of calculation was replaced by an elaborate detachment from the mere mention of money.

Robin made the change in the draft, and the reading continued.

While his clerks were making the several copies needed – one for each party, one for his office, and one for the *mairie*, the administrative office for the district – he brought out the champagne and cakes he had prepared for a celebration. He gave a charming little speech about watching me grow up into a fine young woman – how proud my father would have been at this moment!

I thought, *If Papa were still alive, there would not be this moment. I would not be married off like this.* I gave a little sob.

Maman did not reach out to comfort me. It was Antoine who took my hand and gave it a reassuring squeeze. I realized that I had been transferred to his care.

I signed the contracts where Robin indicated. The marriage was going forward, and I would simply have to make the best of it.

Chapter 5

Toulouse and Paris, 1809-1812

Antoine chose Toulouse for our honeymoon. He had always wanted to visit this, his late father's native city. We spent a happy three weeks here. For the first time I was able to look after my husband without his mother telling me how her son had always liked things to be done – and therefore how they *should* be done. I do not know whether Antoine noticed the difference between one woman and the next as long as they looked after his needs, but freedom from Maman Madeleine certainly raised *my* spirits. At last I felt like a proper wife. We had tender moments. I recall the day he bought me a red silk rose. We also had a chance to discover the pleasures of intimacy in a place out of her earshot. We were excited when I was late and thought I might be pregnant. It was a letdown to find out two days later that I was not. We assured each other that we had plenty of time.

But there was a darker side to our visit, bringing each of us face to face with our individual memories, ones too painful to share, leaving the other without a way to bring solace and comfort.

I had thought, in traveling from Paris and the places Charles and I had spent so many happy hours together, to put him from my mind. Instead, I found Toulouse a staging site for sending troops and supplies into Spain, its barracks full of soldiers. The many foundries powered by the swift-moving Garonne sent thick smoke into the air as they labored night and day to make guns and ammunition for the troops. Army supply wagons full of their manufactures rumbled to and from warehouses. Far from leaving Charles behind, I saw many like him, as raw and eager as he had been. My heart ached for them and for myself.

Antoine, on his part, met up with an old acquaintance from his time in Italy ten years earlier when he had been assigned to the army as one of Bonaparte's gatherers of artistic treasures. Sergeant Desnoyers greeted him fondly as a comrade-in-arms, and they spent an evening in the sitting room of our hotel suite swapping stories and recollections, while I, relishing my new role as wife and hostess, replenished their glasses and listened with wide eyes as I sewed baby clothes.

I saw a new side of Antoine, at home with army men far removed from the salons and museums of Paris. Like everyone else, I had been stirred by his image of the young whip-thin general Bonaparte striding to take possession of the bridge at Arcola during his first glorious campaign in Italy. During our engagement he had told me stories of his travels to Perugia, Milan, and Rome and the works of art he had seen there. But this was the first time I had heard about the hardships of the French retreat and his brush with death in the starvation and disease that gripped Genoa during the British siege in 1801. I learned how close I had come to losing my husband before even meeting him. The years fell away from the men as they talked, and I caught a glimpse of an Antoine almost as young as I.

When Antoine asked Desnoyers about Spain, clearly expecting to hear that the French were triumphing there as elsewhere in those magical years of Napoleon's zenith, my stomach clenched in dread. His friend's harsh reply – "They are a savage people. They do not deserve the liberation we are bringing them. They do not appreciate their privilege of our presence." – confirmed my fears. His face contorted with anger and he spat into the fire. Immediately he looked contrite and begged my pardon. "I forgot there was a lady present."

I nodded gravely, unable to smile. My hand trembled as I drew the thread in and out of the cloth. I fought hard to keep back my tears. I could not help glimpsing again the horrors of Charles's final moments. I did not want to speak to Antoine about the images this conjured up.

Instead I kissed him very tenderly that night and told him how happy I was that he had survived the siege. To my astonishment, he began to cry, my brave husband who only an hour before had shrugged off hardships as though they were one of the pleasures of youth. I held him and stroked his hair and face and murmured endearments, until his crying fit had spent itself. "It was—" Words failed him. His face grim, his haunted eyes looked past me. "When I finally reached home six months later, I swore I would never leave Paris again. It's taken eight years."

"Only to run into old memories," I finished for him. "Are you sorry we came here?"

"No, of course not." But when we went to bed, he did not reach out for me; he rolled on his side facing away and shrugged off the light touch of my hand on his back meant to comfort him. He did not seek out any more of his old comrades, and he watched the military preparations without further comment. It was several days before I could cheer him up again – and cheer myself. Our wedding trip, I thought, was no place for melancholy and I wished he would put it aside. In time he did, but that young vulnerable man I had glimpsed was gone, replaced by the middle-aged one who had built a cocoon of safety in Paris. There was afterwards a degree of reserve in his attitude to me, as if he regretted his tears.

Ours was a marriage of convenience – for our mothers. Could we make it work for ourselves?

Upon our return to Paris, I began married life by redecorating our apartment on the rue des Saints-Pères, the shabby state of which I had noted during my previous visits. Madame Gros, whom I was now allowed to call Maman Madeleine to distinguish her from my Maman, moved out of the largest bedroom, which now became ours. She preferred to keep her furnishings in her new room but was happy to have me take on the rest of the apartment. I was given a generous allowance for the services of house painters and carpenters, as well as new furniture and other decorations, on condition that I was guided in my purchases by Jacques Amalric, Antoine's brother-in-law. This I was happy to do. I realized it was a means of ensuring that at least some of the money would remain in the family, but I respected Antoine and his mother for their prudent handling of the funds.

Jacques, the husband of Antoine's sister Marie was a *marchand-mercier*, a merchant of all those luxury goods so useful in outfitting the homes of the wealthy and powerful. French and Chinese porcelains, crystal punchbowls and glasses, silver flatware and dishes, centerpieces and candelabra, clocks of all sizes, fine furniture with marquetry veneers, chandeliers hung with drops of rock crystal,; gilt bronze wall lights and fire dogs were just a few of the items in his shop. The trade in such goods had suffered with the demise of so many of the old aristocracy during the Revolution but recovered during the creation of a new aristocracy of the Empire.

Together with Jacques, I visited the studios of the *menuisiers-ébénistes* – the makers of both plain wood and upholstered furniture. For our bedroom, I ordered a mahogany wardrobe and dressing table from Bernard Molitor and a new bed from the firm of Jacob-Desmalter – not, mind you, as elaborate as the elegant swan bed they had created for Joséphine, nor with such a profusion of expensive gilt bronze mounts. From Jacob-Desmalter, too, I purchased a settee and chairs for our salon. From Jacques's shop I commissioned a new frame in the current style for the mirror over the fireplace and purchased bronze and porcelain ornaments. I made note of nursery furnishings that I would like when the time came.

When my purchases were delivered and installed in the newly repainted apartment, I could look around me with a sense of accomplishment and take pride in my up-to-date home. I invited Maman, Pauline, and all my friends to tea so that they too could admire it. Fortunately, Maman Madeleine was on her best behavior that day.

Jacques invited me to select a wedding gift from the shop. I chose a tête-à-tête, a delicately decorated porcelain tea service for two made by the Sèvres Manufactory. When I showed it to Antoine, however, he was upset: "But there are *three* of us!" Clearly I had married the mother as well as the son; by then I knew better than to debate the issue. I returned the tea set, knowing that Jacques would be sympathetic. As an in-law he understood the challenges of dealing with the formidable Madame Gros. He made me laugh by referring to her as "Madame Mère," the official title given to Napoleon's mother.

The following Sunday, he brought us a mantel clock surmounted by the gilt bronze figure of a woman painter at her easel, "for the new artist in our family." I was delighted with it and kissed him on both cheeks. Clocks of such quality and decoration were a luxury item far above anything I could have hoped to purchase. Maman Madeleine was torn between admiration of a son-in-law who could afford to give such an expensive gift and disdain for a new bride who started her marriage on a note of such luxury. She hoped I would not think I could continue acquiring items of this sort! I put the clock in our bedroom, moving it after Antoine's death to my painting studio in his mother's old room. There I hoped its extravagant ticking would keep her ghost at bay.

"But there are three of us!"

It was clear from the beginning that the dowager Madame Gros was an all-too-integral part of our married life. She ran the household, and her son's life, as she had done since Antoine's return from Italy eight years before. She knew his tastes, or perhaps she dictated them. She knew how to please him; she'd hired the servants, chosen which local tradesmen to patronize, and conferred with the cook about the day's menu. She kept him up-to-date on his sister's family, who came over every Sunday for dinner at any rate. My role, I quickly discovered, was not the normal prerogative of a bride to create new routines, but to apprentice in the ones his mother had laid down, so that I could take them over when her health began to fail. Even then she ruled the household with the iron rod of the invalid. I could neither manage things to please myself nor carry out her routines well enough to suit her. I appealed to my husband, but his pained expression indicated how much he hated to be bothered with domestic questions. He took his mother's side in any case. Antoine and I married in 1809; his mother lived until 1831. Antoine and I had only four years to ourselves before his death in the summer of 1835.

Nor could I escape by going out to my own studio, as he could. While he produced his larger works in his Versailles studio, he painted portraits and sketches for the large scenes in his Paris atelier, a cell in the former Couvent des Capucines. He had taken me there only once during our courtship. When I suggested that I too might set up my easel there, he rejected the idea without hesitation. Oh, no, that would not do! He had to work alone; only Girodet, his best friend in the neighboring cell, was allowed to interrupt him at will. Besides, all the artists there were men, it would be awkward. "It's a convent," I snapped. "Perhaps it is time to let the women back in." I was rewarded with a wan smile, but the tenor of his objections did not change.

"You'll only need a studio until the children come." I could set up a studio in the room designated as the nursery until it could be put to its intended purpose; it would be so much more convenient for me! *Oh yes?* I thought, *and Maman Madeleine can add her well-meaning comments about my painting to her comments on my lack of domestic skills.* As a miniaturist, Antoine's mother had always worked on a small space, a palette table. She didn't understand my need for a larger space in which my ideas could expand. Besides, any decision made by her son was immediately endorsed.

But I had no choice. Renting a studio of my own would cost more than I could afford, and I had so little of my own, barely enough for canvas and paints. As my husband, he had control, by law, over the income from my dowry and gave me an allowance for my personal expenses. I was forced to paint at home, like a dilettante. Both mothers felt it was a small compromise to make.

I was not the person to whom Antoine opened up easily. In times of worry or extreme emotion, it was to his mother or Girodet that he turned. Although he was not sexually drawn to other men, his closest emotional bond was certainly with them. In the presence of the great, pompous, self-important, money-grubbing Jacques-Louis David, he quivered with suppressed excitement. Rude braggadocio for which he would have excoriated another, he accepted in David without demur.

No, Antoine did not treat me as a helpmeet, a companion, and a source of comfort. I was merely his wife. I had to put up with his sulks and depressions, with long days when he would not speak except to ask about dinner, when tears were never very far from his eyes. I know that his friends found me unsympathetic, that they will say I was a bad wife. But I tried. Truly I did, with all the love of a young bride, a young wife. Maman Madeleine watched us and tried in her own way to give helpful advice, but I think she was secretly pleased that she, not I, was the woman to whom he turned most often.

Nor could my own mother help very much. Not for the first time, I missed my beloved father, thinking that *he* was someone whom I could have asked. Maman told me not to worry, that all couples went through a period of adjustment. Once the children came it was on them that my life would be centered for my emotional fulfillment. "Pray for a beautiful baby who will love you," she counseled. So I did, with fervent hope that dwindled month after month for twenty years, until it died.

I was never very close to Gros's sister, Jeanne-Marie-Cécile, called Marie. Although we spent time together to get acquainted we had little in common. Three years younger than her brother, she was still a generation older than I. She had married about the time that Antoine departed for Italy – just a few years after I was born – and was completely wrapped up in her family, one of those women with whom you can never have a coherent conversation because they are always being interrupted by the children and will not say "no" to them. Marie confessed she was grateful that I would be on hand to look after Maman Madeleine, who had turned sixty that year. "I've been worried because it's always been Maman who looked after Antoine, more than he after her. I'm so busy with my own family that there's really no time to look after Maman at all. It's all I can do to get us over there for Sunday dinner." She did not ask how I got on with her mother; I could sense that she did not wish to know, lest she have to cope with her mother's care instead of me. I was appalled by this attitude at the time; however, I must admit, in all fairness, that I did much the same in leaving my own mother to my sister's care.

One of Antoine's pleasures in the early days of marriage was showing off his connections to the powerful and introducing me to this world that I now shared by marriage. I had already been to Malmaison. Now he took me to the Tuileries, the palace that was the center of Bonaparte's empire. He had a pass that permitted him entry whenever he pleased.

We could easily have walked there from our flat – it was just a short distance across the river – but Antoine felt it more fitting that we should travel by fiacre and enter at the porte-cochere. I was glad of it, as the day was damp and I was wearing my best dress and Joséphine's shawl.

As we prepared for our visit, I watched Gros pin to his lapel the silver *Légion d'honneur* that the Emperor had given him. He wore it always with pride, a badge of honor and the mark of the Emperor's highest approval. I observed, not for the first time, how he stood a little taller and straighter after he put it on. While his battle paintings showed the excitement of heated conflict, he had taken pains to avoid actual fighting after his first taste of it in Italy. He was a little ashamed of this, as though weighed up and found wanting in his own opinion, compared to all those hardened veterans who had gone out year after year while he stayed home. The medal helped soothe him, telling him he too had served in his way.

Our objective that day was to see the Galerie de Diane, the long public gallery on the upper floor of the palace. It was a popular gathering place for the court as well as the site of official receptions and state dinners. The chairs, sofas, tables and cabinets placed along the walls were of the highest quality. Scattered among them were massive, skillfully carved tables and vases of Russian malachite mounted in gilt bronze, gifts from Tsar Alexander. But for me the highlights of the Galerie de Diane were the dozen monumental paintings by the leading artists of France that hung in shallow niches set in each wall. It was in this space in Bonaparte's chosen palace at the heart of the empire that Antoine's *Surrender of Madrid* and *Meeting of the Two Emperors* would hang as soon as he had finished them. Today he had to be content to extol Bonaparte's virtues – clemency, generosity, humane acts, the ability to lead and inspire – as others had rendered them.

My teacher Taunay had contributed an over-door of the *Crossing of the St. Bernard Pass*, a delightful scene of pine trees towering over the army and large clumps of falling snowflakes. Ostensibly celebrating a military feat, it nonetheless had an air of serenity about it that made me smile. This painting gave me heart and hope that I might one day be represented here. I knew I could not carry out a grandiose scene, but the size and subject of this one were within my grasp.

I was distracted from examining this and the other canvases as closely as I wanted to by the bustle of the crowd around me. It was important to attend court even when the Emperor was away from Paris, as his officials kept count of who came and reported this back to him. Thus the rooms were as full with the leading figures of society as if he were present. Some gave amused glances at this plain little *bourgeoise* who actually *looked* at the paintings instead of treating them as merely part of the setting. My fascination with the courtiers, however, lasted only until I overheard the utter banality of their conversation. Then I was able to return to my normal self and give the paintings their due.

The Revolt in Cairo, by Antoine's friend Girodet, had recently been placed in the gallery. It showed a tumult of hand-to-hand fighting between our troops and the turbaned natives that had taken place during the Egyptian campaign a dozen years earlier. A few foreground figures stood out – a hussar in red, white and blue who ran with his sabre upraised to challenge a dark, heroically nude native. This man countered the hussar's attack with a scimitar, even as he tenderly supported, with his other arm, a gorgeously dressed dying pasha. Another native seated on the ground dangled a French soldier's head by its blond braids. There were none of the calm virtues embodied by the other paintings but an energy and delight in the mêlée for its own sake.

A throng of courtiers had gathered in front of this work. The women tittered gently at the nude man, pretending to be shocked, while the men commented eagerly on the surging action and tangle of bodies. As I listened to their excited chatter I could not help looking back and forth between the crowd in the painting and the crowd observing it, imagining how the Galerie de Diane would look should they break out into a frenzy of violence – the shouts of the men, the screams of the women, the utter bewilderment of the liveried servants. An almost hysterical laugh bubbled up within me and would have burst out had I not smothered it in a fit of coughing. "Are you all right?" solicitous voices inquired. A footman appeared at my elbow with a glass of water on a tray.

When I had recovered I went in search of Antoine, whom I found laughing with a flirtatious young woman. I envied her beautiful costume – a dress of dark green silk and a pale green turban shot with gold and silver threads, with feathers that danced animatedly as she spoke. Her *parure* of emerald necklace, bracelets, rings and earrings winked in the candlelight.

"You wretch!" she cried, tapping him with her folded fan. "I heard you married! You didn't wait for me." She pouted to make her point. "She's a dazzling beauty who brought you a great fortune, I hope?"

I winced when I heard this: neither characteristic described me and only served to highlight the difference between us. "She's pretty enough and suits me very well," replied my husband. Not exactly rapturous words on the part of a newlywed, and my spirits sagged a little. I stole a look at Antoine; he too was animated in his charming flirtatious mode. He would no sooner consider marrying this woman than she would truly wait for him, but their banter was a social code they both knew and understood, to which I was an outsider. Antoine now looked for me, caught my eye, and signaled me to come over. I felt shy and tongue-tied, but the other woman put me at my ease with a practiced grace I envied whole-heartedly.

"Pretty enough, indeed!" she scolded Antoine, then praised my face, figure and shawl, and made suggestions for the feathers and jewels similar to her own that she would have had Antoine buy for me.

I was not displeased, but Antoine laughed outright. "One must be rich as your financier husband to afford them."

Again I felt my spirits fall. I had not brought him so great a fortune that he could afford such things. I was too shy to say anything else. It would have been rude to excuse myself to look at the paintings again. I was forced to stand there while their conversation flowed around me.

The woman, in the same teasing tone of voice, told Antoine that she had decided it was high time to commission another portrait. "My husband will be away on the Emperor's business and cannot take me with him. I must do *something* to while away the lonely hours—" with a meaningful wink at Antoine. Immediately he took out the small sketchbook he carried everywhere and made an appointment for her to come to the studio.

Before they could resume their conversation, however, an older but still commanding figure appeared in the doorway. He was twice her age, solid in his figure and balding. Small eyes peered out of a fleshy face. The woman had her back to him, but I could see how impatiently his eyes scanned the room. "Marie-Ange!" he bellowed as they came to rest on the woman. A look of intense annoyance came over her face, to be carefully smoothed away as she turned to smile at him. "Yes, my darling?"

"I've been ready to leave these ten minutes. Where have you been?"

"Standing here in plain sight, my love, waiting for you to find me." Her voice was musical, intending to tease him as she had teased Antoine, but I could detect an edge of tolerance in it.

"Well, let's go. I'm tired, and I have things to do before I leave tomorrow morning."

"Of course. But first, won't you at least allow me to present—"

"Another time, Marie-Ange. *Allons*!" She turned around, made a face at Gros with a slight shrug, whispered "*Désolée*" at me, and obediently followed her husband, whose expression softened into a dour smile as she turned the beam of her charm on him. I watched them thoughtfully until they faded from sight. For all her apparent advantages, she was no freer than I, merely tethered on a longer, albeit a gilded, chain.

Antoine looked pleased. "Another commission. At least he pays promptly."

"How much—?"

"Four thousand francs for a full-length." He said it casually, merely stating his price, but I was stunned.

"If you stopped doing history paintings and concentrated on portraits, you would be very wealthy indeed."

He flinched as if stung. "It's the history subjects that are the important work of a painter – the enduring themes of the classical past and the Bible, and the high moments of our glorious new age. Portraits are mere likenesses. Didn't Taunay teach you that?"

"Don't be angry," I pleaded. This side of Antoine was still new to me. "I'm not greedy but this portrait that will take you a month to paint is as much as my dowry would bring us in an entire year. I wish I had a talent for faces!"

"I painted many portraits when my prices were lower, to get out of poverty. Now I don't have to paint them any more unless I want to."

And you wanted to paint her, I thought, beginning to feel jealous again.

"Did she mean it when she scolded you about not waiting for her?"

Taken aback by the change of subject, he struggled to shift mental gears. When he realized what I meant, he laughed.

"Of course not. I'm a mere painter and not nearly wealthy enough. The four thousand francs that loom so large to us is not a tenth of what her husband spends on her clothes and jewels each year. He'll grumble about my price but pay up in the end because it's what the government paid for the marshals' portraits, and it will make him look good." Whatever charm Antoine had shown the wife was lacking in his assessment of the husband. "Besides, you saw him. It didn't look as if he were about to leave us very soon, did it?"

"No, not at all." I was sorry I had asked, but it was a useful insight into social distinctions that not even a revolution could sweep away. Noble birth and good breeding may no longer have been the deciding factors; perhaps it was merely a matter of economics these days, but the strata of society were still in place. Money had gone from being suspect to being desirable and estimable. Yet, no matter what prices he might command, no matter how much wealth Antoine might accumulate, he would always remain "Gros the Painter." Away from his canvas he would be someone to flirt with but not to take seriously.

And I would always be Madame Gros, the painter's wife, a plain little *bourgeoise* in Joséphine's shawl. Was that really all I wanted from life at twenty? It couldn't be – there must be more than that!

But what? And how to achieve it?

At last, on 12 March 1810, I met Napoleon Bonaparte face to face. Antoine and I were visiting Denon at the Musée Napoléon (the new name for the art collection housed in the Louvre) that day, about eight months after our wedding. Denon gave us a warm welcome. Over a glass of wine in his office with its view of the Seine, he conveyed the latest news from the court. The previous day the Emperor had married, by proxy, the Austrian Archduchess Marie-Louise, the daughter of Francis II of Austria and great-niece of Marie-Antoinette. She would soon be coming to France for their formal wedding in the chapel of the Louvre and then would reside alternately in Joséphine's former apartments in the Tuileries Palace and the newly decorated Château of Compiègne, north of Paris.

Denon then took us down to the storerooms. A new shipment of treasures culled from Prussian and German courts during the last round of conquests had just arrived.

Workmen stood over several open crates in which cloth-wrapped bundles were nestled in sawdust. Denon's personal secretary supervised the taking of inventory that two clerks wrote down at his dictation. One of the men had just unwrapped a footed dish whose golden gleam contrasted with the humble setting. Lovingly Denon took it into his hands and showed it to us.

"It's called a *tazza*, and it was made in Florence in the sixteenth century as part of the dowry of one of the Medici brides. The workmanship is superb." He pointed out the engraved scrolling on the dish and the sculptural qualities of the foot and stem. "The Florentine workshops were unsurpassed for the mounting of the gems around the border." He caressed a cabochon agate with his thumb and returned the *tazza* to the patient workman to be re-wrapped.

"Here we have a cabinet, also made in Florentine workshops, that was part of the same dowry." He led us to it. "The eighteen drawers are mounted with pictures of animals made of inlaid stones of different colors and patterns. The Italians call this technique *pietra dura*. The large panel in the center shows Orpheus playing a violin to charm the beasts. It was used to store a collection of shells and corals and rare stones." He stood back to let us look at it more closely. Each enchanting animal was a mosaic of stones carefully selected to mimic its natural coloring. The whole was encased in gleaming ebony.

We turned eagerly to see what other things he would show us, when a loud commotion in the hallway caused us to turn our heads. A voice was shouting orders in heavily Italian-accented French; muted French voices were making hasty agreement. "It's the Emperor!" the secretary said in panic, as he and the clerks rose from their chairs. The workmen ceased what they were doing and Denon and Gros straightened to attention. I was still wearing my hat, as it was a cold day; quickly Antoine snatched it from my head and laid it down on one of the crates, as Napoleon marched briskly into the room. The men bowed; Antoine tugged at my skirt so that I too should show the proper respect. I curtsied.

"I'm a married man again," the Emperor told us. He caught sight of Gros. "I hear you are, too." Antoine, obviously proud to be singled out by this comment, introduced me. Bonaparte gave me a quick glance and a nod and turned back to my husband. "I got a young one this time. I hope she's a tigress in bed – like yours, eh, Gros?" He gave him a playful shove. I blushed. Antoine, so adept at court banter, was for once at a loss for words.

Bonaparte snorted in delight at having tongue-tied him. "A man needs a son of his own," he continued. "The Archduchess will be here for the official wedding by the end of the month." He turned to Denon. "Now her apartments must be made ready. I brought Duroc to pick out more of those treasures you've been hiding in storage and put them to good use."

Antoine introduced Marshal Duroc, whose portrait he had painted the year before. As Superintendent of Buildings he oversaw the decoration of the royal apartments in the many imperial palaces.

"I assure Your Majesty that I have only put aside those things too delicate or too rare for—"

"Nonsense, Denon! If they fall apart we can have new ones made. It will be even more impressive to show the world we are so wealthy that we can treat these things as mere ornaments. That cabinet, for instance" – he nodded at it – "would serve well for her jewels." The secretary signaled the clerks to make note of his choices. "And that dish would do for sugared almonds. My spies tell me she's very fond of them."

Denon gave an involuntary shudder at the thought of his treasure put to such vulgar use. He attempted a tactful reply. "Sire, these are the treasures of France."

"I AM FRANCE!" Bonaparte's cannon roar made us all jump. His next words had the brisk precision of an artillery volley. "These things are here because of *my* battles, *my* victories, *my* treaties. *I* take the lead and France follows." Abruptly he wheeled his forces to face me. "Am I right, Madame Gros?"

"Y-yes, Sire, of course, of course," I stammered, instinctively dropping another curtsy. I trembled in the direct glare of his attention.

He transferred that glare to Denon and fired another salvo. "Even a mere girl knows more than you about what is due me! Duroc!"

Reinforcements appeared at his flank. "Yes, Sire?"

"Apparently Monsieur Denon needs some assistance in selecting which items from his storerooms would be suitable. Perhaps you would care to assist him? Persuade him to answer *de oui* instead of *de non*?" Pleased with his pun, he guffawed. Obediently we all followed suit.

"It would be my pleasure, Your Majesty."

"Excellent. I am glad *someone* is pleased this afternoon. I AM NOT." With this final bang of artillery, he turned on his heel and strode out, beckoning Duroc to follow.

To my surprise, Duroc winked at us as he left. Denon explained later that both of them had often seen such tantrums before and took them in their stride.

It seemed very quiet in the storeroom after the Emperor had gone. The workmen resumed their unpacking. Gradually my heartbeat returned to normal.

Denon sighed. "When I bring something into the collection, I don't like to let go of it again," he said ruefully. "But if I must, I must." He was a true connoisseur and collector. Works of art and precious objects were not merely things to be used, as they were for Napoleon. To Denon, they had lives and personalities and needs of their own. He remained guardian over his treasures until 1815, when he resigned to protest Louis XVIII's insistence that they be returned to the countries from which they were taken.

That was the first and last time that I had personal interaction with Bonaparte. Crude and inconsiderate of the feelings of others, he was nonetheless compelling in his sheer energy and assumption of command. I could sense in those few minutes what had drawn so many men to him. In the coming years the full folly of their trust in him would be revealed.

Chapter 6

Paris, 1813-1814

In January 1813, Girodet gave a dinner party to celebrate the return of his friend Dominique Jean Larrey from the Russian campaign. Larrey, the chief surgeon of Napoleon's Imperial Guard, had married one of David's students and become a friend of Girodet, if not of Antoine. Nonetheless we too were invited for Madame Larrey's sake.

As we dressed for the evening – I chose a wine-red gown and the garnet necklace and earrings Antoine has given me for Christmas – I asked my husband about her. He smiled at the memories. "The Leroux-Laville sisters, Charlotte and Marie, were two of David's most promising women students. Marie was a year older than I, quite a young lady. I was rather in awe of her. Her father was the King's finance minister, and we had no doubt she would marry well. We were all a little in love with Charlotte. She was younger than I and not so grand. François Gérard was head over heels in love with her, and almost married her."

"Why didn't he?"

"He was an ardent supporter of the Revolution, in the mold of David. One day he came to the studio in

Republican dress, just when Charlotte and her family were beginning to worry about her father's position and the survival of the royal family. She was furious with François. Told him exactly what she thought of him, and threw his ring in his face. We were mesmerized by her fire and passion. We'd never seen a woman erupt in such fury before." His eyes sparkled. He might have been describing an incident from one of his battle scenes, the charge of an Arabian horse or a Turkish warrior intent upon the head of a Frenchman.

I was impressed. "That was courageous of her. People were imprisoned for less."

"Yes," he shuddered. "And Gérard was just the person to denounce those who disagreed with him. He did that to me – that's why I went to Italy when I did. Fortunately, he couldn't do it where Charlotte was concerned – as much for fear of appearing a vengeful jilted fool as for love of her."

"And what did David think of it?"

"He wasn't there that morning. She stopped coming to the studio after that, and David was too distracted by his political activities to ask why. But she remained friends with the rest of us. We heard she had fallen in love with a young army surgeon, and that her father—"

"The minister— "

"—objected to his lack of prospects. But she, too, knew how to fight for a cause she believed in. After they married, we all met Larrey. He and Girodet became friends, but I could never stomach him. He always had too good an opinion of himself, and a lesser opinion of the mere mortals with whom he was forced to associate. Until I started to gain a reputation, of course – then I was a treated as a friend of long standing who would naturally be eager to include his portrait in *Jaffa* or *Eylau*."

"But you didn't," I replied, thinking of my encounter with the artist's model who had posed for *Jaffa*.

"I wouldn't give him the satisfaction – not even to please Charlotte." He said it with the air of scoring a point against an opponent. He smiled. "Tonight, he'll ignore me as much as possible, and treat me as of no importance when he *is* obliged to take notice of me. Just you watch."

Despite my husband's misgivings, I looked forward to meeting the legendary Larrey, veteran of Egypt and Eylau, who was celebrated by everyone from the Emperor to the rank-and-file troops. He defied death – his own and his patients' – by carrying out surgeries on the battlefield itself while the fighting raged around him. On first sight, it was apparent he had not yet fully recovered from the starvation and frostbite of the Russian campaign; even after a month of plentiful food, his clothes hung on him. His face was seamed and weather-beaten, his dark hair going grey. But his black eyes were intent and intelligent and full of life. He retained his society manners, bowing when he was introduced to me and behaving towards Antoine with a minimum of politeness, though I caught him scowling when he thought no one was looking. Charlotte, at his side, was dark-haired and slender, dressed in a gown of deep yellow that seemed to bring a ray of sunshine into the room. Her smile was dazzling, yet in repose her face, too, showed signs of strain. It could not be easy to be separated so often, and for so long, from the man she loved.

Girodet had the confidence that comes from being both wellborn and one of Napoleon's chosen artists, whose originality had made his reputation. He was not only able to purchase his house with family money but also to hire Percier and Fontaine, the leading architects of the day, to decorate it. The walls were stenciled with Percier's signature delicate classical detail but in a bold color scheme that could only be Girodet's. That he was a non-imperial commission they would make time for, in itself spoke of his importance – though, unlike Larrey, he was never one to insist upon it. He carried himself with his usual self-deprecating humor, and I couldn't help liking him.

He greeted me as an old friend. In a quiet moment alone, I told him how sorry I was to learn that *The Revolt in Cairo* had been removed from the Galerie de Diane and placed in storage.

"Yes, Empress Marie-Louise took offense at the nude man who had not the decency to wear a fig leaf. It was even suggested that I *'faire disparaître sa nudité'* – make his nudity disappear – by painting over the offending parts." He shook his head in disbelief.

"You should be honored," I told him, deadpan. "It puts you in the company of Michelangelo."

He stared at me and burst into laughter. "Ah, yes, those poor souls of the *Last Judgement*, not allowed to enter the afterlife unclothed." I was pleased to see I had restored his good humor. "I refused, of course. I paint the bold deeds of men, not cater to the sensitivities of young ladies" – his voice rose to a falsetto as he pronounced this – "even if the lady in question is an empress."

Girodet was, in fact, a good friend to women, like so many of his kind. But this request had offended his professional pride as a painter. The painting was left in its original state. When necessity compelled the governor of the Tuileries to display it again in the presence of the Empress, a potted palm or torchère was always tactfully placed in front of it.

For the party, Girodet had arranged for a cassoulet, a specialty of Larrey's native Toulouse, as the main dish. As fragrant silver tureens were brought to the table following a salad of winter lettuces, Girodet proudly announced that his cook had even gone to the trouble of finding the best Toulousain goose sausage for it.

"All my favorite dishes!"

"I consulted Charlotte when planning the menu." He raised his glass of champagne to her, and she smiled back. Women always smiled easily at Girodet.

Larrey took a forkful and savored it, testing nuances of flavors and textures, closed his eyes briefly in ecstasy and swallowed. He reached for a glass of the red wine that succeeded the champagne. "A feast for the gods," he said to Girodet, with an open smile. As if receiving his benediction, the rest of us began to eat. It was good hearty fare for the cold of the night outdoors but too much for the warmth of the room. I soon put down my fork, as did the woman next to me. It was Charlotte Larrey.

She smiled in sympathy. "Dominique grew up eating food like this, but I've always found it heavy for my taste."

I smiled back. "It's delicious, but the room is so warm." What a stupid thing to say, I thought.

She was gracious enough to ignore my gaffe. "Girodet told me you too are a painter. With whom did you study?"

"With Taunay." My heart warmed to her: she did not assume I was an amateur, painting for a hobby, studying with a drawing master. She nodded approval. Gaining courage, I continued. "Antoine told me about your student days together." Belatedly, I realized that Antoine had told me about her love life and her politics, but not about her art. "What subjects do you paint?"

"Portraits. I was always drawn to people of the here and now, instead of mythologies. And you?"

"Landscapes. I love Paris, but one can feel too shut up here. Painting landscapes lets me leave for a little while, if only in my imagination." I surprised myself when I said this. I had never articulated, before, just how stifling my situation had become, and how much my painting was an escape.

Larrey continued to eat cassoulet with appetite. He beamed at Girodet. "I wish we'd had this in Russia – we could have used something hot and sustaining on the retreat."

Conversation halted at the introduction of this word never spoken aloud during the Empire. Larrey realized too late what he had just admitted – defeat, failure, the lack of warm food of even the humblest kind, such as this – beans, sausage and fat pork. He froze, mortified at what he'd said, a rare moment of discomfiture for this man. Embarrassed, he looked down at his plate. After a moment's silence, we began to eat again, talking a little too loudly to provide cover for his embarrassment and give him time to recover. He continued to sit motionless, hands grasping knife and fork on either side of his plate, staring down at his portion, until one tear drop and then another fell onto the plate. I was amazed to realize that this tough veteran was crying. He lifted his head then, and his face was filled with pain. The sight of it again brought conversation to a halt. "It was terrible," he said in a hoarse voice, staring with eyes that saw not us but unbearable memories. "Terrible."

Charlotte exclaimed "Dominique!" in alarm and started to rise to go to him.

At the sound of her voice, he snapped back to the present, the dinner table and the celebration, shook his head slightly to rid it of memories, like a housemaid shaking a dust mop, and motioned her to sit down again. Putting down his fork and knife, he raised his glass in a toast to her. She summoned up a smile in return, though her eyes were serious and watchful.

Soon after the details of the truth of the Russian campaign started to trickle back to us despite Bonaparte's best efforts to suppress them. Larrey had not exaggerated.

France's armies continued to suffer defeat. Half a million veteran troops lost in Russia could not be replaced. Young conscripts hastily trained and ill prepared for battle were no match for the seasoned armies of the enemies of France. Larrey returned to duty. Bonaparte's star was descending, taking France with him. At home, Antoine grew more and more gloomy and his mother, ever sensitive to her son's moods, followed suit. His drawing of *The Burning of Moscow*, showing French soldiers rescuing women and children from the fires set by Russian boyars during the occupation was turned down as a subject for the Galerie de Diane. Too much of the truth was now known for even Antoine's skills to be able to put a good face on it. Without a major subject to work on, without his beloved Emperor's face to paint and deeds to chronicle, he had lost his main purpose in life. However, portrait commissions continued to come in.

That spring, I was surprised to receive a letter from General and Madame Legrand, with whom I had had little contact since my marriage. They had written to Gros to commission a portrait of their son, it said, and would be coming the following Wednesday to talk with him. They hoped they would see me. They had chosen him not only for his fine reputation but also because of his connection to me. I smiled ruefully – I had brought my husband a commission. I did not know whether to be glad or sad about this particular one.

The Legrands had aged in the five years since their son's death. The General had suffered wounds during the retreat from Moscow, from which he never fully recovered. His hair was completely grey and he moved slowly and stiffly, like a man much older than his fifty-one years. There was a noticeable tremor in Madame's face and hands. I tried not to show the dismay I felt. Madame Legrand smiled sadly when she saw I was wearing the ring she had given me, and I responded with the warm embrace that had been my habitual greeting to her. Both of us had tears in our eyes when we drew apart. She held my arm as we walked the few steps into the salon – even for so short a distance, her steps were slow and uncertain, and my heart turned with pity. She kept me beside her on the sofa as the General, seated in a chair across from my husband, told him they wished to have Charles portrayed full-length in his cuirassier's uniform standing next to his horse. Antoine suggested a landscape background and asked if there were a portrait from which he could take Charles's face. The General turned to his wife, who drew from her bag a miniature wrapped in one of those handkerchiefs edged with black lace she had carried ever since his death. Her hands were trembling so much that I took it from her, unwrapped it, and handed it to Antoine.

"It was painted when he was thirteen," I explained calmly, "and it is a very good likeness." I did not add that I had one Charles had given me.

Antoine studied it gravely for a minute, examining it, I knew, as much for the skill of the painter as for the features of the painted. When he looked up his smile was reassuring. "He was a beautiful young man," he said warmly. "It will be an honor and a pleasure to paint his portrait." Some of the sadness dropped from the old couple as pride took the place of sorrow. I gave Antoine a proud, tender look that seemed to take him by surprise.

There was a discreet knock at the door and the maid entered with tea and cakes. Madame Legrand ate and drank with hearty appetite, I was glad to see, and grew relaxed and animated, more like her old self. Antoine offered the General something stronger to drink and ventured to bring up one of the rare pieces of good news from the front. The visit had turned the corner from sorrow to hope, and the General decided it would be best to take their leave on this high note before their reserves of energy were overtaxed. Madame Legrand leaned on his arm only a little as they walked to their carriage.

Antoine and I returned to the salon, where he reverently wrapped the miniature to take to his studio. He leaned forward to kiss my cheek. "Don't worry, my dear, your old man will do your young man proud." Surprised, I stared at him. There was a wry twist to his smile. "Only those who die remain forever young and dashing. The rest of us decline into prosaic middle age, I'm afraid."

Even as you will hung in the air unsaid.

I could not think what to reply to him. He shrugged slightly and walked out of the room.

"Come to the studio. I've finished his portrait." The invitation came without preamble on a warm July morning as Antoine was getting dressed. He was not even looking at me, but paying particular attention to tying his cravat while looking in the mirror.

I was startled. He so rarely let visitors into his studio. Even I, his wife, could enter this sanctum only when invited. It was the rare colleague such as Girodet who could come at will; but as an old friend he knew how to time his visits.

"Charles's portrait?" I did my best to match his offhand tone of voice, busying myself with laces and garters, not looking at Antoine either.

"Of course." He smiled. "You knew him. I want to be sure I've caught him as best I can, with only the miniature to go on."

I could understand – Antoine wanted his portraits to be more than a likeness, to have insight and the essence of the sitter's character. But why had he waited until now when the portrait was finished, and not asked me before?

"Of course I'll come if you really wish it." Now we looked at each other for the first time. I smiled, and some of the tension went out of his face, but he still seemed wound up. "When would you like me to be there?"

"Now?" It was as abruptly said as his first statement. "I can wait for you."

"Yes, yes, of course. I'll be ready shortly." He nodded his thanks and left our room.

I dressed as quickly as I could, with a sense of occasion, putting on my white dress trimmed with dark red ribbon and the garnet necklace and earrings. Antoine was pacing the hallway when I came down. During the cab ride to the studio, he looked out the window and avoided my eyes. "Antoine," I asked sharply, "what's *wrong*?" He shook his head and would not answer. I shrugged – I could not pry it out of him if he did not want to say. Finally we arrived at the rue des Fossés-Saint-Germain, down the street from the Théâtre de l'Odéon.

"*Et voilà!*"

I gasped. Charles stood before me, young and blond and vibrant, dressed in his uniform with its shining metal breastplate, wearing his gauntlets for riding, supporting his casque with its horsetail flowing against his leg. He leaned nonchalantly against his horse, his legs crossed like an English milord's. He gaze was fixed on something in the distance, but I expected him to turn his head to look at me at any minute. His face, copied from the portrait of him as a thirteen-year-old, was too young for an officer of the Grande Armée, but not so much younger than the impressionable young cadet I had first seen weeping over the doctor in *Jaffa*.

I looked and looked, unable to tear my eyes away. The artist's part of my mind was calmly cataloging parts of the painting – the beauty of the background landscape, the way the hand holding the helmet blended with the horse plume, the sitter's gloves indicating that Gros had not been able to paint the hands from life, the abruptly foreshortened horse, which I recognized as Dagobert, a friend's stallion. The wifely part of me was proud of my husband's accomplishment. The girl I thought I no longer was came rushing back to embrace Charles, to celebrate his life and mourn his death all over again.

I turned my head to tell Antoine how beautiful it was and realized I was crying. I groped blindly in my purse for a handkerchief, until he came to my rescue with his own, with which he gently dabbed at my eyes and cheeks. I gave him a watery smile and took it from him, just as Charles had taken mine the day we met. Antoine brought me a chair and a glass of water. When I had recovered, he apologized, stammering a little. "I'm sorry – I did not mean to distress you – I thought it would be a pleasant surprise for you – I did not mean you to be overcome—"

I thought to reassure him with praise for the painting. "You asked when we were at home if you had caught the essence of him. As my reaction shows, indeed you have.

He was so proud to be a cuirassier. He would have loved to ride Dagobert. The Legrands will be very pleased."

"Thank you," he said in almost a whisper.

Encouraged, I went on: "We met in front of *Jaffa*, did you know that?" and went on to tell him about that day and the encounter with the artist's model afterward. He laughed. I cast around in my mind for other things I could tell him, but there were none. There was the boy I had loved who had become a soldier and died still a boy, while the girl who had loved him had wept and grown up and married someone else, a common enough story at that time. It was the details that made it special, made it our story, Charles' and mine; and I could not give them away, especially to my husband. Then the source of his unease finally struck me, and I said, "Antoine, are you *jealous* of him?"

He turned a tormented face to me. "Of him? No." He waved a dismissive hand at the dead hero as if to say, *he* may be eternally young, but *I'm* still alive. He had to force the next words out. "Of your love for him? Yes."

"He's been gone five years – until now," and I nodded toward the canvas where the nonchalant lieutenant still gazed into the distance as if too polite to eavesdrop on this disagreement between husband and wife. "He died in

Spain before I met you, and I have been married to you for four of those years, and never—" I was alarmed and indignant at this suspicion of infidelity and had risen halfway out of my chair. "Never have I even *looked* at another—" I stopped, choking on that last word. Our marriage may not have been the happiest, but I took pride in obeying my vows to the letter. I was too angry to say more and stood looking at Antoine, trembling with indignation. He flushed with embarrassment; had he been a boy he would have hung his head. I expected him to approach me with a kiss or an embrace; instead his eyes turned to the portrait.

"You're my wife. I knew you had loved him. I knew the Legrands had chosen me because of you. As I was painting him, I could not help thinking, *I am painting my wife's lover. I am reduced to painting my wife's lover. I am being paid to accept the humiliation of painting my wife's lover. I am—*"

"Antoine, stop! You're making yourself ill over nothing. He was never my lover. He was a boy I loved before I met you. And his love for me came only after his loyalty to his Emperor and his dreams of military glory and his love for his parents. It wasn't enough to stop him from going to Spain to be killed." I had never before so clearly admitted this and it hurt me afresh to realize it. I was angry with Charles and angry with my husband for forcing me to face the humiliating truth yet again. "I married *you*, Antoine, and I have loved you as best I could. I'm sorry if it hasn't been good enough for you."

I snatched up my hat and reticule and ran out of the studio. In the street I walked with a determined pace. I was clutching his handkerchief and would gladly have thrown it away, but I was weeping with rage and humiliation and could not go into a shop looking like a disheveled madwoman. Furiously I dabbed at my eyes with the wretched square of cotton. I paused at a café to drink mineral water and proceeded more calmly to the Jardin du Luxembourg.

It was not crowded on a weekday despite the hot weather and the lanes felt cool and private. I made my way to the Fontaine de Médicis and sat on one of the chairs, soothed by the sound of the water and the conversational quacking of the ducks. It always delighted me when one of them dived for something underneath her and presented a backside of feathers to the world. I was glad to be diverted from the painful scene in the studio. It was too horrible to think back upon, but the thought of going home to his suspicions was worse. So I looked at the ducks and tried not to think at all. I wished I had my sketchbook and pencils with me. I was still clutching Antoine's handkerchief. I got up and went to the fountain, dipped it in the cool water to wash my face, and spread it on a shrub to dry. I returned to watching the ducks. Two drakes were courting a female, showing off in front of her by chasing each other with demonstrations of speed and displays of bright feathers. She preened her mottled brown plumage and ignored her suitors, who quacked the more loudly at each other as if irked at her indifference. She appeared to find little to choose between the two and waited patiently for the winner to declare himself. I envied her detachment.

"I thought I'd find you here." My husband's voice broke into my reverie.

"Yes," I said calmly. "I'm watching the ducks do their courting."

He looked at the drake that quacked triumphantly as the other took flight. "I hope he makes a success of it." Before I could respond, he spoke intently. "Augustine, I'm so sorry. Jealousy got the better of me. I know I had no cause. I would never have undertaken the portrait had I known it would result in this bad feeling between us. It won't happen again." I looked at him. As I had given him no cause for his jealousy, I could not give him any reassurance for unraveling it. He would need to come to terms with it on his own.

"Augustine – I was wrong – please – forgive me – can you?" I was touched despite myself and put my hand on his. I realized then that, however much I might hurt, he would always be the one who would need comforting. He lifted my hand to his lips and then clasped it. Two large tears rolled down his cheeks and I brushed them off with my free hand, caressing his cheek as I did so. This caused fresh tears to flow; he groped for his handkerchief, forgetting he had given it to me. I looked to where I had left it. Someone had removed it from the bush, thinking, perhaps, to have found himself a treasure. This struck me as funny, and I gave a long peal of laughter. "It's gone," I told Antoine, lightheartedly. "Never mind!" On impulse I kissed his eyes again and again until his tears had ceased. Two girls passing by giggled to see aged adults behaving like young lovers; I ignored them. Eventually we arose and walked arm-in-arm down the length of the garden toward the Observatory. Antoine sent his mother a note with a messenger to say we would be lunching at a restaurant. After the tension of the morning it was a relief to give way to the pleasures of eating, and to follow that by taking a

room at the hotel next door, in broad daylight. I felt quite–
–

But there are some places the reader may not follow me, and to bed with my husband is one of them.

I brought the Legrands to the studio to see Charles's portrait after it had been varnished and framed. That day was again the cause of tears, but happy ones. Antoine had reverted to his usual charming self in front of clients. However, it was a relief to both of us when the painting was taken from the studio to be delivered. When they sent payment, he gave the money to me "for paints and canvas" as a final apology.

Maman Madeleine was indignant: he was spoiling me; the money should be invested, or put aside in gold, to be on the safe side. If the rumors she heard were true, the Empire was in serious difficulties and it was said the Emperor's luck was running out. "Be quiet, Maman!" My husband's sharp reproof was not at all his usual loving and patient tone and I sensed fear lurking beneath it. His mother opened her mouth to protest, saw the look on his face, and closed it again without saying another word.

"The money is Augustine's to save or spend as she pleases," he continued in a normal tone of voice. But the fear we all lived with had been brought out in the open, and it would not be so easy to send it into hiding again. I took Maman Madeleine's advice and converted the four thousand francs for Charles's portrait into gold coins, taking care to do this a little at a time to lessen the risk of being robbed.

For the news was not good, no matter how the carefully edited Bulletins of the Grande Armée tried to make it appear so. We were all frightened, even those of us who longed for an end to the fighting and the return of the Bourbons. We had been accustomed to success, even while deploring its cost. Now we were a nation in defeat.

For Antoine, who loved Napoleon with his heart and soul, it was agonizing. He lived to paint his hero's accomplishments, but there were no new triumphs to record. His newest commission was not a battlefield scene: in the Dome of the Panthéon, the Church of Sainte-Geneviève, Bonaparte was recasting himself as successor to Clovis, Charlemagne, and Saint Louis, the great medieval kings of France, lawgivers and supporters of the Church. It was a prestigious, well-paid assignment but not an exciting one; its main virtue for Antoine was keeping despair at bay.

The long cold winter of defeat that started with Russia in 1812 never stopped. The months seemed to drag on interminably, alternating between hope and despair. For some, it was hope that Bonaparte would prevail and despair that Paris would fall. For others, it was hope that the Allies would take over without bloodshed and despair that he would insist on trying to fight and cause yet more good men to be killed for nothing. Our minds went back and forth between the realities of that day and the fears of the coming one.

I was surprised to find this same vacillation in myself. The return of the Bourbons to their rightful place on the throne of France was an idea I had cherished since childhood. I detested Bonaparte for the slaughter of the youth of France and the suffering it caused. But his rise had also been the rise of France to a new era of glory not seen since the time of the Sun King, and I could not help but share in the shame we all felt at her downfall.

How symbolic that the surrender of Paris and the entry of the allied troops would come in spring 1814 after Bonaparte abdicated and was sent into exile on Elba. I was one of the many who lined the streets around the Porte Saint-Denis on 31 March, waving our handkerchiefs, to welcome the Tsar, the King of Prussia, and the Austrian military commander at the head of their troops. I wondered how many in the crowd had been part of the cheering mob that had witnessed the execution of Louis XVI. How many now wearing the royal colors of blue and white had then worn the red, white and blue of the Revolution?

For Gros it was the death of everything he had held dear for over eighteen years. I tried to reach out to him, but he shut me out, insisting angrily that he was all right, that everything would resolve itself for the best, that the Emperor – and here his face softened and his shoulders straightened – had faced overwhelming odds before and would pull off yet another miracle. He said it in the way mothers pray for their dying sons, clutching their rosaries, averting their eyes from the reality of the bandaged, battle-scarred figure on the bed, closing their ears to the priests who attempt to assure them their boys would soon depart for a better world. Antoine did not want to listen to anything I said. He fled to the comfort of Girodet and Denon.

Once, a strange sound woke me in the middle of the night. His space in the bed was empty beside me. I sat up and listened more closely – violent sounds of breaking crockery and glass in the kitchen – the servants who slept in the attic couldn't hear it. I went downstairs – Antoine was in an orgy of destruction, weeping – finally, he stopped, and broke down in racking sobs. He pushed me away when I tried to comfort him, and I crept back to bed.

He cried, too, for his paintings, his precious children on whom he had lavished so much care and love. He was terrified they would be desecrated or burned. They were not destroyed – as the government had paid good money for them, they were considered national assets – but they were banished to the dungeons of the Louvre storerooms to languish in darkness for more than a decade.

In the midst of all this came another blow. Joséphine was terminally ill, a matter of months, her doctors said.

He and I went out to celebrate or mourn the events each in our own way. I did not tell him of my activities with the artist friends I met up with, as I knew they would pain him, but once we met on our street as I returned from cheering the Comte d'Artois, the brother of our new king, Louis XVIII, as he rode with the Paris National Guard to give thanks at Notre Dame Cathedral. Antoine took in the blue rosette I wore on my white dress, and my face flushed with the too-rare pleasure of enjoying the day, and was horrified.

"How *could* you?" It came out almost as a hiss.

I stood my ground. "The killing is over. At last! I am not the only one to give thanks for that."

"You don't understand. They died *for* something: for France, for country, honor, and glory. To celebrate the allies' win is to denigrate their sacrifice."

"You don't need to apologize for him anymore, Antoine. He is gone. The truth can come out."

"*Apologize*! The truth is that he brought France its greatest *gloire* since Louis XIV, the Sun King."

"Who also bankrupted France in his search for glory," I replied tartly. We entered the house. I took off my bonnet in front of the mirror in the entry, handing it and my shawl (as Antoine his hat and coat) to the maid who came running at the sound of our voices. We suspended the argument until she had left. I turned to the mirror again to smooth a stray lock of hair. Antoine stared at my reflection, outraged as much by my insistence in continuing as by my opinions. I looked back as calmly as I could, while his venom gathered force. His eyes flicked right and left, looking for something that would sting me as badly as I had stung him.

"I would have thought, out of respect for the memory of your precious Charles," he began, his voice turned lofty, morally superior, and smug, "you would refrain from celebrating. *He* believed in what he fought for."

I might have known he would use that. My reply was bitter. "And died uselessly nonetheless. I faced that truth long ago."

Then Maman Madeleine called reproachfully to me, to break up the argument. We did not speak to each other again for several days.

Nonetheless, Gros went to pay his respects to Louis XVIII, from *politesse* and practicality. Having been painter to the highest persons in the land, he was not prepared to sink back into a purely middle-class portrait practice! His was a talent meant for grand themes, he said, even if the Bourbons were not the most inspiring subjects for his canvas. And the painting of the Dome – what would become of that? Most of it could easily be adapted for Bourbon use. Would the government commission still hold, and could he go ahead? The summer, the only time of year practicable for working in the space, was soon coming up. Who would now have the authority to approve it? He needed to find out. Besides, he was damned if he would let Gérard, dreadful man, get in there ahead of him. All of this came forth as he was dressing for court with special care, but it had the air of a man talking to keep his courage up. I murmured what reassurances I could, and wished I could volunteer to go in his place.

His visit to the Tuileries was awarded, in time, with a commission to paint the King's portrait. Well, it was a start.

Chapter 7

An Interlude: A Gathering of Women Artists
Paris, 1813-1814

Although I have already covered the years 1813-1814 in
the preceding chapter centered on the decline of
Napoleon's Empire, the events surrounding my artistic
career during that time formed an activity apart from the
upheaval and its strain on my marriage. It was to be,
ironically, a time of great productivity and growth. It was
then, too, that I met Josée, who has been my friend ever
since.

When we returned from our honeymoon in Toulouse, I
was no longer a girl and a bride, but a married woman. I
had a household to run, a husband to take care of and learn
to love, a mother-in-law to please, and girlfriends to
impress with my new status. They exclaimed over my
fortune in marrying a man so well established and resident
in Paris, not attached to the army with the attendant
anxieties I had known only too well. Some even inquired if
I might already be pregnant. This always made me blush.

The friends who had been fellow students at Taunay's
studio had other, more pressing questions. "What about

your painting? You won't have to give it up, will you?" Amongst this group, this was always our greatest anxiety – that the new duties of being a wife and mother or the disapproval of a husband and his family would force us to fold away our artistic ambitions with other girlhood dreams. While none of us dared to have as large an ambition as Gros or David, our art was important to us, and the thought of giving it up monstrously unfair.

As I have already related, finding the space and time for it was not without its challenges. When household duties kept me at home, I took up still-life subjects of household objects and flower bouquets, reminding myself that many another artist had kept her hand in by painting what was before her.

My artistic ambition might have withered had I not been welcomed into the circle of Charlotte Larrey and her sister Marie-Guillemine Benoist. Charlotte gave me what I most needed, a friend and colleague. She paid me the compliment of accepting me as an equal. The more I learned about her, the more I admired her. Her sister, prize-winner at the Salons and the only woman artist to be commissioned by Bonaparte to paint his portrait, is the better-known artist; her husband is the Larrey who collected the accolades of soldiers, doctors, and historians;

but Charlotte, I have always thought, was one of the unsung heroines of the times.

"It wasn't easy," she told me one day as we walked through the galleries of the Musée Napoléon. "Dominique was away for thirteen of our first twenty-one years of marriage. He wasn't paid regularly and often had to pay for surgical supplies out of his own pocket. More than once they were stolen. He would come home with several thousand francs in hand all too rarely. I had to paint portraits just to put food on the table and keep a roof over our heads. Once, Dominique wrote to ask me to ask the Emperor's favor by painting and presenting a miniature portrait of His Majesty, so that the back payment of his salary could be expedited. He was the favorite surgeon of the Emperor, praised in his dispatches, but if it were not for help from my sister, we would sometimes have starved. And yet my son – who watched me struggle with all of this – wants to become an army surgeon, just like his father."

I was pleased when Charlotte invited me to attend one of her sister's Thursday studio afternoons. I felt a mounting sense of excitement all week and could hardly eat lunch that day. I was rather intimidated at the thought of meeting Madame Benoist, whose portrait of Empress Marie-Louise had been shown at the last Salon. A smart manservant answered my timid tap on the door of the Benoist residence. He led me to the top floor of the house and stopped before a door behind which I could hear women's voices. "*Entrez*, Madame!" he said with another bow. "I regret I cannot take you in, but men are not allowed." Startled, I hesitated. "*Entrez, entrez*," he urged, almost smiling. I plucked up my courage and walked in.

A burst of light, color, warmth and fragrance flooded my senses. Even now, almost thirty years later, I can close my eyes and inhale the deep, rich rose perfume exuded in the dead of winter by bowls of potpourri, candles scented with attar of roses, and the perfume worn by Madame Benoist herself. Draped everywhere were fabrics and shawls in rose colors – reds, oranges, yellows, and pinks, with here and there the deep green of stems and leaves. Turbans and great ostrich plumes were scattered among them. Candles flickered on tables and shelves. A corner stove gave off welcome heat, and a teakettle boiled gently upon it. An old-fashioned Turkish-style divan stood against one wall with several chairs in front of it; a round table in their midst bore a plate of cakes and several cups and saucers – whose floral pattern I was sure would prove to be rosebuds. Wide-eyed, I took it all in. Easels were there, and a model's stand, sketches for her best-known paintings, plaster casts of ancient sculptures, colors, sketchbooks, and chalks, all the things with which a studio needed to be furnished, and the smell of turpentine could be detected even under the scent of roses. But the setting was intensely feminine, affirming that womanhood and serious art were not mutually exclusive. This was a far cry from the "virtuous" Spartan simplicity of the bare wooden surfaces of Taunay's and David's studios. I drank it in with a quickening sense of delight. I smiled. I threw back my head and laughed, opening my arms to embrace it. The four women at the end of the room, who had been smiling at my childlike wonder, joined me in laughter. Encouraged, I swept up a vast shawl of embroidered, fringed silk and wrapped myself in it, executing a pirouette. In this I was joined by the others, and we spun round the room like dancing couples seen from a balcony, drawn by an invisible centrifuge, until we all ran out of breath and stood laughing. Madame Benoist cast aside her orange silk and came to welcome me with a warm kiss, saying to her sister, "You have brought us *une femme d'esprit*!"

A woman of spirit: I considered the words, savored them. I would not have said that they described the Madame Gros I had become. But they suited very well the youthful Augustine I once had been. "Yes," I replied, "a woman of spirit!"

The others nodded in approval. Charlotte introduced me formally to Madame Benoist – or Marie, as I was instructed to call her, and to Marie's youngest daughter, also named Augustine, a girl of twelve who seemed older than her years, as if she spent all her time in adult company. The fourth guest was Louise-Joséphine Sarazin de Belmont, who liked to be called Josée. She and I were the same age and she was to become my closest friend. Josée had curling red hair and freckles that defied all her attempts to fade them with beauty creams. She had never married. No man would put up with her independent nature, she said. With no family money or state patronage to rely upon, she nonetheless earned her living as an artist, specializing in classical landscapes. My mother and mother-in-law would have sighed in despair at this folly, but Marie and Charlotte were looking at her with admiration, so that I felt free to do so too. We were all part of the sisterhood of *femmes d'esprit*.

So vivid is my memory of that afternoon that I can hear again the rattle of the teakettle lid, drops hissing on the stove, Marie's laugh as she lifted it and poured the water into the waiting teapots. Eagerly we took our seats. Josée, to my fascination, sat back in the Turkish divan, stretched her legs out and kicked off her shoes, with an air of being at home with such informal comforts. She saw my look of astonishment and beckoned to me to sit beside her. I hesitated only a moment, then joined her, removing my shoes as she had done and wriggling my toes to emphasize their freedom. Charlotte handed me a cup of rose-scented tea and I inhaled deeply its perfume. Young Augustine – whose scent, I recall, was tea rose – handed round the cakes. I half expected to find they too were rose-scented, but they were ordinary cream-filled cakes, bland and slightly sweet. Their sensuous delight, I discovered, came from licking the cream in the manner of children who know how to get at the essence of a treat. The others were doing the same – the cakes had been chosen to bring about that response, both sensual and childlike, behavior I had never seen encouraged before – quite the opposite, in fact. Marie winked at me and said, "Here we create our own rules."

Talk turned, as it always did, to painting: what canvases Marie and Josée were working on, what commissions they had in hand, what ideas they had for works to undertake without one. Charlotte, relieved of the responsibility of supporting the family now that Larrey had been paid in full, spoke of portraits of friends. I told them about my latest arrangement of pots, pans, and dead fish. Talk then turned to the Salon. There would be not be one that year, but they were already looking forward to the Salon of 1814.

"And you, Augustine – what are you planning for the Salon?"

I was startled. "I have no plans at all. I'm not ready yet."

"Nor will you be," admonished Josée, who had shown at the Salon of 1812, "until you strive to, and then present yourself as an artist before the jury. They won't take you seriously until you take yourself seriously." She was no longer lounging at her ease but sitting upright, turning to speak intently in my direction, looking me in the eye. Instinctively my spine stiffened and I, too, sat up, unwilling to be caught at a disadvantage. For a moment I knew the thrill a soldier must feel when his general gives his speech in the bivouac the night before a battle. "Well?" she prompted.

A dozen reasons rose to my mind. I had no proper studio and little money of my own to spend on supplies. My mother-in-law would not be pleased that I aspired to the Olympian realm she felt belonged more properly to her son. My own mother would tell me I should give up girlhood dreams now I was married. And Antoine? Could I count on my husband's support? I didn't know – I had never before put it to the test. But I knew that Josée would consider them mere excuses, not reasons.

"Well?" she prompted again.

I drew in a big breath and took the plunge. "A still life," I said, pointing to an arrangement of pink and orange shells and grey-green leafy corals on one of the studio tables. "I will submit a still life to the Salon." I sounded more certain than I felt, but I had made a pledge I could not go back on. At least, unlike yesterday's herrings, the shells did not balefully reproach me with glassy eyes.

"Brava!" Josée said in approval. The others applauded.

"We will help you to be ready," Marie said. Charlotte, who had shown at the Salons de la Jeunesse in her youth, nodded. Augustine looked puzzled at the fuss – sending paintings to the Salon was something she'd seen her mother do all her life.

"I wonder what Antoine would—" I started to say, but a commotion from the others cut me short.

"We don't mention our husbands here," Marie explained, "by the rules of the house. The next time you do so, you shall pay the fine, one franc." I must have looked puzzled, for she continued: "This studio is a space where women exist in their own right."

"So that was why the butler could not show me in." I gave a hoot of unladylike laughter at the thought of that haughty personage being barred from even knocking on the studio door.

"Why, Augustine, you're a merry one!" Charlotte exclaimed. Merry? Me? This made me laugh all the harder, and the others joined in.

A little clock chimed the hour in silvery tones. Abruptly, Marie stood up and began to clear away the cups and plates. "It's time to work, *mes filles*. We have much to do." We picked up our pads and pencils and each chose a corner of the studio to sketch. I settled down to begin my acquaintance with the seashells.

So began the best eighteen months of my life.

The persona of Merry Augustine allowed me to bring out and develop a side of me I had never known before. I had been, in turn, the dutiful daughter, the serious painting student and aspiring artist, the newly grown-up young woman anxious to impress a handsome soldier, the grieving woman old beyond her years who had lost her sweetheart and her father in rapid succession, and the young wife out of place in a middle-aged household. Not until now was I encouraged to be a happy, laughing young woman. I reveled in it. I shook my hair loose, walked with a dance in my step, raised my voice, argued with gusto, laughed belly laughs, and expressed my opinions with vehemence. This carried over into my art – I painted more freely, applied colors more daringly, took risks.

I was not sick once in the whole of that time. I glowed with health. When I met up with old friends, they asked if I were pregnant. More than one wondered if I had taken a lover. Once I caught Maman Madeleine giving me a speculative look, as if she, too, wondered. I laughed out loud at the sheer ridiculousness of the idea and kissed her warmly on both cheeks, startling and pleasing her.

It was the courage gained at the studio that gave me the ability to speak out so strongly to Antoine over Charles Legrand's portrait that year – and to put into our lovemaking afterward a degree of enthusiasm I had not hitherto shown. It helped to break our marriage out of its routine of grave courtesy into something approaching passion, to the gratification of us both.

Because talk of husbands was prohibited in the studio, I could not speak of this with my new friends, but I found myself speculating, sometimes, if it was the same for them. I giggled like a schoolgirl at the thought of their faces, were I to mention it, adding to the merriness of my demeanor. Josée said it was as if I were bubbling over with a joke inside.

We met every week except when Marie was at her country house in September and October. In those months I went to Josée's studio at 13 rue de Condé. Not as ornate as Marie's, it still exuded feminine warmth. We drew and painted side by side and came to be fast friends. I admired the skill with which she painted her atmospheric but finely detailed classical settings. She turned her fierce dispassionate critical eye most often upon herself; to me, she always tempered her criticism with encouragement. We all – Josée, Marie, and I – reworked our subjects several times over that year, before we were satisfied.

At first, I set the shells and corals in front of a neutral background – the colors were true, the forms beautiful, the details faithful (and quite a time I had mastering that lacy coral leaf!) – but the whole was lackluster in effect. My spirits sank, looking at it. Could I do no better than this? Fortunately Marie, correctly interpreting the sag of my shoulders, came to stand beside me. She did not waste time in recrimination but regarded the composition as a problem to be solved, a challenge to rise to. She stood back, assessing it with a shrewd, narrow-eyed glance. "Set them against a black background," she suggested. "It will make your colors appear much more vibrant." I am glad I took her advice.

The studio was our refuge but we could not entirely ignore the growing unease in the city outside. The ban on mentioning husbands was lifted as Charlotte gave reports of Larrey's movements with the Old Guard and Marie of Monsieur Benoist's activities in the government. It became apparent as 1813 progressed into the dire winter of early 1814 that he among others were quietly negotiating with the Bourbons for their return and working to be assured of retaining or improving their positions in the government when this happened. Our talks helped us prepare for the changes ahead, while our work – drawing, sketching, painting – helped us to hold fast to our core selves through the upheaval around us. To our relief, the new government announced that the Salon of 1814 would take place as planned.

Our talks grew more uninhibited as we grew bolder. I did not realize how much so until the day Elisabeth Vigée-Lebrun joined us for one of her rare visits. The doyenne of women painters in France, she had known Gros since he was a boy. Charlotte, Marie, Josée and I proposed to paint heroic topics that should be shown but would not – army wives bringing up their children on their own; women gathered around the dispatches in the newspaper; women scanning the lists of the dead. Josée suggested a scene in a mercer's shop, where a woman at one end of the counter would be buying a length of dull black cloth for mourning clothes while a soldier at the other end considered gold braid for his uniform. Charlotte proposed a variant on Marguerite Gérard's sensation of the last Salon, *The Letter*, in which a young woman read a letter with bad news while seated in a comfortable upper-class interior, with a solicitous maid attending to her faint. Charlotte suggested instead a scene in which the notice of death would come to a woman in poverty with little food to feed the children. Charlotte knew military widows like these: hearing of her husband's death was often the last straw for a woman who had been barely hanging on waiting for his return. As little as she herself had, Charlotte had tried to help them.

I thought of Lucie's sister hearing of the death of her husband. What if I were to paint that not on the small scale deemed appropriate for a domestic subject but life-size, like David's *Hector and Andromache* – the story of

167

another military wife whose husband has been killed and whose son is bereft?

Or on a larger scale still – what if I were to paint, as the pendant to one of Antoine's five-meter-long battle scenes, a scene of the effects of victory at home? I put the question to the others in an excited voice. They laughed and applauded. "Brava!" Charlotte said, and poured another round of champagne into our glasses.

"But who would give you a commission for it?" Vigée-Lebrun asked, bringing our flights of fancy to earth in her practical way. "Could you afford a thousand francs for the canvas and paint without one? And," with a significant glance around the room, "where would you have the studio space for it? Works that size need to be hung on the wall of a palace or a museum. Who—?"

"The King of England."

"The Czar of Russia."

"Francis II of Austria."

"King Bernadotte of Sweden."

"King Ferdinand of Spain."

We all laughed. Working for those patrons seemed as far-fetched as the painting itself.

Vigée-Lebrun who thirty years before had been portraitist to Marie-Antoinette and her circle, smiled and turned her gaze upon young Augustine Benoist. "Perhaps in her time, but I fear not in this one."

Despite Vigée-Lebrun's misgivings, I began to think about the subject I had proposed. How could I distill the scene to the telling details that would have the most impact? I thought, yet again, of the dying doctor in *Jaffa* and that figure's ability to bring forth a powerful emotional response in the viewer. It was a daunting task. There were so few modern precedents for monumental scenes of domestic tragedy. The melodramas of Jean-Baptiste Greuze, so daring a half-century before, now seemed hopelessly old-fashioned. David's wives, mothers and sisters of Greek and Roman heroes had been frank in the suffering caused by the loss of their menfolk, but their tears were shown to disadvantage compared to the stoicism of the men. Try as I might, I could not imagine my modern-dress scene as a monumental canvas. Its subject demanded handling on a more intimate scale, even if the problem was a national one repeated over and over. A woman's weeping, except for the women of myth and history, simply was not heroic.

But why should it be so? I had lived with the conventions of the hierarchy of subject matter all my life, in which classical history and Biblical subjects were the most highly regarded, domestic subjects much less so, and the still life on which I was working, at the bottom; but it was not until now that I had thought to question them.

The grief of women is not ennobling – it is merely a fact of life. It does not spur a man on to heroic action; it reminds him he is mortal and that by following one loyalty he will betray another.

Unwilling to admit defeat, Napoleon fought on. Larrey patched up the wounded as best he could. Paris continued to deny publicly that disaster was imminent, but to prepare for it privately.

The strain took its toll on our marriage. Our closeness did not last. It took all Antoine's energies to stave off acknowledging the inevitable. Even while the litany of defeats continued to grow, he daily climbed the two hundred steps to the Dome of the Pantheon to place his hero among the great monarchs of France. He had no energy and even less sympathy to spare for a wife who accepted reality, and still less did he want to listen to her advice. Antoine and I were never again to achieve that measure of intimacy and mutual appreciation that had been too brief an interlude in our marriage. More and more we judged each other by the shortcomings of what we were not instead of by the strengths of what we were.

Tired of his rejection, I continued to find solace in the friendships in the studio and to throw my energies into my painting. I rearranged and repainted Marie's shells and corals several times before I was satisfied. While I welcomed and adopted her advice to give my painting a black background, finding the right sort of deep, matte black for just the right effect presented a challenge in itself. Lampblack, made from soot, was the easiest to obtain and gave the best effect when wet but was too greasy and failed to dry properly, making the whole of the canvas a soggy mess; next I tried ivory black. It worked so long as I did not attempt to paint over it in lighter colors, to which it lent a crackled texture at odds with the smooth surface of the shells. More than once, I cursed my pigments under my breath. At last I was able to juxtapose the colors as I wanted. The painting was as good as I could make it. Even Antoine gave it a nod of approval, and Maman Madeleine paid it the ultimate compliment when she found nothing in it to criticize. She gave me renewed hope that it would pass muster with the Salon jury, of which Taunay was a member. I wanted him to be proud of me.

On the appointed day, I brought my picture to the Louvre for submission. I went alone, as the painting Josée had planned to send had been sold and its purchaser was unwilling to part with it for the length of the exhibition. There was a long line of us and my hopes quailed before so much competition. What if, after all my efforts, my work would not be good enough? Luckily, I had reached the head of the line before my courage failed me. The secretary and his clerks made note of my entry in the register and wished me luck. I began to feel better. As I walked away past the long line of entrants that waited patiently, it struck me – I was an artist who had prepared and submitted a painting to the Salon! I looked again at the receipt in my hand to verify that what had eighteen months before been unimaginable had become a reality: I was an artist who had submitted a painting to the Salon!

Three weeks later, Marie and I learned our paintings had been accepted. Marie's success had never been in doubt, but it was a tremendous first step for me. Josée and I approached Marie's studio in high spirits, prepared to celebrate.

Usually there was the sound of voices and laughter in the studio, and sometimes the notes of young Augustine's harp. Today, however, it was unnaturally silent as Josée and I climbed the stairs. Instinctively I wondered who had been killed, only belatedly remembering that France was now, supposedly, permanently at peace. Puzzled, we entered without our usual joyful greetings. Marie and Charlotte sat at the far end of the room in the doleful attitudes of the women anticipating disaster in David's *Oath of the Horatii*.

"What has happened?" we exclaimed in alarm and hurried over to them.

Marie was too upset to answer, and it was Charlotte who spoke in a voice that seemed to bite off each word in anger. "She has had a letter from her husband saying that she can no longer show her work at the Salon because it is beneath the high status of his position in the new government." She thrust this document at us.

"Not in keeping with *his* position?" Josée was instantly outraged. "What about *her* position as one of the leading painters of our time? Portraitist to the former Emperor of France, successful exhibitor in the Salon year after year, medal-winner in 1801 for her *Portrait of a Negress*, which was purchased by the State as an outstanding example of the accomplishments of modern French painting? Haven't *her* talents been part of what helped *him* gain his position? And this is his gratitude for them?"

She was splendid in her indignation, her red hair coming loose from its demure chignon like a burst of flame, her eyes throwing sparks. I admired her fighting spirit. Even Marie, warmed by the energy of her defense, was able to smile. Later, we painted Josée as Marianne, spirit of the French, urging her troops to victory.

I was always slower to react, and when I did I was puzzled as much as indignant. "But he has been in the government for years, as long as you have been married. Your father was a government minister before the Revolution, and it was perfectly all right then for you and your sister to exhibit at the Salon de la Jeunesse. No one objected before. Why is it different now?"

A puzzled silence was the only reply.

We did not know then how much the new regime would want not just to return to the past but to invent a new, even stricter etiquette for a society in which everyone knew and kept his or her place. Gros could escape these strictures because the Bourbons needed him to turn his talents to their glorification and remind their sometimes fickle subjects of the legitimacy of their rule. But Marie Benoist, as a wife, could not.

"But what will you do, Marie?" Josée asked, her voice gentle.

She gave a profound sigh. Her shoulders sagged as though all the responsibility of living up to her husband's new status lay heavily upon them. "I will do as he asks. After all, we live in society and must obey its rules. And yet, after all my hard work and success—" Her brave words could not stem the flow of tears.

Charlotte signaled us to go. We tiptoed down the stairs in subdued spirits.

The episode shook me profoundly. The return of the Bourbons was something I had longed for since childhood, and I had never questioned it. I was still glad of it – I could be certain of that. Yet Marie was my friend and a fellow artist who took pride in her work. Her husband's request hurt her deeply and I felt that hurt. Perhaps her sacrifice was a small price to pay for the return of the rightful order. But why should she have to pay it at all?

She continued to paint portraits of the family with her customary skill and polish, but her heart was no longer in her work. Josée and I still came on Thursday afternoons, at her urging, but we felt embarrassed, almost guilty, to discuss our Salon hopes in front of her. She could not bring herself to visit the exhibition. It was a sad end to a fine career.

It was nonetheless exciting to be part of the exhibition on opening day, instead of on the outside looking in. Just ten years before I had been an eager young student attending my first Salon – and now mine was one of the paintings other art students would look at. Pleased with its placement, I attended the prize-giving ceremonies, applauded the winners whole-heartedly, and collected congratulations from Taunay, Denon and Antoine, my mother and sister, Charlotte and Josée, and my friends from Taunay's studio.

The Salon of 1814 was the first one in more than a decade in which big paintings praising Bonaparte did not take center stage. By now we were so accustomed to them that we noted their absence even more than we had paid attention to their presence. It seemed very odd, the exhibition somehow diminished because of it. There had not yet been time to paint the deeds of Louis XVIII, but celebration of the monarchy was everywhere. Kings of the Middle Ages and Renaissance were resurrected and the acts, faults, and foibles of more recent royal families were tactfully avoided. Antoine sent *François I and Charles V at Saint-Denis*.

I turned a corner into the next gallery and found what I had been unconsciously looking for, paintings with an emotional impact. The talented young painter Théodore Géricault had sent a pair of subjects – an eager young cavalry officer charging into battle and a wounded cuirassier leaving it. Antoine stood in front of the latter and I went to join him. It was a figure of tremendous power, raising more questions than it answered. The wounded warrior showed no blood, no gaping tears of flesh, but he looked back warily at the field of battle as he led his nervous high-stepping horse down the slope. The one painting headed with confidence into Russia, sure of victory, the other headed out of two years of decline looking back in pain. I thought of Marie's wounds and how they hurt even if they did not bleed.

The *Wounded Cuirassier* drew many viewers. Some, wanting only to be entertained, shrugged off its effects and walked on. Others turned as somber as the painting's lowering sky as they looked at and absorbed it. An old man looked at it with tears running down his cheeks. He reminded me a little of Charles's father. I went over to him, putting my hand on his arm in sympathy. After some minutes he gravely nodded his thanks and walked away. We had not spoken a word but had shared the emotional bond this painting had the power to evoke. I felt a profound gratitude to the artist.

I knew that painting could do more. I knew that *I* could do more. To be accepted to the Salon was no longer enough. Already my ambitions had grown.

Chapter 8

Paris, March-June 1815

On 10 March 1815, Bonaparte escaped his confinement on Elba and returned to France. As everyone knows, Marshal Ney vowed to bring him back in a cage but returned him at the head of an army. For over a week they made a triumphal progress the length of France, gathering support as they went. Antoine was overjoyed, but my heart sank as I read the reports. To my dismay, the King and the government did nothing to attempt to stop them. Sending Ney had been their one decisive gesture, and they were at a loss to propose another. The change in the country's loyalties from Bonaparte to the Bourbons was too new to be trusted and, as events had shown, could all too easily be reversed.

As Bonaparte neared Fontainebleau on 19 March, Louis XVIII prepared to flee Paris. Antoine, having gone to the Tuileries Palace that night to await his hero's expected arrival, was a witness to the King's shameful midnight flit. Ironically, he was later to do a painting of the royal departure, investing it with pathos, honor and fervent loyalty.

Bonaparte reached the Tuileries at dawn. Antoine came home for breakfast exhausted but glowing, having cheered himself hoarse. He had seen Larrey in the crowd, he said, and for once they were in complete agreement, embracing like old friends.

I groaned inwardly. Not again! Whatever doubts I had had about the return of the Bourbons were swept away by the sure knowledge that the return of Bonaparte was far worse. Not all the battle, all the worry, all the mobilization and expense – not all the change and transition when we had just adapted to the last changes. Poor Charlotte! Just when she thought her husband was home for good. I did not realize I had said it aloud until Antoine looked at me in amazement and asked, "Charlotte? What does she have to do with anything? Is that all you have to say?"

"If Bonaparte is back, there will be war."

"There will be an opportunity for France to regain her supremacy!"

"There will be grievous wounding and killing of men who are husbands and sons. There will be wives and parents left worrying, then grieving. Charlotte and the women of France have *everything* to do with it."

Gros stared at me as if unable to believe his ears. His Emperor was back; the fortunes of France were looking up. He was like a man coming upon sweet water after a drought. Always emotional and excitable, he burned as if with an inner flame. He is in love, I realized, and his loved one, given up for lost, has come home to him. Not for the first time I envied him his happiness even while I deplored its cause. And all I could think of to say was this prattle of the suffering of women! He shook his head pityingly, then shrugged, and went upstairs to wash and shave and change clothes. He did not ask me to accompany him, and I did not volunteer. I could not celebrate. I would stay indoors to express my disapproval of Bonaparte's return.

By mid-afternoon, however, I was tired of being inside, forced to listen to Maman Madeleine enthuse about her son's excitement, unable to ignore the growing murmur of the crowd streaming down the rue des Saints-Pères on its way to the palace. I intended to walk in the opposite direction – to the Luxembourg Gardens, perhaps, to take solace in the Fontaine de Médicis – but it seemed as if all of Paris was in the streets, irresistibly drawn to the Tuileries, delighted to have their Emperor back again, believing new victories to be in the offing. It was impossible to push my way against the human tide. I was carried along, almost lifted off my feet. Was it only ten months since this same populace had welcomed Louis

XVIII and the promise of peace? "Don't you remember?" I wanted to scream at them.

A huge hand slapped me on the back. "Cheer up, Madame!" ordered a rough but friendly voice, as its owner fell in step beside me. "He's come back to us!"

I turned to remonstrate but the words died in my throat at the sight of the empty sleeve pinned to his chest. He grinned broadly. "First Grenadiers," he said proudly. "He pointed me out with his sword after the battle of Iéna as an example for the new recruits to look up to. Twenty thousand troops on the field and he singled *me* out for praise." Tears sprang to his eyes. He blinked them away and lifted his voice in joyous acclaim. "*Vive l'Empereur!*" The crowd responded enthusiastically. "Come, Madame, you've more voice than *that*." He gave me another resounding slap on the back as if to shake it loose from my lungs. Fortunately, we had now crossed the Seine and reached the Tuileries Gardens, already tightly packed with the cheering populace. The Tricolor flew over the palace, replacing the white flag of the Bourbons. My companion took his hand from my shoulder to remove his hat, and I managed to slip away from him. Still, the crowd bore me onward.

At that moment, Bonaparte made an appearance on the central balcony. Flanked by officers resplendent in uniforms lavished with gold embroidery and braid, he stood out by the plainness of his grey coat and black hat, to emphasize that his person needed no embellishments to exert its authority. The crowd roared. A group of young men near me – I recognized Antoine's nephew Paul among them – set up a rhythmical chant: "*Vive l'Empereur*! *Vive l'Empereur*! *VIVE L'EMPEREUR*!" It spread throughout the crowd and my body thrummed with the sound. I alone was silent. Bonaparte spread wide his arms to embrace the Parisians before him, then cupped his hands to bring its love to his heart – like an opera singer shamelessly milking his audience while taking a bow, I thought. The crowd again roared its approval. He inclined his head – he would not bow to the people of France, not him – and went indoors again. Vainly the crowd tried to call him out. Finally, reluctantly, they began to depart, and I could escape.

The royal family and its followers fled to Belgium. Gleefully, Gros stopped painting Louis XVIII and the Duchesse d'Angoulême on the Dome of the Panthéon and applied for reinstatement of his original commission. With luck, he would be able to spend the summer on it. The government, however, had more pressing matters to deal with. The coalition that had vanquished Napoleon once before now sought the opportunity to do so again. A wide plain in Belgium was chosen for the battle site.

As I had feared, France was about to be plunged back into war. In my mind's eye I could see Bonaparte and his Marshals eagerly rubbing their hands, ordering maps to be brought and unrolled, and poring over them to strategize for the coming battle. Here was a business they knew, a course of action they understood. Wellington and his allies were no doubt doing the same.

It was a situation we had seen before – France facing overwhelming odds, France against the rest of the world – but it did not bring the ease of familiarity. Antoine and other apologists for Napoleon claimed that it was all the fault of the coalition. I, among many others, felt that Bonaparte, by his very presence, invited hostility and battle. All that spring, debate raged in Paris – privately, as his government would not admit of any doubts – about Napoleon's chances for success. With his army depleted of seasoned troops, victory was not going to be the certainty it would have been ten years before. It would be, instead, the last throw of the dice by a desperate gambler who had nothing left to lose. France, on the other hand, would have a great deal at risk.

Orders went out requisitioning men and horses. An appeal was made for new recruits – eager French youths who had feared only that they were never going to have the chance to see action. To the dismay of the Gros family, Paul Amalric, then sixteen years old, responded. Having grown up on his uncle's stories and paintings of the Emperor, he believed passionately in the glamour and glory of them. "This is France's last chance for glory!" he told his parents. "The Bourbons will bring us nothing but mediocrity!" His was a sentiment well captured by Stendhal several years later in *The Red and the Black*.

A family conference was called. Of habit, I scanned the Amalrics' salon to see what new treasure Jacques had brought home from the shop – he changed the décor often, according to what was in fashion, feeling it a good advertisement. This time it was a chandelier in the form of a star-covered globe girdled by candle-bearing griffons, but I had no time to examine it closely. Jacques was distraught. It was a father's role to be proud to have a son in the army, just as it was a son's role to make this part of his passage into manhood. But his reality could not hold to this principle. He wanted his son home and safe, and was telling him so at some length when we entered.

Paul was furious. "What would *you* understand? You're just a shopkeeper!" He invested the word with all the scorn with which Bonaparte spoke of the English. Jacques, turning red from the double embarrassment of his son's public rebuke and his own shame, had no words to reply. It was Gros's sister Marie who spoke up to scold their son: "Show respect for your father!"

Paul scowled. Half-boy, half-man, wanting to stand on his own feet but hating the thought of upsetting his mother, he reminded me of how he looked as a small boy in a pout. I would have smiled had the occasion not been so serious. He turned to appeal to his uncle, hope lighting his face, feeling sure of Antoine as an ally.

"Uncle Antoine – you understand. You've served the Emperor for twenty years. You've told the world of all he's accomplished on and off the battlefield. *You're* proud of me for wanting to enlist, aren't you?"

"Yes, Antoine, so he's been telling us. Your paintings have created a patriot." Marie's tone of voice would have blistered the paint off Antoine's canvas. "We thought you should hear it." *This is your fault*, her stony expression said. *Now do something about it.*

Antoine looked appalled. It was the first time such an accusation had been leveled at him – by his family, no less! He was at a loss how to reply. Love for his Emperor and his nephew were, I knew, struggling within him. The "woman's argument" that he had shrugged off as a matter of little importance when I put it to him on the morning of Bonaparte's return now struck home with all its force. As always at a time of crisis, his first instinct was to appeal to his mother for support. His anguished gaze, seeking her out, found her eyes not approvingly upon him but studying Paul's face with an intense hunger, memorizing it feature by feature lest she not see him again.

"No, Antoine," Marie said, "Maman can't help you this time." Years of buried resentment at being the second-best child found their way to the surface and rang in her voice. Being mother of the only grandson gave her a status in the argument that she was not slow to take advantage of.

Gros answered his sister's look with a steely gaze of his own, lifting his head and straightening his shoulders. "I love my nephew," he said, "but I will *not* speak against my Emperor." He turned to the boy. "Paul," he said in a much warmer voice, "it is indeed a noble thing that you wish to do. I would not try to persuade you otherwise."

There was a stunned silence. Then Paul gave a great gulping laugh of nervous relief and pandemonium broke loose. Maman Madeleine made loud wordless laments. Marie screamed at her brother, springing forward with hands like claws, prepared to tear at his face. Jacques tried to restrain and calm his wife. Paul wrung his uncle's hand and tried not to look smug.

No one paid any attention to me. After six years as part of this family, I was still merely Antoine's child bride whose opinion didn't count. Ignored by them, I stared at each one in turn, feeling as though I had dropped into a Dutch painting of a beggars' brawl. Suddenly I had anger of my own to deal with. This boy was not going to become cannon fodder simply because his mother and uncle were engaged in a showdown for his grandmother's affection.

"Quiet!" I ordered.

The cacophony raged as before.

"QUI-ET!" My open palm thumping the tabletop underscored my bellow and brought about the desired effect. I turned to Paul.

"You're enlisting because of your uncle's paintings? The paintings aren't the truth – they're only what Napoleon wanted you to think was true. Antoine has been telling these lies for so long that he's ended up believing them. At least learn the truth of those famous events celebrated in them.

"At Jaffa, he had twenty-four hundred prisoners of war – to whom mercy had been promised – bayoneted to save bullets. Those French soldiers who he's visiting and 'curing' in the hospital? He ordered them to be poisoned so they wouldn't slow down the retreat."

"Lies!" Antoine shouted. "All lies spread by the English!"

"And those wonderful battle scenes of Egypt – the Pyramids, Aboukir?" I continued as if he had not spoken. "We lost that war despite those victories. It was a lost cause after Nelson and the English destroyed the French fleet at that *other* Battle of Aboukir that we don't like to talk about, the one the English call the Battle of the Nile. Only Bonaparte sneaked out early to proclaim a victory, leaving others to the business of surrendering. Denon can confirm this – he came home with Bonaparte and Murat.

"Then there was Eylau, and that famous scene of compassion for the enemy troops he hadn't quite managed to slaughter." Antoine gave a low moan but did not speak. "That battle was fought in the midst of a blizzard. No one could even see who or what they were firing at, but they still managed to kill ten thousand men on each side. When the weather cleared, the French declared victory – and then departed! They had to fight for it all over again the next summer. Do you want to give up your life for a tactical retreat – for Bonaparte's mistakes? Think about it for a minute before you rush off."

"But Uncle Antoine served in the army!"

"As part of the art-collecting commission in Italy, not as a fighting man. He nearly died in the siege of Genoa. Having got home safely, he hasn't served in the fifteen years since. He has been painting those so-called victories and great moments from the safety of his studio in Versailles, where he need face nothing more hazardous than rheumatism."

Antoine flinched and turned red. Maman Madeleine stared at me open-mouthed, too shocked at my outburst to come to her son's defense.

"But we *can't* lose!" Paul cried passionately. "We'll win! We *must* win! And I'll be able to say I took part in that victory."

"And after it? Do you think one battle will do the trick? That the Allies will give up and go away? What about the battle after that, and the next, and the next? Have you thought of that?"

Judging by the sharp intakes of breath around me, none of them had.

Paul appealed again to Gros. "She's just being mad and spiteful. It's not all true, is it?"

Antoine looked stunned. He opened and shut his mouth several times. "I – he—" The words would not come. Wildly he scanned our faces, seeking support but finding none. The fight went out of him and his shoulders sagged. "Yes," he told his nephew. "It's true, all of it."

"You're just saying that because they want you to!"

"No," he said calmly, looking Paul in the eye. "It's true."

The boy, ashen-faced, clearly held it as a betrayal: "You and your paintings – you've been lying to me! I *hate* you!" He ran out of the room. Marie started to follow him but her husband restrained her. The boy would need time on his own to sort things out.

There was nothing left to say. We took our leave.

Shattered by the encounter Antoine slumped exhausted during the cab ride home. The rush of energy of my outburst had drained me. As my glow of triumph faded, a reaction set in, and I, too, was exhausted and sick at heart. In the process of trying to save our nephew I had torn my husband's most important works to shreds – paintings that had delighted me, inspired me, moved me to laughter and tears. I had betrayed my own belief – carefully nurtured by my training in the studio of Taunay, himself an occasional apologist for Bonaparte – in the power of art to uplift and transform and better mankind. I had betrayed both of us as artists.

When we arrived home, Maman Madeleine went to her room. Antoine stumbled, dazed, to the salon, where he sat down heavily on the sofa, his face in his hands, and burst into tears. I knelt before him, my own eyes damp, wishing I could give comfort and restore some of what I had taken away. "Antoine," I said as gently as I could, "Antoine." I reached up to put my arms around him, but at their touch his hands lashed out to push them away and he sat back, eyes glaring out of that tear-streaked face. I, too, shrank back from the impact of that gaze.

But I need to try again to make things right between us. "Antoine, what I said – it was to save Paul's life. Your paintings are magnif—"

"How could you?" His voice was rough and hoarse. "How could you? It's been hell these last two years, watching his defeat" – he pressed one hand over the *Légion d'honneur* in his lapel – "and with it the fall of France. I've been so worried for him, for our future, for

France's future. Some days it has been all I could do to get out of bed and make my way to the studio, hoping I would be able to call on some unknown inner reserve to enable me to put paint to canvas."

I shook my head in sorrow and pity. I had not known the depths of his despair. "You never said."

"I did not want to acknowledge it – to the world, only to hide it from myself. The thought of putting it into words was infinitely worse." He shut his eyes in pain. Two tears fell from beneath the closed lids. He opened his eyes and drew a shaky breath. "And then the nightmare was over – my beloved Emperor was again among us!" He sat up straight, eyes shining as they reflected an inner vision.

The hope died out of them as they came to focus on me. "Your words cut like knives to my heart. For my own wife to attack me in front of my family like that! How *could* you?" he demanded again.

I was deeply distressed to see him in so much pain and know that I had caused it, however good my intentions. "I was thinking only of Paul and his parents. I didn't say those things as a gratuitous attack on *you*. I wanted to save his life." My voice was soft, a plea for his understanding.

"GET OUT OF MY SIGHT!" I was truly afraid for him then and feared he would become even more enraged if I stayed. I ran from the room, from the apartment, and stayed away for several hours. When I returned, I did not go to our room but slept on the sofa.

I was awakened there the next morning by Maman Madeleine. She hissed as she bent over me: "How dare you call my son a liar?" She slapped my face.

At breakfast, Gros was more like his old self, but the rift that had opened in our marriage was now irreparable. We lived in the same house, ate our meals together with Maman Madeleine, even slept in the same bed, but more and more, we became strangers to each other.

From that day he could not paint any more battles, no matter how much the new government wanted him to. He went back to the classical subject matter of his youth.

It was also the beginning of the Gros family's rift with me. Forgetting that I had said these things in an effort to save Paul, and remembering only that I had said them about Antoine, their ire shifted from Antoine to me.

However, my words had the desired effect. Paul stayed safely at home and the Empire came to its weary end without him. He has never quite forgiven me, and I am happy to say his dislike has lasted for over twenty-five years.

Chapter 9

Paris, 1817-1819

After his defeat by combined English and Prussian forces at Waterloo, Bonaparte was safely sequestered on St Helena. All artistic reminders of his presence were banished to the storerooms of the Louvre. Artists were commissioned to create new works to take their place. Gros reluctantly took up his brush in praise of the Bourbons. In the Salon of 1817 he exhibited a large painting of Louis XVIII's departure from the Tuileries to which he had been a witness.

Marie Benoist resumed her studio afternoons, but the old *joie de vivre*, the attitude that "the opinion of men does not matter here" was gone. It was all too apparent that Monsieur Benoist's dictates did matter. Still, Marie liked to encourage other artists. I continued to attend faithfully. As I got less and less support from my marriage, the studio and its friendships became my emotional lifeline. However, I felt more comfortable about expressing my Salon ambitions when working alone with Josée. We each had paintings accepted in 1817. I had turned from still life to landscape; Josée continued to exhibit the landscape subjects inspired by classical history and mythology on which she was steadily building her reputation.

Théodore Géricault did not send anything to the Salon that year. He had been in Rome and was preparing a monumental painting of the horse race at the Roman carnival. He came to dinner one evening shortly after his return. Before, he had been a youth with talent. Now he was a man of maturity and assurance, with a tall, lithe body and an arresting face – full sensuous lips, strong chin, dark eyebrows, and short, curling brown hair. He brought such energy to whatever he did, whether it was covering acres of canvas or conversing with a friend. He was only two years younger than I. Next to him Antoine looked subdued, prim, and old-maidish. I could not help comparing the two. Théodore did not mean to surpass the older man but he could not help pushing ahead of him artistically to pursue his vision.

Not since Charles had I felt so alert and alive to a man – and Charles had been a mere boy in comparison.

After Antoine's outburst over Charles's portrait, I did not want to give him any cause, real or imagined, to be jealous. Even if our marriage had not been a success, I had never been unfaithful to him and had no intention of betraying him in the flesh. However, I could not help acknowledging my attraction to Géricault and playing out alternatives in my imagination.

Of course, having made up my mind not to act upon my attraction, I began to run into the man everywhere: at the art supply shop, in the galleries of the Louvre and the arcades of the Palais-Royal; at the Champ de Mars and the Champs-Elysées; in restaurants and cafés; even at my own dinner table. For someone reputed to be hard at work on an immense masterpiece, he certainly spent a great deal of time away from his studio. Like Girodet, he had inherited family money and did not need to sell paintings for a living. Nor did he relish the solitude of the studio the way Antoine did. He loved the company of other artists and their animated intellectual debate. Josée was a particular favorite of his. They were both intrigued by the new printmaking process of lithography, less labor-intensive than engraving and etching, and its potential as both an original and a reproductive medium.

One day he joined Josée and me at the Salon for a lively discussion of works in the galleries. Paintings depicting the historical kings of France were as popular in 1817 as they had been in 1814, particularly the illustrious deeds of those Louis who had preceded the current king of the same name – Louis VI, Louis IX (Saint Louis), Louis

XII, XIII, XIV, XVI and XVII were all well represented, as were those perennial favorites, François I and Henri IV. Géricault was scornful of the so-called Style Troubadour, with its meticulous prettiness. Josée, more tolerant, laughed and replied with robust good humor that called forth the same in him.

"And what do *you* think, Madame Gros?"

I was startled – not as quick-witted as my friend, I was content to follow Josée's lead. I rarely took part in these debates outside of Marie's studio, but my practice there stood me in good stead as I found my voice. "Why should the Middle Ages and Renaissance, given their prominence in France, be considered less worthy than ancient Greece and Rome? You are an admirer of Antoine's work. Do you think the worse of his painting of François I and Charles V – the one he calls his 'bouquet' for the beauty of its colors – because it is not of, say, Alexander and Porus?"

He paid me the compliment of listening closely and replying with respect for my opinion. It was a gratifying, all too rare experience. Antoine's contemporaries never talked to me about art – even Girodet only inquired after Gros – while I was always relegated to the group of wives and mothers and sisters at these gatherings. As I talked with Josée and Théodore, my Merry Augustine persona came out. Théodore accepted it, not damping my spirits as Gros and Maman Madeleine did. I found my heart expanding with gratitude. It gave my attraction to him an added dimension: the same fulfillment I felt after an afternoon with my friends.

Soon after, Géricault came to our house again for dinner, and he and Antoine fell to talking about Rome. My husband envied him his ability to come and go to Italy as he pleased, and the length of time he could stay there.

Afterward, I asked Antoine, "Why don't *we* go to Rome for six months? We can afford it! I want to see firsthand the masterpieces by Raphael and Michelangelo and Bernini. I would love to attend services at St Peter's."

Gros shook his head and frowned. "I'm too old for such a tiring trip. Travel is for young men."

"Nonsense – you're only forty-eight. Denon was fifty-five when he went to Egypt – and that was far more strenuous and hazardous than Italy."

"Denon's an exceptional man. His intellectual curiosity overrode the prospect of hardships. I prefer my creature comforts in Paris. Besides, Maman wouldn't want to be left alone."

I looked at him with distaste. Who *was* this middle-aged man I'd married, smug with satisfaction at the self-imposed limits of his life, who expected me to live within them as well, and who seemed incapable of imagining that I might want something more? I felt like a goldfish swimming round and round in its bowl, forever seeing the outside world without being able to reach it.

"But *I* want to go. I'm one-half of this marriage." (Only one-third, really, but I wasn't going to admit that now.) I struggled to fight back tears. "Don't my wishes count?"

"Of course they do, in many things. But asking me to prove my love by taking you to Rome is going too far. I wish to be here and no place else." He opened his newspaper and hid behind it. The argument was over as far as he was concerned.

I was seething. The Empire was gone; a new world was opening up; one's vistas could expand if one let them. My ambitions had expanded since joining Marie Benoist's group. I had shown my work at the Salon not once but twice. I longed to find other places and experiences where I could spread my wings.

If Théodore were my husband, he would take me seriously, I thought. *More to the point, he would take me with him!* I laughed at myself and shook my head to clear it, but the idea would not go away. I tried to imagine what it would be like to have a husband my own age, young and strong.

It became a full-blown fantasy for me, elaborated in private moments. *Théodore, thé-adore, thé-t'adore. Théodore, thé-adore, thé-t'adore*. The silly rhyme I had composed would repeat itself, over and over, in my head. *Théodore, I adore you.*

I would close my eyes against the realities of Paris, where our love would be hemmed about with restrictions and worries about word of it getting out. I imagined being lovers in Rome, away from the impedimenta of family and society, where I could become Merry Augustine all the time. We would make love in our studio and have long conversational meals with friends where I would join in the discussion as an equal. I would set a course of study for myself, sketching in the galleries and monuments and streets, painting in the studio, growing as an artist both in skills and scope.

This new-found freedom would make its way into our bed, where I would display a passion I had only rarely – too rarely! – known with Antoine. Imagining his mouth on mine, his rough hands running over my smooth naked body, rousing me to a pitch of desire I had never experienced, feeling his own, but always holding back until the last possible moment, an explosion of pleasure for both of us. Then, afterward, sated and content, we would sleep in each other's arms.

My fantasy existed outside real time – I knew that eventually Géricault would want to return to Paris and that when we did, all the censure of family and society would fall upon me. I refused to think that far – it would only spoil it.

I was too embarrassed to try out any of my imagined lovemaking with Antoine, and I was afraid lest he think I had taken a lover for real. I could not confess it to anyone, not even Josée. I tried my hand at painting the images in my mind, but they looked so amateurish that I burned them. Confession in church brought penance but no relief from my desires, only the forgiveness of past thoughts.

One late autumn day Josée and I were painting in her studio when Géricault arrived unannounced. We each wore an old dress and a paint-stained smock, our customary working attire. My hair was bundled under a scarf and Josée's red tresses were in glorious disarray. I was dismayed to look so bedraggled, but consoled myself that perhaps it was no bad thing to be seen as a working artist. I envied Josée her lack of embarrassment, but of course her heart was not fluttering as mine was. He had come to tell us he would soon be leaving for Rome. Before I could stop myself, I blurted out, "Oh, I wish I could go with you!" His eyebrows shot up. I blushed deeply, wanting to explain that of course I meant it for the sake of Rome rather than for himself, but I was afraid an explanation would make matters worse. I tried anyway, couching it in terms he would accept: "When you and Antoine spoke about Rome that evening, I urged him to think about taking me there and spending several months this time. He wouldn't even consider it – he says it's too strenuous for him at his age." Despite my effort to keep my voice neutral, I could not help injecting more than a trace of contempt into it.

"It would be an honor to view the galleries of Rome in the company of your husband, Madame Gros. I would learn a great deal from the experience," he said formally. I winced – it was not *my* company he looked forward to. "But you must remember the circumstances of his first visit. He was there on the orders of Bonaparte to select the greatest of Rome's treasures for France. Despite the promise of restitution made by our present King, few items have in fact been returned. It has been twenty years but Monsieur Gros's name is still remembered with great

203

bitterness. He would not find himself welcomed were he to return."

"Oh," I said meekly, my indignation deflated. "I had not thought of that."

"I tell you this in confidence, Mesdames." He looked at Josée before turning back to me. "Your husband is a sensitive man and I would not wish to hurt him by repeating it. As he has no desire to go, there is no point. I urge you, Madame Gros, do not press this visit upon him. It would come to no good."

There was nothing I could reply to that.

"I fear I have introduced too somber a note into our pleasant discussion. I will take my leave of you now." He got up, bowed to us, and left.

Josée and I were silent for some minutes after he left. I closed my eyes in exhaustion, hearing his voice and the passion with which he spoke, seeing the large ungainly hands as they gestured to emphasize his point. The passion had not been for my sake, but a wave of desire washed over me nonetheless. Tears of humiliation burned my eyes.

"Augustine." I opened my eyes with a start; I had forgotten Josée was there. "Why don't *we* plan a trip to Rome, the two of us?" She smiled and reached forward to squeeze my hand.

I felt a small spurt of hope before practical considerations arose to counter it. "Do you think we could? Neither of us has much money." The four thousand francs Antoine had given me for Charles's portrait had been spent long ago, and I knew that Josée was dependent solely on her art to bring an income.

"True, but if we wait for these men to take us, we will never get there! I feel more confident taking matters into our own hands." I managed a small smile at that. "Besides," she continued, "if – I mean *when* – we go, I want you there with me."

Her kind words achieved what Géricault's brusqueness had not. I cried in earnest, while she stroked my hair and murmured comforting words. When my tears subsided, she brought me a glass of cold water and a clean handkerchief so that I could wash my face.

"I apologize for weeping," I said in a low voice. "It's just that it felt so good to have someone care about *my* feelings." I blinked back more tears. The need to indulge in self-pity was gone. I wanted to stay close to this marvelous creature who cared about my feelings, held my hand when I was upset, and encouraged me to dream.

A nearby church clock struck six. Wearily I sat up and thought of the dreary evening before me. "I need to go home to give orders for supper." I had no appetite, but Antoine and Maman Madeleine would want a full meal as usual.

"You can't go in this state. I'll go out to get something to eat. Write a note for your cook and I will see it is delivered."

While she changed into her street clothes, I did as she instructed, suggesting our cook make a dish that I knew was a favorite of Antoine's. I hoped this would make up for my absence.

It was pleasant being alone in Josée's studio, which was both living and work space for Josée. A large folding screen and curtain at one end served to create a bedroom with a simple iron bedstead and battered armoire, and a plain cotton rug underfoot. I changed my clothes there as usual and hung my studio dress and apron on their hook. The studio part, its walls hung with drawings by Josée and her friends, including a portrait sketch of her by Géricault, doubled as salon with a threadbare sofa and upholstered chair. A plain wood table and chairs served as dining space, desk, and drawing table, while a stove in one corner provided heat and a minimal cooking surface. Large windows faced north – good light for a painter, but they would make it cold in winter. I shivered at the thought. It was a far cry from the fashionable furniture and ornaments I had purchased upon my marriage. Clearly Josée chose not to spend what modest funds she had on the comforts of a bourgeois home. But she had generosity and independence of spirit.

I wished I had taken her path, managing my own money and devoting my time and energies to becoming as good an artist as she, instead of turning them all over to the Gros household to be frittered away. But I had not known, at nineteen, that such a life was possible. Even if I had, would I have had the courage to pursue it, without Josée to show me the way?

I stood for a long time at the window watching the sky change from blue to aqua with a golden haze on the horizon as dusk came on, while the clouds went from white to orange-red to grey – effects Josée captured time and again in her landscapes. In the houses below on the rue de Condé, I saw lamps and candles being lit, people moving about, meals being prepared. I felt as if I were standing outside myself, watching my ordinary life go on out there.

I came out of my reverie when I heard Josée's step on the stairs. I lit candles and began to set the table. She brought with her the makings of an informal supper –

bread, ham, cheese and apples – and held aloft a bottle of champagne. We opened our supper with a clink of glasses in a celebratory toast.

In the following months, Josée and I made detailed plans of what to see, whom to contact, and where to stay. We bought the latest guidebooks, calculated the amount of money we would need, and set up a moneybox in her studio to which we contributed something each week, with a ceremonial clink of coins. I took great comfort from this activity.

Elaborating my travel plans with Josée did not quite blot out the thought of Géricault, who stayed in Rome for several months and resumed his place in our circle of artist friends upon his return to Paris in the summer. I found my attraction to him was as strong as ever. He had never completed his panoramic Roman horse race and was now, in 1818, planning to use that canvas for a subject inspired by the recent scandal of the wreck of the ship *Medusa* and her abandoned passengers. Despite his excitement over this new subject, he revealed few details about it. "Last time I dissipated my energies in talk instead of work," he told us. "I don't want to make that mistake again." Gros was one of the few whom he invited to his studio to see it in progress. As the invitation was given at our dinner table, it was extended to me as well. Clearly I was an afterthought, but it was an opening I was determined to take advantage of.

I let a week go by, waiting for a day when Antoine would be at his Versailles studio, occupied with his monumental canvas of the Duchesse d'Angoulême. As soon as Maman Madeleine had gone to her room for her after-lunch nap, I dressed with care, choosing silk undergarments and a filmy cotton dress.

Because of the warm weather, I took a fiacre most of the distance. I had the driver drop me off at a little distance from my destination and walked uphill the rest of the way. Géricault's studio on the rue des Martyrs, near the top of Montmartre, was almost at the edge of Paris. I could see and hear the creaking windmills that dotted the landscape beyond it and the huts of those who worked in the city but could not afford to live there. The conditions and population of the street were better than that, but not by very much, I thought, wrinkling my nose at the smells that assailed it. I wondered why the wealthy Géricault had chosen to live in an area so far below his means. It must be because of the studio, I realized: spaces that could accommodate so large a canvas were difficult to come by in the better neighborhoods.

Arriving, somewhat out of breath, at number 23, I hesitated, but only for a moment. Telling myself it was now or never, I let myself in the unlocked street door. As I crossed the courtyard, I took off my hat and shook my hair free of its pins, as I had imagined wearing it in my Roman fantasy – long, luxuriant and brown, abundant and curling. I reached a hand to the bodice of my dress to reposition my breasts to make a more seductive neckline but decided against something so obvious. I knocked tentatively on the studio door.

There was no response. I knocked more firmly.

"Just a moment!" A long moment, as it turned out: he was still wiping paint off his hands as he opened the door. "I'm coming, I'm coming!" His face broke into a big smile at the sight of me and my heart leapt. "Madame Gros!" he boomed, looking around for the husband he assumed was at my side. The look of welcome faded, to be replaced by concern. "Monsieur Gros is not with you? Is he ill? Have you come for my help? Just give me a minute to clean up––"

"No, not at all, he is quite well, painting at Versailles. I came to see – to take up your invitation to see – the shipwreck scene you told us about."

"Oh." Clearly he was taken aback. "Is Josée coming, then?" he asked.

My heart sank, but I forced myself to smile and speak lightly. "No, not today – you will need to find me sufficient on my own."

He winced at this implication of his rudeness. "Of course you are welcome by yourself," he said formally. "It's merely that I am used to seeing you in the company of others. When one catches sight of Melchior, one automatically looks for Gaspard and Balthazar."

I laughed at the analogy to the Wise Men and the tension between us dissipated. "*Entrez, entrez,*" he urged me, holding the door wide so I could do so.

"Who is it, Théo?" called a masculine voice.

Damn! It had not occurred to me that he might have company.

"It's Madame Gros, Eugène. Are you decent?"

"As long as I am lying face-down, yes." The amused reply came from a youth with a shock of wildly curling black hair and a smooth expanse of back and buttocks who was posing for one of the figures on the raft.

"I will ask her to face the other way for a moment."

I obliged, and there was the rustle of silk fabric behind me.

"You may turn around," said the youth. I did so.

"Madame Gros," Géricault said formally, "may I present Eugène Delacroix?"

It is a name the world now knows, of course. At the time, however, he was merely Géricault's friend, and his presence threatened to thwart the purpose of my visit. Despite this I could not avoid drawing breath in pleasure at the sheer beauty of him. He knew it and instinctively struck a pose that showed him to best advantage. He wore his dressing gown naturally, without embarrassment. The thought crossed my mind that it was a pity it was not *he* whom I had come to seduce, for I suspected he would be much easier than his friend.

"Gros – as in the painter of *Jaffa*?" he inquired, his eyes lighting up.

"That is my husband's work. I, too, am a painter, under my own name, Augustine Dufresne." His eyes did not light up this time.

"I am a painter also, but I am here for Théo." He gestured at his figure on the canvas, and we turned our attention to it. It lay face down on the raft. Around it, other dead and dying men trailed limbs in the water. Drawing the eye upward, a pyramid of finely muscled men signaled to something in the distance, a ship so small in that vast ocean of canvas that Géricault had to point it out to me with the long handle of his paintbrush.

The wretched tale of the *Medusa* – how her incompetent captain wrecked her and set most of her passengers adrift on a raft, and the harrowing struggles of the few survivors, who were forced to resort to cannibalism – had shaken Paris considerably the year before. The one hundred and fifty deaths that would have been deemed the casualties of a mere light skirmish in the time of Napoleon assumed during the peace the stature of a full-blown massacre. Those in opposition to the government pounced on it as symptomatic of the blundering Bourbons in general and Louis XVIII in particular. Even I, with my strong loyalty to the Bourbons, had been repulsed by the newspaper's illustration of the ragged band of almost skeletal survivors in their tattered clothing and wondered how Louis XVIII so readily managed to squander our good will again and again.

The newspaper engravings were in my mind as I beheld the unblemished well-muscled flesh of the men in the painting, like marble sculptures of antiquity or of Michelangelo brought to life. Sketches for some of the figures hung on the walls of the studio. A severed head and limbs, painted in one of the hospital dissecting rooms, brought to mind the legend of Saint Denis, walking from the center of the city and up this very street after his execution, holding his head in his hands. I remember also the head of a drowned man with grey flesh and opaque unseeing eyes and a portrait of the Negro who posed for the pinnacle figure of the human pyramid – but the whole painting went beyond these details. Radical though Théodore may have been in some ways, his painting, like *Jaffa*, was cast in the academic tradition, transcending "mere" truth to create an image that took its place in the traditions of art. *The Raft of the Medusa* reduced the struggle to its most elemental – man versus the wind and waves. Gone were the politics that had been so prominent a part of the newspaper accounts. I doubt whether anyone would even remember the scandal today, a quarter-century later, were it not for the painting.

So absorbed was I in looking that I had forgotten the two men until Géricault brought in three glasses of wine and Delacroix came to stand beside me. He had changed from the dressing gown into a dark green suit and applied cologne with a pleasant lemon smell. Charles would have envied his beautiful boots of supple brown leather. He smiled easily at me. "Théo's conception is extraordinary, is it not?"

214

"Indeed," I agreed warmly, turning my head and smiling in return. It was impossible to look away from this beautiful young man. He wore his hair rather long and unkempt, but his mustache and van Dyck beard were neatly trimmed, and his eyebrows had a natural arch many women would envy. The almost hypnotic gaze of his black eyes held the promise of much but the offer of very little. He was, I was disappointed to realize, one of those men for whom the pleasure of the conquest was not so much in bedding a woman as in eliciting from her the desire to be bedded. I had met his kind before and knew better than to be flattered by his attentions. It was not so much that he found my person attractive as that my married status was a challenge. There was only one way to reply to such games: I yawned.

He dropped his eyes. I turned my attention back to the painting.

"Théo has benefited greatly from studying your husband's work," he said, pointing out figures whose poses I recognized. There was even a group of father and son inspired by the dying doctor and his patient in *Jaffa*.

"So he has – Antoine will be pleased," I replied. Privately I wondered how truly flattered Antoine would be by this admirer whose imitation so often led to surpassing his idol. There is a limit to the patience of even the best of mentors.

"I regret I must leave now for another appointment. Please tell your husband, Madame, how much those of us who admire his work regret it had to be put away for political reasons. We hope that one day it will again claim its rightful place on the walls of the Louvre." He gave us a small formal bow in parting.

"I wish he would not so firmly *Madame* me," I said to Théodore afterward, as he refilled our wineglasses. "I am not so old as *that*."

"Ah, do not underestimate the attraction, for a very young man, of someone he considers an older woman." He smiled and raised his glass in a toast. We drank.

I took courage from the wine. It was now or never. "What about the attraction for a man of a woman his own age?" My heart was thudding in my chest. I had to force myself to look into his eyes.

"Well, yes, of course," he replied, beginning another easy laugh that stopped abruptly as the meaning of my words and look sank in. He spluttered in his wineglass, inhaled some of the liquid by accident, and surrendered to a fit of coughing that would not lessen until I had thumped him on the back several times. It was not how I had envisioned laying hands on him.

At last the spasm subsided and he could speak.

"Madame Gros," he croaked, "you forget yourself." A milder fit of coughing took him; this time I kept my hands at my sides and let him deal with it himself.

"You are asking me," he gasped, "to dishonor the man I revere more highly than any other painter in France." More highly, it was clear, than the painter who now offered herself to him. He started to cough yet again.

"No," I would have liked to tell him. "I do not 'forget' myself. I have come here fully consciously, knowing what I want." But it did not seem likely that saying this would bring me any closer to achieving what I desired. Or had desired, for the moment had passed.

"Thank you for showing me your painting, Monsieur. I wish you a speedy recovery from your cough." The noise of it followed me out the door, across the courtyard and into the street.

Outside, I began to shiver despite the warm sun. I walked away quickly, not caring which direction I took. I was churning with emotions I could not express out loud in public: furious at myself and him, ashamed of pursuing a lover, yet proud of having the courage to do so. I did not for an instant think he would tell Antoine, but could he resist the temptation to tell his friends? Would my name become something for Delacroix and others to snigger about?

"Do you know why she was really here, Eugène?"

"Oh, I think that was obvious from the start!"

I walked even faster to get away from the mocking laughter that seemed to follow me, feeling more and more a fool with each step. I did not think about where I was going, but my feet of their own accord found their way to the rue de Condé. Josée was not there, but the concierge, who knew me, let me in. Safely hidden from the scrutiny of others, I could let loose the tears I had been holding back.

Josée found me huddled on the sofa when she returned. "Augustine! What has happened?" She knelt in a graceful movement and took my hands in hers.

I shook my head.

"Tell me," she urged.

I poured out the whole sordid tale, half-afraid she would recoil in disgust. She said nothing when I finished but got up to bring me a glass of water. Her face was grim as she sat down by my side.

"Don't be angry with me," I begged.

"Angry at you? Why should I be? No, it's that pious Théo taking shelter behind the sanctity of marriage." She turned to face me. "The truth is, he has been having an affair with his uncle's young wife. She gave birth to Théo's child last year. He really loves her. Only he can't talk about it because of her situation."

"You mean – after all he said about dishonoring—"

"Yes, and for two years now."

"That hypocrite! Taking the high moral ground to make me feel ashamed, when all the time—" I was spitting mad. "Why didn't I know? How do you know? Why didn't you tell me?"

"It's an open secret and the family relationships make it even more awkward, so he never talks about it."

"Then how do *you* know?"

She shrugged. "People tell me things. They know I don't betray confidences." She smiled at me. "As I will never breathe a word of this conversation to anyone else."

"Thank you," I whispered. "Do you think he would tell—"

"Antoine?"

"No, I'm sure he would not – he has too high a regard for *my* husband's feelings," I said ironically. "I was thinking of Delacroix and his other friends."

Josée considered and shook her head. "No. He would not want it to get back to Antoine. Nor would he be very successful in playing the role of the young man of outraged virtue. I'm sure he'll let the matter drop."

This proved to be true. On the few occasions we met, we were formal and polite to each other. He did not accept any more invitations to dinner at our home, though he and Antoine would sometimes meet at a restaurant.

It was my first and last attempt at taking a lover.

Chapter 10

Paris, 1819-1822

Unhappily, I had to abandon my painting. After having a group of landscapes accepted for the Salon again in 1819 and seeming well on the way to modest success, I was like many other women claimed by family duties. For once it was not Antoine's demanding mother – she achieved much more satisfaction from laying exclusive claim to her son's attention, in order to complain the more loudly that I was ignoring both of them. It was my own that needed help.

Maman had not done well in the years following Papa's death. Her eyesight began to fail, though she was only a little older than Antoine, whose vision stayed keen until the end. Ordinarily I, as the eldest daughter, would have taken her into my home, but Antoine and I were already caring for Maman Madeleine. So it fell to my sister Pauline and, nominally, my brother Henri to help her. This situation was not without its problems.

Pauline had married the year after me, in 1810. Her husband, Jacques Carbonnet, was the son of a family friend and an agent de change like our father. He had a clubfoot and a pronounced limp, so that he could not be conscripted; he was cheerful about it, recognizing the advantages it gave him in a war-mad world, when he otherwise would have been no woman's first choice. He admired Pauline and wanted to marry her despite his parents' misgivings that he would inherit our mother and brother as part of the marriage. His parents had made prudent inquiries of the notary and found that our mother's portion of Papa's estate would not come with her but had gone to me. This only made Jacques feel closer to my sister, as he himself was a younger son. He, too, had been second choice until his brother went into the army.

Pauline was grateful for his interest. I had been the favored sister who had married well; Henri was the only son, while she had too often found herself taken for granted. Soon Pauline and Jacques had three children, none of whom inherited their father's condition. She loved being a mother, something I wholeheartedly envied her. Antoine got on well with Jacques and enjoyed playing with his niece and nephews.

Pauline shared the Dufresne family artistic talent. In her case it took the form of designing and executing elaborate embroideries, work for which she did not need a studio but could do at home. Moreover, embroidery was a raised and tactile art form that our mother could feel with her fingers even after the colors had become indistinct shapes. After finishing two sets of table linens, drapes, and other domestic items, Pauline made a dress for herself. The dressmaker who later restyled it exclaimed at the fineness of the stitching and inquired if she would be interested in working for her, apologizing profusely lest her spontaneous offer have offended someone so clearly a *bourgeoise*, not a working-class seamstress. Pauline accepted for the dual pleasures of having her talent acknowledged by someone outside the family circle and earning her own money. She did not tell Jacques, who would have been appalled to have it thought that his wife needed to "take in sewing." Maman, who now lived with her, and Henri and I were so accustomed to seeing her embroidery, we never noticed that this parade of garments came and went unworn by any of us. Had Henri suspected that she had a supply of francs to "lend" him, he would have laid claim to a share of it. She converted her earnings into gold coins whenever she could and kept them among her embroidery silks in a beaded purse she had made herself. She took them out to look at and count now and then when her spirits were low. The gold was her personal insurance against hard times. So well did she keep her secret that I did not learn of this until years later, long after the seamstress had retired.

Henri was sixteen, feeling newly grown-up and important, when he stood in my father's place to sign my marriage contract. A year later he served as witness for Pauline as well. He lived with her and Jacques until he gained control of his inheritance at twenty-one and moved to lodgings after their first child was born. The baby's crying got on his nerves, he said, as did, I imagine, the fact that his mother's and sister's attention had been diverted from himself to the newcomer. If there was no one to look after him in lodgings, at least it was quiet. His fifty thousand francs of capital earned two thousand francs a year, enough to keep him but not enough to support a family or contribute to our mother's support.

When the ten-year-old Henri had visited the Salon of 1804 with the rest of the family, he had been impressed by the art he saw there, but even more by the acclaim and admiration and accolades given to the artists. He did not understand the hard work that must go into one's practice to earn them. He studied painting with a succession of masters who acknowledged his talent but deplored his laziness. Unlike Géricault, who had pursued a rigorous course of personal study in the galleries in the Louvre, Henri took it for granted that his renowned brother-in-law would help him achieve artistic fame and fortune. Gros, having seen many young men of ambition come and go over the years, made introductions for him with an air of taking no responsibility. His friends gave him work, I could see, mostly to oblige Antoine. Henri congratulated himself on the launch of his career not by getting down to work but by getting drunk, an omen of what was to come. He did not have the discipline to produce a steady stream of paintings. However, two or three clients liked his work well enough to ask for further pieces, so that his painting earned enough for him to claim he made his living from it.

Henri was generous in compliments and gallantries but guarded about the substance of his life. He always said he was working hard but privately we women doubted it. We predicted that marriage would be the making of him and shook our heads in humorous dismay as we despaired of any sensible young woman taking him. He fell in love from time to time with actresses and spurned the shop assistants and friends' younger sisters who openly expressed their admiration of him. He grew quite friendly with one of the female students at the master's atelier, but she worked hard, had ambition for herself, and made him see his excuses for what they were.

Maman was blind to all these shortcomings even when her eyesight was still strong. Henri was her adored son.

One day he would surely be an artist of note, and she praised his talent loudly at a dinner party at our house that included not only Girodet but also Denon and David. Even Henri looked abashed in such august company and blushed at his plate, not daring to meet their eyes. After a painful silence, David raised his glass to salute my mother and said mildly to Henri, with only a little of his habitual stammer, "You are fortunate indeed, young man, in the loyalty of your family." I stole a glance at Maman Madeleine as he said this. She sat mute with a virtuous look that proclaimed *she* had no need to boast; *her* son had already proved his worth. My exasperation with my mother overflowed into a longing to smack my mother-in-law as well. I rang the bell for the next course and talked brightly of lamb roasted with rosemary. After that we were careful to invite Maman and Henri only when we were *en famille*.

My relationship with my brother and sister was complicated by Maman's gift to me of her share of Papa's estate. The four thousand francs a year earned by my dowry became part of the Gros family income managed and invested by Antoine and Maman Madeleine. As a result I rarely saw cash in hand from it: my lament to Josée that I had very little money of my own was genuine.

However, I arranged that the income from Maman's contribution would be paid to my sister for our mother's support. It was only fair, I thought, and I carried my point over the objections of my mother-in-law, who reminded me of it every time I complained of being short of cash. Maman's money had become mine and in turn my husband's; as a result, the income from it became a gift from Antoine to me and thence to my sister for our mother's upkeep. In this process the income had gone from a right to a gift, with a sense of obligation on both sides – an uncomfortable situation. While Maman still had some income from the dowry she had brought to her marriage, she was now largely dependent on her children. That and her deteriorating eyesight led to a great deal of self-pity that no amount of loving words could lessen.

The brunt of our mother's care fell on Pauline. No one expected Henri to take the responsibility; in our experience, young men needed looking after, not the other way around. Too, as Maman grew older and physical infirmities set in, she needed a woman to help with dressing and bathing and going to the toilet. The less she could do, the more short-tempered she became. Servants can escape but daughters can't.

I was surprised to receive a note from Pauline in April 1820 saying that she wished to call on me "for a private talk." Maman Madeleine was entertaining a group of friends that afternoon, so I suggested we meet at Galignani's café instead. It was one of the first warm days of the spring and it would be a pleasure to sit in the sunshine in the garden. I arrived first, and as I waited for her I realized with a pang of conscience how long it had been since I had visited to see Pauline instead of Maman or talked with her as we had as young sisters. Her life was wrapped up in a happy marriage and a growing family. With no children and only a lukewarm relationship with my husband, I could not follow her down those conversational paths. It saddened me now, how much we had drifted apart, for all we saw each other often. Her arrival in a charmingly embroidered dress of deep blue saved me from further unhappy thoughts.

"Pauline!" We embraced. She smiled but it was clear she was troubled. Could it be something about her own health? I shivered. When the waiter came, I ordered coffee and an assortment of cakes that I knew would please her.

"Pauline, what's the matter?" She gulped and shook her head, fighting back tears. I took her hand, squeezed it hard, and waited.

"Tine, I think – I'm certain – Maman is going blind."

Relief that Pauline was all right flooded through me, before the impact of her words hit home in a second cold wave of shock. Both her hands now gripped mine, and some of the tears she had been holding back spilled down her cheeks.

Of course, the waiter chose that moment to return. Pauline released my hands to fumble in her bag for a handkerchief. I poured a cup of strong coffee, added hot milk, and put it and one of the cakes in front of her. "Eat this, you'll feel better. Then tell me." I took just coffee myself – I had no appetite. Pauline must not have had breakfast or lunch, I decided, and said as much when I put a second cake on her plate. She nodded and made short work of it and a third before putting down her fork and accepting a second cup of coffee. She looked better now, more resolute, ready to face the crisis. She smiled her thanks.

"Pauline, what makes you think so?"

"Little things – at table, she always runs her fingers over the utensils before she uses them, as if to make sure of what they are. Sometimes she asks the maid what's in the serving dish even as she looks directly at it. Once, when Jacques asked her to pass the saltcellar, she couldn't

229

seem to find it, and one of the children had to help her. Then last night, I asked her to hand me the gold thimble that was on the table next to my chair. She peered at the tabletop closely, said, 'I don't see it,' and groped with her hand like a blind woman until she found it, carefully felt it to identify it, and held it out to where she thought I was. That's when I knew." She sighed. "I suppose I've known for some time but didn't want to acknowledge it, so I wouldn't need to face it. But now I have, and I do."

"*We* do, Pauline. *And* Henri. It's not fair for you to have to face this alone." Even as I said it, I realized just how much she had already coped with by herself. I paid over Maman's money and made the occasional visit. Henri had long since lived on his own but visited his mother, we knew, all too rarely for her liking. It was Pauline who took care of her day in and day out. A sharp glance from my sister implied that she had read my thoughts.

We both fell silent. I ordered more coffee and wrapped my hands gratefully around the warmth of the cup. The day no longer seemed as sunny as it had been.

Blind. As a painter that condition had always had a particular horror for me. To live in darkness with only the memory of colors, to lose one's skill with hand and brush, to never again see a landscape, a fine horse, the face of a loved one (one can feel the contours of a face, but not the color of the eyes), a skyscape of scudding clouds, the heart-stirring sight of a troop of hussars on horseback, nor all the beauties of Paris, its buildings, gardens, and river: those were the things I should miss. To walk hesitantly, groping one's way, or be led everywhere by a guide, helped in so much you were once able to do for yourself. To be pitied by fellow artists with whom you once strove side by side. To have no diversion from your own thoughts and self-pity at the end of the day.

"Poor Maman!" I exclaimed, shuddering.

My sister gave me a surprised, slightly censorious look. She, I knew, would not be taking an emotional inventory but thinking along the practical lines of running her household, taking Maman's condition into account as she would the addition of another child or the need to hire a new cook. My squeamish imaginings were a luxury she could not afford to allow herself, and it was plain she had little patience for people who did.

"What can I do to help you, Pauline?" My offer was sincerely given. I was unprepared for the bitter outburst it provoked.

"Take Maman to live with you, so *I* can be the one with the luxury of visiting her from time to time. Don't 'help,'

Augustine, take the problem over, take it away from me! Since you married I've had eleven years of taking care of Maman, and Henri too for five years of that, and I've a family of my own now. You don't have any children—"

"Pauline!" I was shocked and frightened. I had had no idea such bitterness lurked beneath the surface of my practical sister so adept at coping. Her accusations stung, especially the taunt about having no children of my own. Had a stranger said such things, I would have lashed back. But this was a beloved sister who was feeling the strain of a burden about to be doubled, who clearly needed respite.

"Pauline." I said her name low and firmly, to bring her back to the present – the garden café, the sun, the presence of others at the tables around us. "Pauline," I repeated, "look at me."

She turned her head, brought her eyes into focus, and realized what she'd just said. "Oh, Tine, I never meant it to come out like that! I know how much you've wanted children and tried for them! Don't hate me, Augustine," she begged.

In reply, I dipped my handkerchief into my water glass and wiped her teary face, making soothing noises as I did so. How many times over the years must she have done this for a child? It brought back memories of our mother doing it for us, soothing away hurts and troubles. I would need to take Maman's place, I could see, in taking care of my sister. When Pauline was calmer, I told her, "I can't change the past, but I can help, starting now and going forward."

We sat quietly for some time absorbing the impact of the news when we were approached by a pair of slightly tipsy hussars in dress uniform who offered to cheer us up, saying two such pretty ladies should not be sad. Before we could recover from our surprise to decline their offer, the waiter and manager came over to hustle the men out: "This isn't the Palais Royal!" Pauline and I collapsed with giggles: here we were, old married women of thirty and more, being approached as pretty young things. It broke the tension of our serious discussion and brought a smile to our faces whenever we mentioned it in the months to come.

I signaled the waiter for two glasses of wine to calm my sister and put color in her cheeks and warmth in her stomach, as well as – I must confess – to give myself courage. Maman was not easy to deal with at the best of times. I had been glad to leave her care to Pauline, but I, too, was her daughter and should share the responsibilities.

"I can't take Maman into my home," I told her. "Not with Maman Madeleine in charge of the household." Pauline gave me a surprised look. "Oh yes," I told her, "I'm Antoine's wife, but it's never really been *my* house. Antoine's always been happy with the way his mother manages things and never wants me to change them. Every change I've tried to make in eleven years has been countermanded by one or the other of them. When I married him, I didn't realize just how much I'd be marrying her as well." I took a large gulp of the wine and said, "I sometimes wonder just why he married. Because he wanted a wife? Or because he thought his mother needed an assistant to make sure all the work was done to her dictates?"

"Augustine! Surely he loves you?"

"As best he can, after his mother and his Emperor and the late Empress and his best friend Girodet and..."

"Tine! Surely he's not one of those!"

"In bed, no. Emotionally, yes, like the rest of Monsieur David's students. Thank God that dreadful man has been banished to Brussels!"

"Oh, Tine, I never guessed."

"It's not the kind of thing I want to admit even to myself, much less to a sister whose marriage has been so

234

happy." Tears of self-pity welled up, but I refused to give in. "Enough. I did not meet with you to talk about my problems, but to see how I could help with yours. If I cannot bring Maman to my house, as things are, how can I help you?"

I helped by visiting Maman four or five afternoons a week. Often Pauline took this opportunity to go out or to give time to her children, and Maman and I were left on our own. When she was in a good mood, she would talk about her childhood and youth and the days when my father came courting. It was then that she told me about the night the Bastille fell. I heard tales of my grandparents that I had not heard in years. Her face would be animated and I would catch a glimpse of the girl she had been.

Antoine sometimes came with me. He painted a portrait of her asleep in her armchair. It was highly gratifying for Maman to be painted by an artist of such eminence even if she could not see it. Painting her brought out a different side of him, the portraitist flattering the client, jovial and easy to get along with. It was a role he found easier than son-in-law.

As her condition progressed, however, black days of self-pity became more frequent. Her loss of sight was her principal complaint; she lamented the loss of colors, of seeing what went on around her. She complained about how difficult it had become for her to do the simplest things – drink a bowl of soup, dress and undress, or use her chamber pot. Her sense of isolation grew so intense that she complained of being abandoned even when Pauline, Jacques and I were present. Assured of our presence, she would ask why her friends Sophie and Beatrix had deserted her. When we gently reminded her that they had died some months before, she envied them. She alternated between wishing she, too, were dead and accusing us of longing to be rid of her. It became harder and harder to reassure her, not to mention ourselves, that we loved her and wanted her still with us. She countered our assertions by saying that she knew she was a burden in our lives, and it would be better if she were out of it. It was chiefly for my sister's sake I persevered.

I paid dearly for the privilege of this familial duty – with my painting. The friendships I had formed in Marie's studio slipped away as I was drawn into the world of my sister's household. Once, when I missed a visit to Maman to see Josée, my mother's laments drove me nearly mad. She no longer rejoiced I was an artist but resented it and tried to make me feel guilty for being able to see. My sharp reply annoyed Pauline: now she would have Maman's complaints about me to deal with on top of everything else.

I tried to be content with "keeping my hand in," by sketching in the Tuileries gardens on my trips to and from my sister's home, but it was painful not to have anything to send to the Salon in 1822. That was the year of Delacroix's first great success, *Dante's Boat*. He had chosen a scene from the *Divine Comedy*: the boatman Phlegyas taking Dante and his guide Virgil across the River Styx, while the souls of the damned attempt to climb on board and one bites the stern of the boat in frustration. The conception was unlike anything else at the Salon. He had clearly benefited from his study of classical sculpture as well as of Géricault's heroic nudes. I could not find any trace of Antoine in it. Antoine, however, admired his use of color, particularly the tiny rainbows he had inserted into the drops of water seemingly flecked onto the canvas. I was boiling over with envy for Delacroix's accomplishment.

Antoine moved away to look at other works, but while I continued to examine the painting, Delacroix came to stand to one side of it to collect congratulations. I introduced myself to him a second time, reminding him of the first time we had met, also in front of a painting of a boat. His face clouded. Théo was very ill, he told me quietly, tubercular disease compounded by a series of riding accidents. He had not sent anything to the Salon but had embarked upon a remarkable series of portraits of the insane.

I was no longer in love with Géricault – that passion had burnt itself out – but I regretted deeply that so great a talent should be short-lived. I knew what pain Delacroix must be feeling at the prospect of losing his friend. I extended my hand, intending to put it lightly on his arm, but he grasped it firmly in both of his for a moment.

When I had recovered my composure, I left the Salon Carré to go in search of the smaller works amongst which mine used to hang, but that felt even worse. There were a fair number of women artists among them, other women who no doubt had domestic obligations of their own but who managed to make time to paint and draw and submit their work. I was jealous of them, angry at myself, my sister, my mother, my husband, my mother-in-law, and my brother, who had been of so little help with our mother, using his studio as his excuse and his refuge. I had to leave before resentment choked me. I marched resolutely home, snatched up my sketchpad and pencils, and headed out again to the Jardin du Luxembourg. As the walk calmed my emotions, my thoughts turned from resenting others to planning what I would draw. I sat down at the Medici fountain but it failed to have its usual calming effect. I opened my sketchpad and, inspired by Delacroix, started to draw demons of the kind biting Dante's boat, internal ones – Envy, Disappointment, Despair – external ones – Maman, Henri, Pauline – giving vent to an interior landscape as I had never done before. I filled sheet after sheet, working in a trance. I came out of it only when the garden attendant approached me at dusk before locking the gate. My hands were almost black from the pencil. I washed them in the fountain and dried them on my petticoat. At home, they would be wondering what had happened to me, but I could not return yet, feeling as I did. I found a restaurant in the area of the Panthéon and sent a note that I was eating out. Gradually, as I worked my way through the courses of the meal, I regained my calm.

When I looked at the drawings I had done, I was amazed and dismayed. They were tangible proofs of the darkness that had been seething inside me, now brought out into the open. Of course their execution was not as skilled as Delacroix's – he was and is something exceptional – but they had life and power. Girodet might appreciate them, I thought, as his work so often hovered on the edge of the acceptable. Did I even dare to show them to anyone? They were so personal and not the sort of thing painted by a woman. Women drew subjects celebrating domesticity; my drawings vilified my family. Could I afford the alienation they would cause? Women are supposed to be the nurturers and supporters. Would anyone outside the family circle find these drawings any more acceptable? Or would I find myself labeled a madwoman, like those sad lost souls painted by Géricault? I shivered.

What do you do when you have discovered the truth about yourself and know it to be unpalatable? I shut the sketchpad quickly – I didn't have an answer for that, and I was too exhausted to think just then. I paid my bill and left.

It had grown dark and the moon had risen, illuminating the Panthéon. The majestic bulk of Soufflot's dome made me catch my breath at the beauty and drama of the scene. Yet I knew what labor and anxiety the interior of that dome had cost Antoine over the past decade, and it was not finished yet. As if in response to my thought, the moon hid behind a cloud. I laughed ruefully and hailed a passing fiacre to take me back to the rue des Saints-Pères.

When I got there, I found a note from Antoine: he was dining out with friends he had met at the Salon. He would not have noticed my upset state or my absence at dinner, nor wondered what caused it. He had been celebrating with other artists but had not invited me to join them. I was furious all over again and cut short Maman Madeleine's lamentations at being left alone all day. I retired fuming to our bedroom.

Antoine was surprised at finding me awake when he returned at midnight. "You waited up for me? That's sweet," he said absently. "It was a *wonderful* evening." He went on to tell me about it, his voice slightly slurred with drink, punctuating the narrative with huge yawns. Girodet was there, of course, Gérard, Isabey with his son, Horace Vernet, Géricault and young Delacroix. They drank a toast to the Emperor's memory (Bonaparte had died the previous year and it was safe to do so without being reported to the police) and went on to dinner at Le Grand Véfour in the Palais Royal. The wine continued to flow and the rabbit stew, made from game bagged that morning, practically leapt from the plate to the palate. He had been undressing all the while, folding his clothes neatly as was his habit, and now he slipped his nightshirt over his head and gave a last contented sigh in memory of a day well done. He still had not asked about me. He would be blissfully asleep in five minutes unless I spoke up now.

"I know one artist who *wasn't* there," I began mildly enough.

"Who?" He yawned, not much caring what the answer was.

"Your wife."

His attention sharpened. "I looked for you when we left the Salon, but you had gone."

"Your note didn't invite me to join you later, either."

"None of the others invited their wives."

"None of the other wives are painters. I don't care about not being invited as a wife. But I *am* an artist."

"You've hardly painted at all since your mother fell ill, and you didn't send anything to the Salon this year."

"Is that the true measure, the Salon? Is one not really an artist otherwise?"

"Well, yes, but an amateur." Too late, he realized the danger of this pronouncement; he looked horrified at what he had let slip out.

"Even if there are good reasons for her not to paint, such as taking care of her mother?"

"But it's in a woman's nature to make sacrifices to take care of others. Look at Charlotte."

"And you men count on it, don't you?" I could not keep the sneer out of my voice. His using Charlotte as an example stung. All that talent and training gone to waste in supporting a husband who, however much he was a master surgeon on the battlefield, was a self-regarding braggart. Antoine disliked the man, yet he applauded Charlotte, who had also been a star pupil of David, for her sacrifices to take care of him. Antoine had no great fondness for my family, but he would take it for granted that I would make sacrifices on their behalf.

And what sacrifices had he made on behalf of his beloved mother? I was about to ask when the unlovely answer hit me with all its unwelcome force. He had married *me*. He had given up his comfortable bachelorhood so that his mother would have someone to run her household and take care of her while he continued to turn his full attention to painting. He had given up his weekly visits to those accommodating women whose business was pleasing men, to take on someone who had dreams and ambitions of her own, who would expect to be considered, loved, and made to feel important. *I* was his sacrifice, and he had married me with a set of assumptions based not on who I was, only that I was a woman. Thirteen years of marriage, thirteen years of learning who I was, what talents and ambitions I had, three showings at the Salon, five years as a member of Marie Benoist's studio group, countless hours of drawing and painting outside it – yet his assumptions remained as they had been on the day we met. My stomach lurched. I wanted to ask, who *was* this man I had married? – but I understood him all too well.

"Augustine," he said plaintively, "I don't want to fight. It's late, and we're both tired" – or you wouldn't be so bad-tempered, he meant – "can't we leave this until another time?"

As if you would understand better what I was upset about. "Yes, you're probably right," I said. We got into bed, and he was snoring peacefully within five minutes.

It took me a long time to fall asleep that night. My dreams were disturbing – I was mounting the grand staircase of the Louvre, eager to see the next Salon in which my work once more appeared, but when I reached the top of the stairs I took a wrong turn and found myself wandering for hours through other galleries, unable to find my way. Sometimes the galleries had many paintings, the accomplishments, the fulfillments of other artists. But a long series of rooms had only curling picture wire hanging from the molding, dark patches on the wall fabric to indicate where paintings had once hung, floors gritty underfoot, and a general air of neglect. I hurried through, dismayed and frightened by the desolation I felt. When at length I managed to make my exhausted way to the Salon, it was closing for the day and guards were directing visitors to the exits. I caught only a glimpse of a well-filled gallery through an archway before I found myself again at the top of the stairs. The crowd was thick; I lost my footing and started to fall forward. Just as my temple made contact with the cold stone edge of a step, I jolted awake. My heart was beating rapidly, my breathing was shallow, and I was infinitely relieved to find it had all been just a bad dream. But its meaning was clear.

When I awoke again, it was full daylight. I had slept later than usual. Antoine had gone out, evidently not wishing to continue the discussion I had started, in which he had already made his opinions clear. Maman Madeleine would expect an apology for my brusqueness last night, and my sister and mother would expect one for my absence yesterday. No one would think of offering an apology for sapping my creative lifeblood with their demands. Any solution to be had for this situation, I would need to find for myself.

I dressed quickly in clothes I did not mind getting dirty, and assembled a new portfolio of sketching paper, pencils and chalks, as well as the drawings of the day before. I was not yet ready to have the members of the household look at them, and I wanted to see them again with a more objective eye.

I decided, on impulse, to visit Josée. I had not seen her for several months but now I wanted very much to re-establish our friendship and re-affirm my identity as an artist.

The concierge confirmed that she was home, adding, "You're just in time to say goodbye."

I wondered about that as I climbed the stairs to her studio. It had been cleared of everything but the landlord's furniture and Josée's clothes. She was packing the latter into a trunk and greeted me a little uncertainly, not her usual wholehearted welcome.

"I just heard you're leaving – are you moving to another address?"

"No, I'm giving up the studio while I'm traveling." Josée hesitated, eyes down, looking guilty as she wondered how to continue.

I realized what her destination must be. "You're going to Rome, aren't you?"

"Yes. I was paid last week for the series of paintings I did for the Duchesse de Berry." The young sister-in-law of the Duchesse d'Angoulême was a generous patron of women artists. "That and what I've saved will be enough."

"But it was going to be *our* trip!" My anguished reply was out before I could stop myself and reframe it as delight in her journey for her sake.

"We started our plan because we could not wait for the men to take us," she reminded me. "Then you had to care for your mother. I've seen you hardly at all these past two years and I realized I could not afford to wait for *you*, either. I need to take care of myself. No one is going to drop everything for me."

I could hear the hurt underneath the stinging words.

"When do you go? How long will you be gone?"

"I have a place reserved on the Toulon coach, the day after tomorrow. I have enough to live on for a year, or even longer if I can find clients while I'm there. The English are particularly fond of souvenir portraits and views, and Monsieur Ingres has given me letters of introduction. So it might work out I can stay even longer." Her eyes were shining. Clearly she had left behind the wistful travel plans we had begun in 1817. And she would be leaving me along with them.

247

"I'm happy for you, Josée." I was in fact sorry for myself rather than happy for her, but pride would not let me say so.

She took something out of the depth of a wardrobe and held it out to me. "I was going to come to see you tomorrow to give you this." It was our moneybox. "That's your half of what we saved until you stopped – I mean, until you started taking care of your mother."

I would not take it from her. "Keep it as an emergency fund. You can give it to me when you come back. I won't be going anywhere in the meantime," I added wryly.

"It's not your money I wanted with me!" She thrust the box at me; I took hold of her hands instead. The box broke into a heap of coins and shards at our feet.

We stared intently and unhappily at each other for a long minute. Gently, I let go.

"I'm sorry, Josée. I wish with all my heart that I could have gone with you, but for now this money is the only part of me I can send. Bon Voyage," I said softly, kissing her on both cheeks. "Bon Voyage."

I left as quickly as I could.

Chapter 11

Brussels, December 1823

At last I had my chance to travel when I accompanied Antoine to visit Jacques-Louis David in Brussels in December of 1823. Visiting his beloved master was one of those rare circumstances that could persuade Gros to leave Paris. It was not the most comfortable time of year to spend three days each way in a public coach, but it was too cold to paint in the Panthéon or his studio. I think he took a sort of proud pleasure in proving his devotion by the hardship of the journey. He invited Girodet to accompany him but his friend was ill and had not maintained the close ties to his teacher that Gros did.

"Why don't you take Augustine?" he suggested. The three of us were dining together that day. "She has always wanted to travel." He winked at me. Antoine invited me in that tone of voice that expects a refusal and was surprised when I promptly accepted.

When I later thanked Girodet, he said, "Take care of Antoine, I'm worried about him. David won't let up on him – whatever he does isn't enough, or isn't the right thing. He can't see all the good in Antoine and acts as if it is of no account. And Antoine takes it to heart. He'll need someone to console him. I'd go if I felt better, but I can't. Please, go with him and take care of him. I know David is a trial for you, but Antoine will need you there."

Impulsively, I embraced him. He was a true and loving friend to my husband, knowing his faults and weaknesses and accepting them with much better grace than I. It's too bad Antoine couldn't have married you, I thought, only realizing when Girodet gave a startled laugh that I'd spoken the thought out loud. I gave a gasp of embarrassment and covered my mouth with my hand.

"Oh, I did ask him, in a manner of speaking," he confessed, "years ago. The affection was there on his side but not the physical inclination. He remained my friend anyway. Many men would not have," he added, his face darkening as a troubled memory passed across it.

I stood on tiptoe and kissed him on the cheek. "Whomever that frown was about, he's not worth it," I told him. Dear Girodet! He died the following year, but my good memories of him are very much alive.

It was a sunny but cold day when we set off for Brussels on the public coach. We brought fur lap robes to keep us warm and I was glad of my fur muff as well. I brought my sketchbook and pencils and amused myself by drawing en route, fixing the outlines of the landscape in my memory; the faces of our fellow passengers (I gave these away as gifts); one of the coach horses eating his oats; even Antoine, once, when I was sitting across from him and he had fallen asleep. He slept very decorously, with his mouth closed and his hat tipped rakishly on his head. My fingers grew cold and stiff outside the muff, but it helped to pass the time.

On the last day we were joined by a mother and two young children who were on their way to visit those loyalists of the Revolution and Napoleon who had emigrated to Brussels, just as we were. The woman's father-in-law had been a member of the Old Guard; her husband had died at Waterloo; her daughter had been born eight months after the battle. The boy, she said, was her orphaned nephew. It was a struggle to keep the farm going on her own, even with her husband's pension. She and the children were barely adequately dressed against the cold. I sat the girl on my lap under the fur robe, felt the shivering body gradually relax and fall asleep, and had the keen pleasure of pretending for a little while it was my daughter I held there. When we parted in Brussels, I gave the fur robe to the mother for their return journey.

"I don't take charity!" she said, and made to give it back to me.

"It's not charity," I smiled, "it's a Christmas gift for you and the children."

Her face softened, then crumpled for a moment before she regained control of herself. "Thank you," she whispered.

Antoine watched this from a little distance with an air of tolerant amusement. "Are we so well off that we can just give these away?" he asked, gesturing toward the other fur that lay neatly folded over his arm.

"As a matter of fact, we are," I replied, tucking my arm in his. "You earned the money for these painting the deeds of Napoleon and his soldiers. They are the widow and children of those soldiers. Who could be a more appropriate recipient?"

"True," he said shortly and hailed a cab to take us to our hotel. Usually Antoine stayed in a modest establishment in the émigré quarter, but because it was my first visit to Brussels, he said, he had arranged for us to stay in one of the comfortable hotels on the Grand Place, the main square of the city. I was glad that he did. After three days of indifferent meals it was a pleasure to eat fine food in a restaurant and be served and soothed by solicitous waiters.

After an early dinner, wanting to stretch our legs, we went for a stroll through the Grand Place. It was our first long holiday to a far-away destination since our honeymoon in Toulouse, fourteen years before, and the first time I had traveled outside France. I looked around me with delight – the variety and beauty of the painted buildings of past centuries, their gilding picked out here and there by the lamps and torches that lit the square at night, the village of Christmas market booths selling toys and trinkets, snatches of conversations in French, Dutch, English and Scandinavian languages I could not identify – I felt I truly had been lifted out of my everyday life. A brass band was playing at one end of the square, and the delicious smells of hot coffee and hot chocolate, roasting chestnuts and crisp waffles added to the holiday atmosphere. Snowflakes began to fall, gently at first and then more thickly, adding their beauty to the scene. I held out my muff to catch them so that I could examine their brief crystalline perfection before they melted from the warmth of my hands. I laughed with sheer happiness and looked up to find Antoine regarding me with a curious expression.

"I haven't heard you laugh like that for a long time," he said, a wistful note in his voice.

He's right, I thought, remembering the days of laughter and satisfying work in Marie's studio. I pushed those thoughts away and returned to the happy moment in the present. I put out my muff to gather more snowflakes and held it out for him to examine. "Look how beautiful they are!"

He looked, nodded, and smiled back at me. We returned to our hotel arm-in-arm.

Antoine had dispatched a note to David to say that we had arrived, and a reply had come while we were out, inviting him to lunch the next day. I was not included – David knew only too well how I felt about him and he had never been one to tolerate a challenge to his authority. Wives, he believed, should make themselves useful, not interfere in a man's real life spent away from them. Certainly he had never taken Madame David's feelings and opinions into account. Antoine was apologetic but I assured him that I would welcome the chance to go Christmas shopping. The exercise would do me good, I said, after sitting in the coach for so long.

The snow had stopped overnight, leaving an inch of clean whiteness that made the Grand Place even more beautiful in the daytime. With my stout boots, I made the rounds of the shops and stalls, bargaining for my purchases: handmade lace scarves and gloves for Pauline and a man's cravat suitable for Antoine's appearances at court. (He wore it the following year to Charles X's coronation.) I visited *chocolatiers* and other luxury food shops, enjoying the sweet smells, the velvety textures of the chocolates, the grainy nature of the marzipan, and the bright jewels of the candied fruits. One bakery offered rich, rum-soaked fruitcakes from England, and I bought two on impulse, surprised by how heavy they were. More than once I returned to the hotel to deposit my purchases.

The crowd was different in the daytime, more children with their parents or grandparents. Young voices filled the air with their excitement, their wistful – or demanding – requests for a particular item or treat, and the occasional howl of disappointment when it was denied. Sellers of hot chocolate did a brisk business as did the man who served thick, crisp waffles spread with *confitures*.

One little boy took off like a flash with his in hand, his eyes so intent on it that he did not notice where he was going. He ran straight into me and dropped his waffle, leaving a sticky trail of jam down the front of my coat. He lifted his face in fear of a scolding and then lowered it in dismay at losing his treat. Before he could emit a wail of sorrow, I leaned down and said, "That's too bad. Let's get another one, shall we?" Happiness returned and he nodded eagerly, taking my hand and pulling me to the stall. His mother came up to apologize. Had the same thing happened in Paris a week earlier, I would have snapped and growled, but I was on holiday here, and happy. I assured her my coat could easily be wiped off and bought waffles for the three of us. We parted with wishes of *Joyeux Noël*.

I was still laughing as I walked back to the hotel. The little boy had stirred old longings for a child. I was only thirty-four. Perhaps Antoine and I could try again, tonight. Smiling, I requested at the desk that a pot of tea be sent up to our room.

The manager gave my order to one of the assistants and then told me, in a low voice, that my husband had returned a little while before. "Pardon me for saying so, Madame, but he did not look well. I suggested a brandy but he refused it. I thought you should know. We can, of course, send for a doctor should you need one." I thanked him and mounted the stairs to our room, my good humor gone, thinking grimly, "David."

Antoine was asleep when I came in. He had not bothered to draw the curtains against the dullness of the day, and his face was wretched in the grey light, looking much older than his fifty-two years, with the tracks of tears on his cheeks. He awoke when the maid came with the tea. I poured him a cup English style with milk and two spoons of sugar. He made a face as he drank the syrupy stuff, but he looked better afterwards and reached eagerly for a cup of strong black tea to wash away its taste. I lit the lamps and the fire the maid had laid and drew the curtains against the now gathering dusk. Antoine joined me in the upholstered chairs by the fireplace, as I sipped my tea and we watched the flames take hold.

"Do you want to tell me about it?"

He shook his head but after a few moments started to talk in a dull monotone. "It was the same as the other visits. He welcomed me warmly at first, introduced me proudly to his assistant Navez, asked eagerly after my work, and nodded approvingly when I told him about the Biblical and historic subjects I have in hand. 'You have taken the right path,' he told me. He showed me the painting he's working on, a scene from Roman history. He likes to hold forth on the superiority of its subject matter, a speech I've heard him give for over thirty-five years, since the day I entered the studio. I'm older now than he was then, but he's still giving me the same speech." He shook his head ruefully.

"When it was time to eat, Navez took his leave. The housekeeper brought up a tureen of boeuf bourguignon. David poured burgundy wine for us. He ate sparingly, saying he had little appetite these days, but he continued to drink the wine, opening another bottle to give me my second glass. By the time the housekeeper returned with fruit and cheese, I realized he was drunk. I could tell by the expression on her face that this was not the first time. She shot me a worried glance with a warning in it; but I was relaxed with food and wine. David had been pleasant and complimentary, and I did not see what was coming.

"He started by saying how good it was to see me and hear the news straight from Paris. He missed France. Life in Belgium would always be exile for him, no matter how pleasant. He was first and foremost a French patriot and he was proud of the work he had done. Changes were needed, he said – in France and in the way she was governed – and only difficult decisions could bring them about. He was proud to have been part of the Parlement that crafted the changes and unrepentant at having voted for the death of Louis XVI even if it meant his exile now. France was better off without the Bourbons. Even though they had returned to power after the Emperor's defeat, their tenure could not last forever. France would grow tired of them again – I would see! He hoped he would be alive to see that. Then he could return.

"'You can return now if you like,' I reminded him. 'I've worked it out to obtain a pardon for you. Louis XVIII regards you as one of the treasures of French art and would like to see you on French soil again. All you need to do—'

"'—is sign a paper saying I repent of my vote for the death of his brother. I have told you before and I tell you again, I will *never* sign such a paper! *You* may have been bought by the Bourbons and their patronage,' he sneered, 'but *I* remain true to my principles.'

"After scolding me for being a turncoat to the Bourbons, he turned his scorn to my paintings. I had never done a true history painting from mythology or the Bible, merely political works that showed the transitory triumphs of mere mortals—"

I had to speak up. "This from the man who said of *Jaffa*, 'One could perhaps do as well – one could not do better.' I was there that day; I heard him. The man who painted the *Coronation* and the *Distribution of the Eagles* and the *Crossing at Saint Bernard*? He was willing enough to do those subjects at the time – and demand exorbitant prices for them. How *dare* he look down on you?"

My husband gave me a long wondering look when I had finished my outburst. His face had lost that grey, drawn look, and there was some pink color in his cheeks. The hint of a smile played around his mouth. He reached out and squeezed my hand, saying "Thank you, my dear."

I was startled. Such moments of agreement and sympathy had become all too rare in our marriage.

"How much more of this did you have to tolerate? Or did you just leave?"

He sighed. "He finally stopped when I started to cry. He always does. He clapped me on the shoulder, told me to take courage – things could still be put right if I make the correct choices henceforth. Then he grew maudlin, blamed himself for causing me pain, reminded himself of all the good things I had done, and looked so miserable I found myself reassuring him that what he'd said hadn't been so terrible after all."

"What a shameless manipulator!"

"Finally, I was able to leave. I don't know how I found my way to the hotel – I was exhausted physically and emotionally." Two tears rolled down his cheeks. "Perhaps a brandy would have helped, but I had seen enough of the effects of drink for one afternoon." He held out his cup for more tea and drank it eagerly, then fell silent, watching the flames in the fireplace. I picked up the novel I had purchased that morning and began to read. When next I looked at Antoine, he was asleep.

We were at breakfast the next day when a letter arrived for Antoine. My heart sank when I saw the large D in the sealing wax. Antoine opened it with some trepidation but his face cleared as he read it.

"He asks to see me again today. He apologizes for his behavior yesterday and blames it on the wine. He wishes me to come to lunch so that he can make amends."

So that he can be reassured you'll keep running back to him, I thought.

"Will you go?" I asked.

"Of course." He sounded surprised that I should ask.

"Then I'm coming with you." He started to protest, but I held up my hand to stop him. "I'll bring my knitting, I'll sit quietly in a corner of the studio. But after yesterday, you shouldn't have to face him alone." My coffee cup made a determined click as I set it in its saucer.

He stared at me for a long moment but in the end he said simply and quietly, "Thank you."

Antoine sent a note to say we would both be coming. I went up to the room to change into my best dress and its matching red coat, so that Antoine would know I was properly honoring the occasion. I busied myself wrapping the gifts I had bought and Antoine sketched me as I worked. Neither of us mentioned the pending visit.

David's home and studio occupied a modest brick building with a typical stepped gable in a quiet, middle-class neighborhood that Antoine told me was a particular favorite of the *émigrés*. The names of some of the shops and restaurants we passed – Au Vieux Paris, Le petit Véfour, La Joséphine – confirmed this. A maid opened the door to our knock and took our coats. A young man then came forward to welcome us, greeting Gros warmly, saying what a pleasure it was to see him again so soon. Gros presented him: "Monsieur François-Joseph Navez." Navez had the easy manners of the professional portrait painter. Antoine must have been like this at his age, I thought, and smiled at the young man. He led us up the stairs to the studio.

Here David came forward to greet us, embracing Gros like a son, hesitating how to greet me, then kissing me on both cheeks like a daughter. I received his kisses with the same false enthusiasm with which he gave them, but the occasion seemed to call for it. It was the first time I had seen him in eight years. His hair had gone from grey to white and his face, in repose, fell into lines of disappointment. His figure was slightly stooped and thickened, but his person and his clothes were clean – he was well looked after.

Several of David's paintings hung on the walls, chief among them the *Death of Marat* of almost thirty years before, which he had brought with him from Paris. Easels held several students' paintings in varying stages of progress. The master suggested to Navez that he show them to me while we waited for the food. Antoine gave a brief nod in response to my inquiring glance: he would be all right. As I moved off with the young man, I heard David make his apologies. Perhaps his good behavior would hold for the afternoon; but if not, I was ready for him.

I was disappointed as I examined the canvases. The application of paint could not be faulted, but none of them had the breadth of subject or theme I would have expected. Whatever he was berating Gros for not doing, his current students were not doing either.

Navez pointed out with pride the sole canvas on which David himself was working, a scene of ancient Roman honor that seemed to require, as they so often did, the death of someone at the hands of his best friend. The drawing and brushwork were so loose and sketchy, lacking his usual tight control, that I could not make more of it than that. I was dismayed.

A table had been set with four places for lunch; Navez would be joining us, as Madame David was indisposed. Perhaps my presence at Gros's side made David feel he needed reinforcements on his. I was glad of someone whose speech was easier to understand – the impediment caused by a dueling wound to his mouth had grown worse with age. Listening to some barely coherent words, I wondered how Gros could have understood half of yesterday's tirade. Perhaps, I thought uneasily, what he told me *was* just the half of it.

Our lunch was a delicious pot au feu of winter vegetables, chicken and potatoes. Gros and Navez, applying themselves to their food, were busily not noticing David apply himself to the wine. He drained his first glass with the grim eagerness of one who needed a drink. Despite the tense knot in my stomach, I ate two large mouthfuls and said encouragingly, "You really should eat more of this delicious food, Monsieur David. Your cook has made a true feast for us!"

The two men grunted their assent with their mouths full. David gave me as much of a smile as his mouth could manage. "Alas, dear lady, I have not the appetite I once had, but it is a pleasure to see you enjoy yourself." He refilled his glass almost to the brim and raised it as if in a toast – but his eyes were cold and hostile, and he defiantly drained it in one noisy gulp.

Antoine caught my eye and shook his head slightly. Clearly the old man did not want us to notice how much he drank. David had noted our exchange and leaned forward to refill Gros's glass with a small cold smile of triumph – Gros was on his side and had put me in my place.

Navez, coming up for air after his first plateful, remembered his duties as co-host and turned the conversation to other topics. David helped himself to a third and fourth glass. When he had finished the bottle he selected another vintage and, bringing fresh glasses to the table, insisted we all try some. It was a light, delicate white wine and I could not hide my pleasure in it.

"I'm happy Madame approves," David said dryly.

"You are a kind host," I replied in the same tone of voice.

The last course was a hazelnut torte. The housekeeper, who brought it, admonished David, "Be sure to save a slice for Madame – it is her favorite." He made to cut a generous piece for her to take to his wife, but he could not manage it. The knife trembled in his grasp, spoiling the immaculate surface of the frosting, and he could not bring enough pressure upon it to slice even so yielding a substance.

I realized then why the studio was so empty of his work and the dictatorial impulse to control the work of others was so strong, why a lifetime's careful habit of sobriety was eroding. He could no longer lift and control his right arm and hand to wield a paintbrush. Painting and politics had been the twin passions of his life; now neither was left to him. No wonder he drank to dull the pain. I could have pitied him had I not remembered how he had treated Antoine the day before.

I pulled the torte toward me and said, in my best hostess voice, "Let me serve." David seemed a trifle apprehensive at handing over the large knife, but of course he could not say so. I felt a small spurt of triumph as I distributed the filled plates. He permitted me to pour the coffee when it arrived, and the meal ended peacefully.

One cup of coffee would not go very far in countering all the wine, I thought, and remained on the alert. I brought out my knitting, prepared to fade into the background while the men resumed their conversation. Navez left soon after – his wife was expecting their first child, he said, and he would like to make sure she was all right. The room seemed colder and duller after he had left.

My needles clicked on. When Gros got up to add another piece of wood to the stove, I remembered the afternoons at Marie Benoist's studio, the colors and flowers and music and laughter. This bleak masculine space rejected all softening. Gros and Navez may have been at home in surroundings like these, but I missed the warmth and encouragement of my friends. My thoughts wandered from the men's conversation when a change in David's tone of voice made me look up sharply. It had neither warmth nor encouragement nor laughter in it; Gros was ashen as his teacher's bile poured over him.

"—licking the boots of the Bourbons to celebrate their so-called triumphs, as if running away from Napoleon were something to boast about. But you always were a political opportunist if you could get a commission out of it—"

"That's enough, Monsieur David." I spoke quietly but firmly. He turned to me in surprise; he had forgotten I was there.

"Eh? What was that?" He turned back to Antoine. "Are you hiding behind your wife's skirts now as well as your mother's?"

"He is hiding nowhere. He has come here to offer his love and respect and admiration, and the results of his labors on your behalf with the French government, and he has sat quietly while you have only heaped abuse upon him. I find it ironic that you, who despite your Revolutionary principles embraced an Emperor and painted a tremendous canvas of his coronation, should level charges of opportunism against my husband. I have not heard you express regret for your actions, nor apologize for the exorbitant fees you charged." He looked surprised. "Oh, yes, I heard all about them from Denon. He's an old friend of my family, you know."

He glared at me. "That self-important paper-pusher! I would have been First Painter had he not interfered. What masterpieces has he painted for France, eh? I have been France's greatest painter for the last forty years!"

"You *were* a great painter, Monsieur David." I nodded toward his recent pathetic effort. "But I would not harp upon Antoine's faults unless I was sure I had none of my own."

"As a teacher, it is my duty to take a paternal interest in my students and guide them upon the right path."

"When they are in your studio. Antoine has been an adult these thirty years."

"Ah, but he always comes back asking for more. It's one of the predictable pleasures of him. Like that statement of regret that he's so eager for me to sign. I know it disappoints him when I refuse, but when larger issues are at stake, I can't be worried about the petty disappointments of individuals."

"Is that really why you value my husband, Monsieur David? The depth of his personal disappointment is the measure of your success in sticking to your precious principles?"

An instinctive denial rose to his mouth – one could see it on his tongue, ready to cross his teeth – it died there – honesty won out. He could *not* deny it. I felt like Charlotte Corday after she had just stabbed Marat, triumphant in the blazing light of truth. I glanced at the painting of Marat and back to David.

"Antoine will hate you for pointing this out," he said in a sly, confiding way. "He so desperately needs to believe in me, you know." He grinned at his own maliciousness.

Antoine had not uttered a sound. An indescribable mix of emotions crossed his face: he resented David for his insults, instinctively defended him against attack, and seemed unsure whether to praise or berate me.

David gave him a look of disgust. "If you can't speak up for me against this – this harridan – just *go*. Take her and get out of my sight, once and for all!" He sprang from his chair as fast as his advanced age would allow and threw open the door of the studio with a tremendous crash that brought the servants running to see what was the matter. "Monsieur and Madame Gros are just leaving," he told them. "Please see them out." He went back into the studio and shut the door with another loud bang.

We walked down the stairs with the best aplomb we could muster. Gros thanked the housekeeper for our lunch and kissed her cheek. To her inquiring look he replied calmly, "I upset him, and my wife spoke up in my defense." Knowing how David hated to be crossed, she nodded sympathetically. Antoine turned to me and said, "Come, my dear, let us go."

He was acting so mild that I had a twinge of worry that he might explode with anger when we were alone, but he did not, just squeezed my hand with a faint smile. At the hotel he handed me out of the fiacre and told me to go in: he wanted to do an errand and would be back in time for dinner. Worried, I asked, "You're not going back there, are you?"

He smiled and shook his head.

"You'll be all right?" I persisted. He nodded but didn't offer an explanation.

That evening he handed me a jeweler's box at dinner. "To my knight in shining armor," he said. Tears came to my eyes as I opened the box and put on the gold bracelet.

Chapter 12

Paris, 1827-1831

As I have written of my life, there is one topic that has been too painful to discuss fully until now – the lack of children in our marriage.

As a girl, I dreamed of the children I would have – at the very least, a boy to carry on my husband's name and be his mother's pride and a girl to be my companion and her father's delight, as I was to my father. Visiting my friends' older sisters, I cooed over their babies, rejoicing in their happiness, knowing it would one day be mine as well. While I waited for Charles to return from Spain, I would wonder sometimes, as I studied the youthful face in the miniature, whether our son would look like his father at that age. The child was so real to me that when Charles was killed, the loss of the son I had imagined was part of my grief.

When I did marry, children were no longer hypothetical but sure to come. Antoine and his mother, discussing the matter at length, let me know they wanted a boy who would be the third-generation artist in the family. They would name him Jean-Antoine after his grandfather; he in turn would have a son he would name Antoine-Jean, and so it would go on for generations. Maman Madeleine, coming from a family of goldsmiths, had the strong pride of the skilled artisan; if the boy were to show more of an inclination toward her father's profession, so much the better! Their discussions left me with mixed feelings. While I would be happy to give my husband a son, it was clear that the boy would be taken over by his father and grandmother to be molded into their family traditions. What I longed for most was a daughter for myself to love, a little girl who would belong to me and love me.

I began to prepare a layette during our honeymoon. Stitching and embroidering the tiny garments, I fell into a dreamy reverie that even Antoine's mother's comments about my slipshod supervision of the housekeeping could not penetrate. I imagined purchasing an elegant mahogany cradle to show off our baby to all who would come to congratulate us. I gave much thought to what to name a girl. Her two grandmothers were both Madeleine, so that was a given for one of her names. For the other I preferred Giselle. I spent hours at the window stitching into the garments of the layette my dreams of the things Giselle and I would do together. My layette was complete before our first anniversary, but the child had not yet come. I continued to hold out hope, only to be disappointed, month after month, year after year. Even the passionate afternoon that followed the argument over Charles's portrait in 1813 did not have the outcome I desired so much.

"Don't worry," everyone told me. "You're still young. There's plenty of time. Just relax, and enjoy trying!" They always winked as they said this, and it never failed to make me wince. They meant to be encouraging, I know, but came across as heartless.

Even when I met Charlotte and Marie and became part of their circle, throwing myself into my painting, I never stopped hoping for a child. It was one of those superstitious bargains one makes. Perhaps, if I looked as though I was happy doing something else, a baby would come. It continued to be the first and chief desire expressed in my prayers. I could rely on my talent and efforts to help me succeed at my art, but conceiving a child clearly required divine help. I sound flippant, even sacrilegious, I know, but the issue was painfully serious to me.

I was desperate enough to try advice that I now recognize as old wives' tales: food and drink to feed to Antoine or have him abstain from, a small vial of blessed water to sprinkle on myself before intercourse, a piece of ribbon specially blessed on Annunciation Day to wear around my neck. In my desperation I even consulted a midwife who supposedly could help me, a woman rumored to be nearly a witch; but I couldn't bring myself to use the strange powders she offered. How ironic that a daughter of the Enlightenment should turn to such resources! Our superior learning becomes a thin veneer in times of distress, when superstition comes flooding back.

As all my efforts met with failure, I began to wonder – was it bad luck, or was one of us unable to conceive a child? Was I barren? I shuddered – what an awful word! – not a mere adjective but a harsh judgment on one's most basic capacity as a woman. Antoine's mother hurled it at me more than once. Pushed beyond forbearance, I made a tart reply that it could just as easily have been Antoine's fault. It was not something I would ever have said to my husband, but she made sure he knew I had said it. Recriminations and counter-charges flew through the household, wreaking further havoc upon our marriage.

Josée was still traveling in Italy, so that I did not have the haven of her studio to retreat to. Attempting to find consolation in prayer, I spent many hours in church. I was only in my thirties, but I began to feel as old and forlorn as the black-clad widows around me.

Then came the worst blow of all – Antoine fathered a child. The question of who had been at fault for our childless state was settled. Maman Madeleine was triumphant in the vindication of her son.

The discovery of his lovechild came at a particularly vulnerable time for me. Josée had come back to Paris only briefly and was now traveling throughout France. Antoine had suffered a nervous collapse following the deaths of Géricault and Girodet in 1824 and David and Denon in 1825. I, too, was hard-hit by the death of Denon, our lifelong family friend; it was like losing my father all over again. After I had nursed Antoine through his crisis and seen him restored to health, Maman fell ill. Coping with all this illness enforced my neglect of my painting and added up to an unrelieved round of drudgery. Then Maman died. No matter how much a death comes as a blessed relief for both afflicted and caretaker, it still calls forth grief and mourning.

Without the presence of Maman, our most consistent unifying force, my relationship with my brother and sister changed. Henri, who had done the least to help us with her care, now expected his sisters to take over her role in caring for him. When we declined, thinking it high time he grew up, he reproached us with indignant self-pity. Pauline and Henri then found a unifying cause in their lingering resentment that I had been given Maman's share of Papa's estate when I married. That I had always turned the income over to Pauline for Maman's care made no difference. Pauline grumbled that it shouldn't have been mine in the first place, and Henri, I knew, brooded that it would have been easier to get his hands on more of it had it been Maman's to dispose of instead of mine. Eager to wash my hands of this long-running dispute, I arranged for my brother and sister each to receive one-third of the income. By tacit agreement we all needed a vacation from each other.

Lifting myself out of my family preoccupations, I began to notice that Antoine was happier than I had seen him in a long time. He added touches of color to his habitual black and white – a bright red cravat, a blue scarf. Two new shirts appeared in his armoire, the flowing kind affected by poets, a style he had always disliked, yet now he wore these gladly. He stood up straight and walked with a spring in his step, even running upstairs at times. And there was a change in his behavior to me that I could not understand – kindness with an undertone of pity, as though I were a newly widowed client seeking a memorial portrait. I puzzled over these things but could not make out their source.

Then, one day in June 1827 I went to his studio to surprise him with lunch at a restaurant. While I was still a little distance away, I saw him coming out of the building. The greeting I was about to call out died on my lips when I saw that he had his arm about the waist of a woman who carried an infant in her arms. Before they had gone many steps, he took the baby from her while she bent down to remove a pebble from her shoe. "Who's Daddy's little girl?" he said, smiling fondly at the infant and kissing her forehead. His face alight with animation and pleasure, he looked years younger. They were so obviously a family group that I, his wife, was left standing on the outside. I was too shocked to cry out. They did not see me but turned up the street away from me. Once they were out of sight, I came back to life, stumbling a few steps. My stomach heaved and I retched into the gutter. Passers-by gave me a wide berth, assuming I was drunk. Their suspicious faces were the last straw to complete my humiliation.

Somehow I made my way home again and lay wretched and shivering for the rest of the afternoon. I had the maid make up the bed in my studio – the room that had been, ironically, intended as the nursery. I could not bear the thought of lying in our marriage bed, with its familiar smell of Antoine. I could not help wondering if *her* bed now smelled like him. I lay with my eyes open, staring at the ceiling – whenever I closed them, the scene on the rue des Fossés Saint-Germain came sickeningly to mind. Oddly, I couldn't remember the woman's features, and I hadn't seen the child at all, only Antoine's face as he spoke to her. I had no sense of time passing until the maid tapped on the door to inquire if I was well enough to come down for dinner, or if she should bring me something on a tray. I sent her away – I had not eaten since breakfast, but I was not hungry. I continued to stare at the ceiling until weariness overcame me and I slept.

When I made my way downstairs the next morning in my dressing gown, pale and lightheaded from lack of food, Antoine and his mother were at their places at the table as usual. Antoine stood and pulled out my chair for me as was his courteous custom, then went on dipping his brioche into his café au lait, eating with good appetite and a self-satisfied air. I longed to punctuate it, to give *him* something to worry about. My resentful air grew as I ate and drank, with what I thought were covert glances in his direction.

Suddenly his mother's voice cut across the breakfast table: "Stop sulking, girl! You've got something to say – *say* it." It was the voice she used to flay a servant who did not quite measure up to standard, and it implied that my illness was certain to have been merely a fit of pique.

"Ma*man*," my husband said in mild protest.

"Well, she *is* sulking – there's no reason—" she started.

That did it. "I went to your studio yesterday to take you to lunch," I began.

"I'm sorry I missed you," he murmured.

"I arrived there just as you emerged from the building with your touching little family group."

"Oh." He lowered his eyes to the crumbs on his plate.

"You were too busy cooing to 'Daddy's little girl'" – here I gave a savage imitation of his tone of voice – "while Mademoiselle Arm-about-her-waist bent down to fix her shoe. That's why you didn't see your *wife* coming toward you."

"My dear, I—"

"Just think," I continued brightly, "you could have introduced us, and then I wouldn't be asking you about them this morning." He had given up trying to interrupt and waited for me to finish. "So – who are they?"

"My granddaughter's name is Françoise-Cécile," Maman Madeleine said proudly. "Cécile is *my* middle name. Her mother is Françoise Simonier. Cécile was born in March, and a finer birthday gift than Antoine could have hoped for." *From you* hung unspoken in the air. I stared at her, and she looked calmly back.

I turned to my husband, but now he was busily buttering a slice of bread, as though the conversation bore only the vaguest relationship to him.

"Antoine!" I protested.

"Yes, my dear?" He raised his eyes to meet mine with an expression of aggressive tolerance that I hated: by not engaging in an emotional battle, it made me out to be the unreasonable one. He hated arguments, especially the running battle between wife and mother that forced him to pick sides. He preferred to deal with domestic issues not with the hot-blooded emotion of his youthful battle scenes but with the cold sterile Neoclassicism of his recent paintings.

I rose and left the room, shutting the door behind me. As I started toward our bedroom, I could hear Antoine's voice raised in furious reproach to his mother. "I was hoping to find a way to have her come here to live with us as our ward. Augustine has always wanted a girl. When

Cécile was older, I was going to propose her as an infant I had heard of who needed a home. Françoise could have come as her nurse, and then I could have had them here every day."

His voice quavered on those last words, and I knew he was crying. He continued in a stronger voice. "I could have thought up some explanation for what she saw yesterday, brought her around. But you had to put your foot in it, stating things in black and white. There's no way she'll accept Cécile now." He was crying again.

I expected to hear his mother murmuring her usual words of comfort and support, but he had shocked the old lady into silence. I could see her in my mind's eye, struggling between her need to comfort him and her desire to take umbrage. A chair scraped back and her heavy footsteps approached the door. I fled to the bedroom.

Antoine came to speak with me. "I'm sorry you had to find out this way," he began. Not that it happened, nor that it would be any less painful any way I heard about it, but that I'd found out in such a way as to thwart his plans. I looked at him coldly. He wasn't sorry for me so much as he was sorry for himself. I stopped listening and finished dressing.

"I'm going to visit Père Martin," I told him. "Perhaps it would do you good to come with me."

He winced. "I've already been to confession this week."

"And got off lightly, by the look of it," I said tartly. I left.

It was a beautiful early summer day and the short walk along the rue des Saints-Pères to the Chapelle Saint-Pierre on the Boulevard Saint-Germain would normally have raised my spirits, but my emotions were too turbulent to be readily soothed. Out of habit I glanced in the window of Debauve et Gallais, the confectioners shop, only to have my eye fall on a display of those cornets of sugared almonds given to new mothers. I hurried onward, almost running, as if I had just witnessed a horrible crime. I yanked open the door of the church and stumbled inside.

Once there, I forced myself to stop, breathe deeply and evenly, and marshal my thoughts. I dipped my fingers in the Holy Water, made the sign of the Cross and genuflected to the altar. In my haste to leave the house, I had neglected to notice the time and now I had arrived in the middle of the weekday Mass. Normally I would have joined in, but I was in no frame of mind that day to be worthy to receive Communion. I slipped into the chapel dedicated to the Virgin Mary and knelt to pray, but words would not come. I looked to the painting on the altar for inspiration, but the calm serene face of the Virgin looked as if it had never felt anger. Joy, acceptance, foreboding, suffering, sorrow – I had seen her display all of those in various works of art. But never anger. *Didn't you at least rage at those who tortured and killed your Son*? I wanted to ask her. She went on smiling fondly, a little sadly, at the baby who reached for the thorn-eating goldfinch, accepting His fate. I looked up at St Joseph, who had found himself married off not to a capable widow who could help him, a lusty woman his own age with whom he would have had something in common, but to a slip of a girl already pregnant with someone else's child. He had acquiesced to all of it. There would be no sympathy for me there either. Finally, I found myself drawn to a painting of St Peter, the patron saint of the church, cutting off Malthus' ear in a fit of rage, then denying Christ thrice before the cock crowed. Thinking about his very human temper and frailty calmed me.

Compassionate, white-haired Père Martin sought me out when Mass was over: "I can see that you are troubled, daughter." That also helped: someone who was considerate of my feelings in the matter as Antoine and his mother were not. In fact, his kind words and welcome were enough to bring tears. He asked if I wanted confession and absolution. I bridled – I was not the sinner here! No, I told him, I wanted to ask his advice. He nodded and took me to the vestry, where we could be alone at that hour. He composed himself to listen. "Tell me, daughter."

The whole unhappy tale came out: the years of wanting and trying to have a baby, the discovery of my husband's lovechild, the hurtful attitudes of Antoine and Maman Madeleine, the assumption that I would accept it all without complaint. I needed advice that would bring me some peace of mind now and point the way to handling this in the future. To leave my husband was not an option, nor to divorce him (divorce, permitted under Bonaparte, had been outlawed by the Bourbons). My husband's mistress and child were something I was supposed to shrug off and accept with good humor. If I were to leave him, everyone would think I was overreacting.

The priest sighed as he removed his glasses and rubbed his tired face. He had to get up early and hadn't had his after-Mass coffee yet.

"It is a tale I have heard often, over the years, and I am sorry to hear it again. The message I need to give you, to accept and forgive, is never a welcome one. Nor, I am afraid, do acceptance and forgiveness come quickly and easily, but they are necessary for your peace of mind. I have seen too many women who profess them on the surface but who seethe and turn sour with resentment inside. I don't want you to become another of them. I know you have had much to deal with these last years – your husband's illness, your mother's death and the strained relationship with your sister and brother. I know this isn't the advice you want to hear now, but believe me, it is the only way."

I sat with my head bowed, absorbing Père Martin's words, wincing at times. He was right. I did not want to accept this advice – at least, not yet. Then another thought came to me. "Perhaps, if I went to see the woman, to talk to her—"

He sighed. "The damage is done, daughter. It is not the woman with whom you have the quarrel, it is the fact of the child." Involuntarily, unable to deny the truth, I nodded in agreement, and a small sob escaped my lips. "Even if she and the child were to disappear tomorrow, that would remain." His voice was gentle but firm, forcing me to face facts. I started to cry in earnest then. He said gently, "You would not wish the child harm, would you?"

"No!" My denial was quick and heartfelt. I raised a shocked face to the priest. "You do not think I would—"

"No, of course not, but I wanted you to realize it, too."

I was silent for several minutes. "Why *her*, Father? *I'm* the one in holy wedlock with the blessings of the Church. I've prayed so long and hard for a child. Why *her*, Father? Why not *me*?" I pounded my fist on the vestry table to emphasize my point. Evidently the old priest was familiar with such vehement protests, for he did not look particularly surprised, nor give the disapproving sniff Maman Madeleine would have.

"I cannot speak for God's intentions in this matter, my child. You must ask Him yourself."

So I did, at length. God must have grown impatient at my ceaseless questioning, for I never received a satisfactory answer. Perhaps, Josée later suggested when she had returned to Paris, it wasn't God's intent so much as a matter of luck. She meant to be kind, I know, but the thought of a random universe was too frightening to contemplate – it was that chaos that had led to the self-determination of the Revolution and the turmoil that ensued.

Then an idea came to me. Perhaps the answer was in the child. I hired an agent to make discreet inquiries.

Françoise Simonier was unmarried and was herself the daughter of an unwed mother. She had moved to Paris several years before from Valenciennes and found work in the linen trade, starting as a laundress and progressing to seamstress. I realized it must be she who had made the new shirts of which Antoine was so fond. She and the child lived in the rue des Prouvaires in the Faubourg Saint-Honoré on the right bank of the Seine.

Plucking up my courage, I set out to find it. It was one of those small bustling streets behind the grand hôtels, the luxury residences of the district. As I passed one, I had to step back to avoid a briskly moving, smart-looking carriage and pair emerging from the gateway. The rue des Prouvaires contained *marchands-merciers* and other shops that furnished the smart hôtels and buildings housing the working-class residents that support the luxury trades. There was even a shop specializing in flowers made of sugar, for table decorations. At the same time, a reassuring whiff of the countryside came from the nearby vegetable market of Les Halles. Casting glimpses through windows and doorways at ground-floor workshops as men and women cut and stitched sheets, towels, and tablecloths, I began to get an idea of what Françoise's life had been like.

I did not stop to browse as I usually would, afraid I would lose my nerve. As I passed places selling embroidered cloths, my sister came to mind; but embroidery was a skilled occupation even a middle- or upper-class woman could be proud of as a hobby. Françoise, I understood, did plain sewing. As I stood in front of the address the agent had given me, a tenement building five stories tall where the inhabitants would be tightly packed, a family to a room, a woman came out and introduced herself as Madame Mauvre, the concierge of the house. She was in her forties, thin and bustling. She asked if I was looking for one of her tenants.

"Mademoiselle Simonier. I heard she was good with linens, and I have some that need mending. My housekeeper recommended her, and since I was shopping in the neighborhood—" The lies came plausibly.

"Ah, Françoise! Yes, she used to do such work, but she hasn't for the past year. Her gentleman friend insisted she stop working and stay home with the baby."

"How fortunate for her." Said neutrally, politely, as one does about a stranger.

The other woman nodded eagerly. She clearly enjoyed the knowledge she had of her tenants and the feeling of power it gave her. "She came here from the country five years ago to get a bit more out of life. Followed her young man only to find he'd taken up with someone else. It hasn't been easy for her, getting too old to be married and working all hours with the linens, pricking her fingers, her back aching from lifting the materials. Then she met Jean, her gentleman friend." Jean? Was this the wrong woman, then? "He may be a famous painter to Kings and Emperors, but he's not a snob, treats her nice. Lifts his hat to me, and says, 'Bonjour, Madame Mauvre,' whenever he sees me. And doesn't mind treating to a round of drinks in the café." She nodded towards a working-class café on the corner, Aux Beaux Echecs.

"He goes there to play chess – some of the best players in the city come here." I hadn't even known he liked chess.

"About a year ago, she came in with me one evening for a drink, and they liked each other right away. He's been good to her, treats her nicely, paid for the midwife, and he's that fond of the little girl." She shook her head in wondering admiration. "He bought her a teething ring of real coral set in silver – would you believe it? And she hasn't even started to get her teeth!" She laughed, displaying how many of her own she had lost.

"Why doesn't he marry her, if he's so fond of them both?"

Madame Mauvre shrugged philosophically. "He's married already. Not happily, I'd say, or he wouldn't be looking elsewhere. But he won't leave his wife." Clearly, she admired the man's integrity. I was speechless, as well I might be, but she seemed to take that for assent. Then, as if sensing the shift in my mood, she said, "Well, can't be gossiping all day, got to get my shopping done. It's a pleasure to talk with you, Madame." She smiled again, and nodded, and went on her way.

I had been prepared to go to Françoise's flat to confront her, but the conversation with Madame Mauvre had made me pause. As I hesitated, Françoise herself came out of the building, pushing an expensive English pram, a sort of baby barouche that was an anomaly in that neighborhood where working-class mothers carried their babies wrapped in shawls.

She smiled hello to me, "Bonjour, Madame, a beautiful day, isn't it?" She radiated happiness, goodwill, and contentment with her lot in life. Startled, I had to agree that it *was* a beautiful day and smile back at her. After that, attack was impossible.

Françoise was full-cheeked, with a naturally ruddy country complexion grown pale in Paris. She had the build of the farm girl, too, stocky and buxom, not at all the trim petite figure of the Parisienne. She was dressed in a simple cotton frock and bonnet, old-fashioned and respectable. Pushing the pram, she appeared to be a nursemaid for one of the wealthy families of the district.

She was older than I had thought, already in her thirties, only a few years younger than I. Antoine had turned for comfort to a not so young woman of lower class, who weighed more than he by a few kilos. He was not the first to seek solace and pleasure with such a one, in such surroundings, but I felt contempt for his lowering himself. I could not let myself sink to his level by confronting his mistress as an equal. I straightened my spine, dusted off my gloves, and turned my back deliberately on the rue des Prouvaires.

I next saw Cécile at a family gathering at the Amalrics' house in celebration of what turned out to be Maman Madeleine's final birthday. She asked Antoine to bring his little girl, then four years old. She spoke tenderly to the girl, who was shy and uncertain in this crowd of strangers, looking to her father for reassurance about what to do. Should she let herself be kissed by this old woman? He smiled and nodded and spoke to her in a voice of such tenderness – "It's your grandmother, angel." It was a tone of voice he had not used toward me for so long that I had forgotten it until then. I could not help myself; I started to sob. Everyone looked at me in astonishment. Maman Madeleine said, "Control yourself, Augustine!" in a sharp annoyed voice, before addressing the child again in a sugary one. Disgraced, I fled into the garden, where I could cry as much as I wanted: no one would disturb me there or, heaven forbid, come to comfort me.

Ironically, it was Cécile who found me when the Amalric children brought her out to play hide-and-seek. She came across me half-hidden in a corner of the garden. At first she thought she had found one of the hiding children. Her look of triumph faded to the uncertainty she had displayed earlier as she realized that, instead, it was the cross-looking lady who got scolded for crying by the old woman who was supposed to be her grandmother. I must have looked woebegone, for on impulse she came up to me and gave me a kiss and said, "Don't be so sad." Before I could speak in reply – I just looked at the girl in astonishment – one of the other children found her and pulled her back into the game.

"Who was that sad lady?" I heard her ask.

"Oh, that's just great-aunt Augustine. She's married to Uncle Antoine, your papa. Don't mind her; she's never much fun." They resumed their game.

I was merely Tante Augustine, not much fun, dismissed out of hand by those who knew me – but the little girl, a stranger, had not hesitated to give the "sad lady" a kiss. I touched my hand to my cheek, as if to implant her kiss there forever. It made me smile whenever I thought of it and gave me the courage to go on in the days ahead.

Chapter 13

Paris, 1830-1835

And now I come to the most painful memory of all, the one that takes all my courage to recall and write about: Antoine-Jean Gros – painter in turn to the Republic, the Emperor Napoleon, and the Bourbons of the Restoration, one of the best-known artists of his generation, and recipient of the *Légion d'honneur* from Bonaparte's own hand – threw himself into the Seine on the night of 25 June 1835.

His act was clearly a suicide. At the time, I said he had suffered an aneurysm, a burst blood vessel in his brain that had caused him to lose his footing and fall by accident into the water. I persuaded his doctor to confirm this story to ensure that his body could be buried in hallowed ground at Père-Lachaise, with no notoriety attached to his memory. I must confess also that I did not want the shame and embarrassment of his act to attach to me, his widow, especially as his friends held no fondness for me.

Now I wish to tell the truth.

Paris was again in turmoil, with barricades in the streets and fighting between the King's troops and the citizens of Paris. Again, the Bourbons were forced out, this time for good.

Charles X seemed to have learned nothing from the misfortunes of his brothers Louis XVI and XVIII. He had gained public sympathy when his younger son, the Duc de Berry, had been murdered ten years before, and there had been rejoicing over the birth of Berry's son six months later. But now he squandered the goodwill of the people. Perhaps after Napoleon's death he felt he had nothing left to fear and could act as he pleased.

A particularly unpopular reform desired by Charles X was to take away the right to vote from the merchant middle class. As a shop owner, Antoine's brother-in-law Jacques Amalric was a member of this class. His and the Gros family's disappointment with the monarchy, to which they would otherwise have been willing to be loyal, had been a topic of Sunday dinner discussion through the spring and early summer. He had signed his name to one of the petitions to the King and admired the members of the Chamber of Deputies who stood up to him.

Antoine sympathized with Jacques, but Charles X had been appreciative of him. The King had attended the opening celebration for the Pantheon Dome; conferred the title of Baron on Gros as a reward; and invited him to the coronation at Reims. Antoine had received the commission to paint several gallery ceilings in the Louvre, which he fulfilled with scenes in a cold Neoclassical style of which David would have been proud. He did not want to lose such an important patron.

Unrest mounted through a spring and summer of food shortages, unemployment, and unrest. Paris finally erupted for three days at the end of July. Eugène Delacroix, catching the sentiment of the moment, celebrated this second July revolution in his *Liberty Leading the People*.

My experience of those days was different. I felt a virtual prisoner in our apartment, afraid to go outside, to open a window, even to look outside lest I fall victim to a stray bullet. I thought of my mother in similar circumstances in 1789 and realized just how terrifying a time it must have been for her.

Antoine was wretched. Having been through so many political ups and downs over the years in France and Italy, and approaching the age of 60, he yearned for enduring stability. He was angry at Charles X for being so politically obtuse as to bring about the unrest.

Jacques Amalric, who had been among the protestors at the Tuileries Palace, came to see us on the third evening.

"We've won! The King has agreed to abdicate!" He picked me up and swung me around in his exuberance.

I smiled at his enthusiasm. "Who will succeed him?"

He shook his head. "It is not yet decided. The Chamber of Deputies – a chamber elected by *all* classes – will decide."

"Perhaps they will invite the King of Rome to rule as Napoleon II," Antoine said, hope lighting his face, his hand touching his favorite talisman, the *Légion d'honneur* pinned to his lapel.

Jacques shook his head again. "Even if they wished it, the rest of Europe would never allow another Bonaparte to come to power."

Antoine's shoulders slumped.

With that, Jacques bade us farewell and went home to break the good news to his family.

In the end, the Duc d'Orléans, a member of a lesser branch of the Bourbons, was invited to ascend the throne. He took the name Louis-Philippe.

Once again, Antoine presented himself at court, fully confident that the new monarch and his ministers would honor his talents and his long record of service. He was to be severely disappointed. The new arts administration scorned and ridiculed Antoine. For the first time in a quarter-century he was out of favor for official commissions. It left him adrift in a sea of self-doubt.

The following year, an even heavier blow fell upon him – his mother's death at the age of eighty-three. She had always been the great prop and constant in his life, his one unfailing source of support and consolation. She kept her strong will in all things until the end. Her mercifully brief last illness was too short to prepare her son for her death. He walked through the funeral Mass and burial in an uncomprehending state, mouthing the necessary things by rote, shaking the hands of the mourners with a weak grasp and blank eyes that saw nothing but his inner landscape of grief. It was only after we had returned from placing her in the family vault that he broke down in floods of tears, locking himself in her room and repulsing all my attempts to comfort him.

Antoine had always been subject to bouts of melancholy. Girodet taught me how to tease him out of them: tell him they were part of his creative genius as an artist, according to the ancient philosophers. This would earn me a slight smile at first, then a more genuine one as he shifted his view to see his ailment in a positive light and no longer felt alone with it. But now, nothing that any of us could say could lift him out of his depression. Only little Cécile could bring a smile to his face and relax its habitual lines of disappointment. Once, on a day when he had not the energy to stir out of doors to visit her, I even went so far as to fetch the girl myself. On our return, I found he had shaved and dressed for the first time in days. He put on a bright face and animated voice so the little girl should not be frightened.

Our life together continued to deteriorate. Any illusion I had that it would improve without his mother was soon dispelled. We had left that adjustment too late. I could not even run the household to suit him. Released from the old lady's tyranny, our cook started to add strange flavors, experiment with new cuts of meat. I enjoyed the change, but Antoine whined and complained like the fussy old man he had become. I would often grimace with distaste for this aging stranger. All our married life, I had looked forward to having my husband to myself. Now that I had, I did not like him anymore. I felt cheated and angry and stubbornly refused to "correct" the household to his mother's ways. It sounds petty now as I write. But at the time it gave me a feeling of power and control, a bit of revenge. Antoine, seeing his complaints did no good, started to eat dinner out with his students or his mistress more often.

These students became his greatest source of support. He was much less dogmatic and dictatorial with them than David had been with him. Teaching provided both a sense of continuity and pride in leaving a legacy in the next generation. His love for his students and theirs for him helped him to keep going through the darkest days.

Even so, it was difficult for Antoine to handle the scornful attitude of the arts administration towards him. Unlike his predecessors, Louis-Philippe allowed the memories of Napoleon and his army to resurface and be honored. *Jaffa* and *Eylau* and other official works of the Empire were brought out of storage and hung in the galleries of the Palais du Luxembourg. In the fifteen years since these works had last been seen, Antoine had tried to live down the contemporary history painter he had been and remake himself into the artist David had hoped he would be. The work that resulted, cold, stiff, and formal, was not suited to his talents.

Once when I compared his current works unfavorably to *Jaffa*, he yelled at me, "I am sick of hearing about that painting! I saw the error of my old ways, and I've moved on since then! Why can't you recognize it? Why can't everyone else?" The last words came out almost a sob. He had done all this at tremendous cost, persevering in the face of the jeers of the critics and the public's dislike.

Now these pictures he so regretted were on display again, delighting the public. *Jaffa* still had the power to cause a sensation, even after nearly thirty years. I went to see it again for the pleasure of remembrance. While I was there Antoine – who had sworn he would not come to see it – entered with a group of his pupils who had evidently cajoled him into coming. He did not see me. For all his assertions of indifference or hostility to it, he looked at his old masterpiece with tears running down his cheeks, overwhelmed by the memories it brought forth. A voice called out, "It's Maître Gros!" Even across the years, I recognized the mock-reverent tones of the model for the figure of the doctor. The crowd burst into applause, and Gros was visibly moved by the tribute.

The government, finally taking notice of him, wanted him to return to painting such subjects. When Louis-Philippe decided to transform the Palace of Versailles into a public museum, his administration requested *The Battle of Iéna* for the new Galerie des Batailles. My husband's refusal contained a reproof: "Having already done so many paintings of this kind, I feel the necessity of concerning myself with subjects more appropriate to the study of art."

After that the government wanted nothing more to do with him. Antoine was written off in the cruelest possible terms as nobody, passé. The odious De Cailleux, the new administrator of the arts, said disdainfully, "Gros is a dead man; he is no longer good for anything." He was immediately scolded by Louis-Philippe for his lack of charity, but the words, once said, made their way to Antoine.

Ironically, it was his loving students who repeated it to him. Although they did so out of indignation rather than a desire to wound him, the effect was the same, destroying his self-confidence. "Then I'm no longer good for anything?" Antoine would ask. "There's nothing left to do but drown myself." It sapped his confidence so much that for a time his creativity was paralyzed and he could not paint. Not even the kind words of pupils and friends could pull him out of his downward spiral.

I had few words of sympathy I could readily summon, they were so long out of use between us, but I managed to say, "That man is a fool, Antoine! You must not believe him."

He looked pleased. "Thank you, my dear," he said, but then lapsed into an even more mournful expression. "Even *you* pity me, it seems – I must be in a sorry state." It was the sort of thing we said to each other all too often then. "I miss you, Maman," he sighed.

He rallied, however, and vowed to do another monumental painting, one that would show them all he was not merely a relic of the Napoleonic era but a living painter. The Salon of June 1835 would be the perfect opportunity. He determined to find a subject that would combine the best of the Neoclassical style and subject matter to which he had devoted his art with the heroic action and spirited horses that everyone so admired in his battle paintings. Each evening he read the classical authors, seeking an exemplary subject. Each morning he went to his studio to find his way, through sketching and drawing, to the idea that would best inspire his brush. After two weeks he returned excited, bearing a small pen sketch that he laid before me in triumph. The subject he had chosen was one of the labors of Hercules – the conquest of the flesh-eating horses of Diomedes and the feeding of that wicked king to his own animals.

Antoine worked on *Hercules and Diomedes* more intensely than I had ever seen him, putting into it all he had learned and believed in. For three months it became his whole life, his hope and vindication. The assured success of this work would restore his reputation. It would make up for the frustration of those last fifteen years, his finally admitted disillusionment with David, and the lack of support from his own wife. "The only two who really understood me were Maman and Girodet," he would cry – tears came to him more easily than ever. So much was riding on this painting – everything, everything. "It *cannot* fail, it *must* not!" He was almost hysterical in his frequent assertions. "Surely this heroic physical combat of horse and man resulting in the triumph of good over evil will have something to please everyone."

In a burst of confidence, he wrote to the Ministry of the Interior to request that it purchase the work and place it in an academy to serve as an example to the young. I had a shiver of apprehension. What if the response to the painting did not live up to his hopes? I was afraid for him but could not respond to him, help him. Too many years of being pushed to the side of his life, of having my own wishes, hopes, ambition discounted and neglected – I could only look on with contempt and dislike, and turn my back on him and his ranting. Our embedded habit of antagonism had left us with little to say to each other that was not steeped in bitterness.

He finished the painting in time for submission to the Salon. I was surprised and touched when Antoine invited me to be the first to see it. He spoke to me tenderly for the first time in weeks as he ushered me proudly into the studio. *Hercules and Diomedes* stood on an immense easel in the middle of the room. I examined it attentively, then with growing dismay, desperately racking my brains to discover something, anything, to say about it. Its sheer awfulness left me speechless.

The outlandishly sized figure of Hercules, bulging with muscles from head to extended foot, dominated the canvas. The absurdly smaller Diomedes struggled in his arms while the diabolical horses tore at his chest. His captor seemed neither pleased nor disgusted, triumphant nor sympathetic, but gazed to one side, not meeting the viewer's eye, with as indifferent an air as if he were killing an insect by drowning it in a basin of water. I have known men to show more agitation waiting for their dinner. The supposedly moral hero demonstrating stoic fortitude clearly had not a thought in his well-proportioned head.

The coloring was cold, the outlines firm, the overall effect appalling.

I turned my gaze from the Herculean alter-ego on the canvas to the mere mortal so desperate for vindication in the eyes of everyone who mattered in the art world – all the while claiming that they did not matter, that he was only doing what was right. He had turned his gaze to the canvas, a look of shining pride on his face. The desperate expression I had seen so often of late was gone. He *liked* his dreadful creation, saw nothing wrong with it, and expected me to do the same. I saw him clearly for the first time in years as though he were something I might want to paint – the small stature, trim figure, the well-fitting clothes and immaculately tied cravat, the hair curling gently onto his collar, and above all the fine brown eyes, large, warm, easily given to tears. Would I set him in his studio, in this imagined painting of mine? No, I thought, I would put him in the Dome of the Panthéon, painting what would seem like a vast area until one noticed the immensity of the space around him. A modern Sisyphus undaunted by the task before him and at the same time condemned by it. Or a modern knight tilting at a dragon, armed only with his painter's brush. It was so ridiculous a fancy I wanted to laugh – or cry, I wasn't sure which.

The contempt I had so long felt for him cracked, then shattered. Deluded, ridiculous, pathetic as he might have been, staring proudly at that disaster of a painting, he was also more human, more vulnerable, than he had let himself be seen for many years. I had looked for the chinks in his armor in our warring days, but having found them now, I felt perversely as though I had been handed a gift of trust to cherish him. I felt overwhelmed, humbled and shaken, cracked out of the cold shell of bitterness that had imprisoned me for so long. Tears came to my eyes.

"Well?" Antoine demanded, turning his gaze back to me.

"I think you're splendid," I said warmly, and darted forward to kiss his cheek. He recoiled, startled, but recovered himself and looked not unpleased. He accepted the kiss then, and bestowed one of his own.

"Not me, you goose, the painting. What do you think of *Hercules*?"

At last he had turned to me, not to his mother, for validation – but as an artist I could not give it to him, however much I wanted to as a wife. Frantically, taking too long about it, I tried to marshal words while he looked at me in happy expectation. When I could finally say something, it sounded hollow and false. The old lines of disappointment replaced his happy expression of pride in his work. He shrugged with an eloquence that implied he had realistically expected nothing better from me. Silently he led me out of the studio to the street, where he hailed a fiacre and sent me home by myself.

When the painting was accepted for the Salon, he was in a fever of anticipation to see where it would be placed and how well it would be received. Once I came in upon him practicing a rebuttal speech to those – "even my dear wife" – who had written him off as dead or at least good for nothing further. He had not seen me. I retreated quietly and closed the door behind me. His life had narrowed its focus to waiting for his vindication.

But for all my belief in the futility of his hopes, at least he had them. I had nothing to hope for, no fame, no recognition; my brief Salon career was long over; my marriage long incapable of repair; my one true love long dead and buried – what was there to look forward to? God help me, I envied Antoine his optimism, however unlikely it might have been! I never saw that so clearly before now. He was miserable, he was tottering on the edge of a precipice mentally and physically, but I envied him then.

Hercules and Diomedes was a dismal failure at the Salon. It was hung so high, catching the glare from the windows, that visitors could barely see it. The critics were even more vituperative than before. Antoine plunged from the heights of optimism to the depths of despair.

The night of 25 June 1835, four months after the opening of the Salon, was warm and oppressive. After our usual silent dinner, Antoine dressed with care and went down to the street. The sound of his footsteps grew faint as he walked away. I never saw him again.

It was too hot to sleep. I lay awake all night waiting for him to come home. I no longer cared very much about his sleeping in another woman's bed, but his coming home at night was part of my daily routine. I grew uneasy. In retrospect it would be easy to claim I had a premonition, but at the time I was more concerned that he had been attacked and robbed. I put on the bracelet he had given me in Brussels, turning it round and round my wrist as I prayed for his safe return.

Finally, a Commissaire of Police came at daybreak. Antoine's body had been found floating in the Seine outside the Paris suburb of Meudon. His neatly folded coat and hat were on the riverbank, with his calling card placed in the hat. It gave every sign of being a deliberate act; there was no suspicion of foul play.

As I sat absorbing the news, my mind and heart were a jumble of thoughts and emotions. Sorrow for Antoine – amazement that he had finally found the courage to commit the act – worry that the shame of it should tarnish his memory – dread that his friends and pupils, who had never liked me very much to begin with, would say I had played a part in driving him to this extreme – anger at De Cailleux and the others who had never appreciated his true worth as an artist – and a belated stab of guilt that I had, at times, been among them. I put that last thought away. Confirmation of the policeman's diagnosis of suicide must be avoided at all costs. I marshaled my thoughts and spoke calmly and deliberately.

"My husband complained of headaches for some time. His doctor was of the opinion that they were caused by a weak blood vessel in his brain. The doctor said it was a condition that had stemmed from the time of hardship he faced during the siege of Genoa, when he served with the army." I was inventing as I spoke, but I managed to put the right amount of pride into my voice, making his death a consequence of service to France, something to be commended rather than censured. "I think we will find this blood vessel burst in his time of mental distress and caused

311

him to fall into the water by accident." My strong voice and direct gaze challenged the policeman to say otherwise.

He was not fooled but he was willing to take direction. "As you say, Madame." He bent his head obediently to write down what I had said in his notebook. I gave instructions for the delivery of Antoine's body to the same funeral service we had hired for Maman Madeleine. The policeman bowed and left.

I sent for Père Martin. Together we prayed for my husband's soul. We set the funeral for three days hence, enough time to put a notice in the newspaper and notify all those who should attend. I asked him to break the news to the Amalrics.

The funeral Mass on 29 June was well attended. All the most prominent artists in Paris were there, including Madame Vigée-Lebrun, who had known Antoine as a child, and all his students, those hopefuls of the next generation, unusually subdued and decorous. The Amalrics brought Cécile. Josée was at my side. The service was a comfort to me, bringing Antoine back from the shameful, solitary manner of his end to the ritual of honoring the dead. His soul wandering in Purgatory would at least be accompanied by our prayers. Afterward the doleful procession made its way out to Père-Lachaise

312

where a chamber of the Gros-Dufresne family crypt stood open to receive the coffin. The sepulcher had been built after Girodet died, when Gros was beginning to feel his own mortality; my mother was the first of us to be buried there. I touched my fingers to the inscription on Maman's tombstone.

Eulogies were said while we sweated in the summer sun. Over and over I heard that Antoine was loved and would be missed. I hoped that he could hear this and be comforted. As always, there were the regrets that he could not have heard them and taken heed in his lifetime. I thanked the speakers.

The funeral repast took place at a restaurant next to the cemetery. Because of the warm weather it was held out-of-doors. The young men from Gros's studio soon regained their native high spirits. I marveled that Antoine, whom I had known only in his middle and old age, should once have been as young as they, a mere lad in David's studio before the Revolution. Josée and I sat at the head table with Antoine's sister and her family, as well as Madame Vigée-Lebrun, her niece Eugénie and the dreadful man she married, Tripier-Lefranc, who had idolized my husband and could only with difficulty be civil to me. My sister and her family were also there, but Henri was probably sleeping off a hangover. I was grateful for his absence, as his feelings for Antoine were chiefly resentment that his famous brother-in-law had not done more to help him.

Reluctantly we returned to the city in the late afternoon. Needing solitude more than solace, I dismissed all those who would have come home with me.

The maid had cleaned and aired the house while I was gone, putting away the black cloth of the mortuary chapel where the coffin had stood, sweeping out the dead flowers and leaves. In the bedroom, she had put Antoine's personal effects into the armoire that held his clothes and made up the bed with fresh linens. I looked at the unnatural tidiness of the room and realized it was a widow's bedroom now. For the first time that day, I burst into tears.

Oh, Antoine! All those wasted bitter years we spent together – I am crying again as I write. Père Martin came the next day to give me comfort, and I took it, but for the wrong things – not for my sorrow for your final action but for my self-pity for being a suicide's widow. Looking back, I realize how hollow it all was and how wasted were the years of bitterness, eating away the best part of me for far too long. May we both find peace.

Chapter 14

Paris, 1835-1840

I did not linger for long in sentimental regret over the failure of our marriage. This period lasted precisely one week, until the reading of Antoine's will.

As on the day of my engagement, we gathered in the notary's office, the Dufresne family on one side of the table, the Gros-Amalric family on the other. Even after a quarter-century of marriage, we were and always would be on opposite sides of the table. I had asked Pauline to come with me. Henri was there at his own insistence as the man (and therefore supposedly the head) of the Dufresnes. I had no illusions about him: he wanted to make sure I inherited well so I could continue to support him when needed.

In contrast to his customary obsequious air, Monsieur Sorel, the notary, had an unusually nervous manner and found it difficult to look me in the eye. I thought it was because of the unhappy circumstances of Antoine's death, until he cleared his throat and began to read out loud the terms of the will.

"What?" I exclaimed, my sharp voice cutting through the lawyer's hushed tones. "That *can't* be right. Read it again!"

"I assure you, Madame –"

"Read it *again*," I insisted.

"I, Antoine-Jean Gros, bequeath my entire estate to my ward, Françoise-Cécile Simonier, daughter of the late Françoise Simonier, deceased in March of this year residing at—"

"No, it's not possible. I was his *wife*. He wouldn't do this to me!"

"I drew up the will myself, Madame, according to his explicit instructions. Monsieur Gros's signature was witnessed by two of my clerks. The document is genuine." The integrity of his conduct defended, he softened and shifted to a tone of professional sympathy. "I understand this is painful for you—"

"Oh, you do, do you? Then why didn't you use that understanding to point out its painful nature to Monsieur Gros?"

"I attempted to do so, Madame. Monsieur Gros was most insistent that the child should be the chief beneficiary of the estate. He has also named you as one of the three executors of the estate, to make sure she receives her due. He said you would understand."

I gasped and choked. He leapt to his feet to pour a glass of water from the carafe on the sideboard. Pauline pressed my hand in sympathy while Henri gave me the sort of resounding slap on the back he would give a drinking companion. This crude treatment worked; the coughing spasm stopped. I wiped my eyes and looked up to see Antoine's sister and nephew shaking with barely suppressed laughter. I glared at them, which only made them laugh outright. A scandalized Monsieur Sorel scolded them.

"Am I to have nothing, then?" My voice had risen in the excitement of my indignation and took on an edge of panic.

"You are to retain the one hundred thousand francs you brought into the marriage and all income deriving from it. You may keep all personal effects and any gifts from your husband. Although ownership of the apartment in the rue des Saints-Pères passes to Mademoiselle Simonier, you are entitled to live there rent-free for as long as you wish." His tone had shifted again and he was using his best conciliatory lawyer voice. It set my teeth on edge.

"You expect me to be grateful to be allowed to live in my own home and spend my own money and keep my husband's gifts of twenty-five years of marriage?" I was happy to see him wince. Let him feel some of the pain of the situation!

I rose. "These terms are unacceptable. You will be hearing from my lawyer." My new black silk dress rustled as I left the room. The sound of the Amalrics' renewed laughter followed me.

Pauline, Henri and I returned to my home for what was to have been a family luncheon, but I had no appetite. In addition, I now had my brother to contend with. "*I* am the man of the family," Henri told me. "Let me take care of this."

I knew better than that. After twenty-five years of attempted dictation by my husband and mother-in-law, I had little desire to put myself under new direction. Responsibility, I knew, was something he assumed only when it would be to his advantage, not when it would put him out for the benefit of others. "I will make my own arrangements, thank you," I said wearily.

He started to argue with me. Pauline cut him short. She had no illusions about our brother either.

"Neither of you has ever appreciated me properly!" he fumed.

"Oh *yes*, we have!" Pauline responded, with a straight look that let him know she appreciated his worth only too fully.

Furious, he stormed out – to get drunk, no doubt. Pauline and I looked at each other in mutual sympathy and exhaustion. His attitude was too familiar to us to need any discussion.

"Would you like me to stay?" she asked.

"No." She looked hurt, and I smiled at her to soften the effect of my abrupt refusal. "I really appreciate your offer, but right now I need to take a nap. Then, I'll need to decide what steps to take next. And I need to start learning how to do it" – I took a shaky breath and my voice quavered – "alone."

Mollified, she kissed my cheek and took her leave.

Once again alone in the home that I had shared with Antoine for so long, I burst into tears. The manner of his death and the terms of his will had exposed so much about our lives that was difficult to admit to myself, never mind to the world: his unhappiness, his mental instability, the unhappy truth about our marriage, my barrenness, and the fact of his daughter, who was the real object of his love.

When I was not burning with humiliation, I was seething with rage. How could Antoine *do* this to me? Afternoon gave way to evening and evening to night, and still my thoughts centered on the horrible scene in the notary's office.

When dawn at long last began to edge around the curtains into the house, I rose from the chair where I had spent the night and went to wash my face. Looking in the dressing-table mirror afterward, I was appalled. The strands of grey hair I usually kept carefully tucked beneath the brown were all too plainly in evidence, standing out as if I had touched Monsieur Lavoisier's electrical cage. The angry fixedness in my eyes and the grim set of my mouth were like Antoine's in his last years. Were these, too, part of his legacy for me? I shuddered and made the sign of the Cross. Grabbing the shawl that hung over the back of the dressing chair, I threw it over the mirror, as though doing so would erase the look on my face and not merely its reflection. My heart was beating wildly.

My maid appeared at the door of the room. "Are you all right, Madame? Shall I bring your morning café?"

"No, I am going out." I needed air.

"Let me help you change your dress, and I'll take this one away to press."

"No, it doesn't matter. I need to leave *now.*" I could not bear to stay in that room another minute. I needed to escape from that house and its ghosts. As always in a crisis, my first thought was to talk to Josée. She would know how to bring me back to my right self.

Josée had recently moved to a smart studio on the Boulevard Saint-Germain, a short distance away. A few minutes' walk brought me there. It was hot and sunny, with little breeze. Housemaids and shopkeepers armed with pails of soapy water cleaned windows and scrubbed doorsteps. Street sweepers were busy collecting the horse droppings that had accumulated overnight; the air was pungent with that and other more pleasant early morning smells: baking bread, roasting coffee, fresh cheese at a dairy shop. When I arrived at Josée's address, number 11, the concierge, yawning and brushing crumbs off her dress, let me in and waved a hand in the direction of the studio. "She is still at home, Madame."

I thanked her and apologized for the early hour. Belatedly, I wondered whether Josée might be awake yet, although I knew she habitually arose early, the better to catch the effects of morning light. I was relieved to smell coffee brewing as I approached her door.

When Josée opened the door, her smile of welcome quickly faded to a look of dismay. I realized how frightful must be my appearance. The concierge hadn't appeared to notice, or perhaps she was accustomed to the peculiarities of her tenants' visitors.

"Augustine! What has happened? Should I send for the doctor?"

"Do I look that bad?"

Josée looked me over critically. "In a word, yes. If I were to paint you now, I would call the canvas *La Malade*, the sick woman."

I gave her a wry smile. "No, I'm not ill – not physically, anyway."

"Oh, my dear – is it – about Antoine?"

I nodded, my eyes filling with tears. As I had so often before, I sank down on her sofa and burst into tears, burying my face in the handkerchief she held out to me.

She sat next to me and put her arm around my shoulders. "You must not blame yourself. His actions were entirely of his own choosing. You have nothing to reproach—"

I shook my head and turned to face her. "It's not that. It's—" I took a deep breath to steady myself. "Yesterday was the reading of the will. He has left everything to

Cécile, and made me an executor, to see the terms are carried out."

Josée's draw dropped. She stared at me in disbelief. I nodded to confirm what I had told her. When she could speak again, she asked, "*Everything*?"

"Oh, I'm allowed to keep my dowry and its income, and the gifts he has given me personally. But the apartment, its contents, the contents of the studio, the money in the bank – it all goes to Cécile." Tears spilled down my cheeks. "After twenty-six years of marriage. Could he really have hated me that much, Josée?"

She did not reply but crossed the room to pour a bowl of black coffee, tempering it with a little cold water so I could drink it straight down. She looked on as I did so and took back the bowl with a nod of approval.

As usual, she was right. I started to feel better at once, even more so after I had eaten the brioche she brought me. She refilled her own coffee bowl and drank it slowly, deep in thought, and set it down with a decisive click when she had finished.

"What you need to do is consult a lawyer of your own, who will look out for your interests."

"But I don't know any," I started to say.

"Oh, but I do. I have several among my clientele. And I think I know just the man to help you."

That very afternoon, freshly bathed and dressed in a different black gown, I went to see Maître Derville, a frequent visitor to her studio. Josée recommended him as a man of sharp intelligence, fearless in argument, who would look out for my interests. Only Josée came with me, at my request. Henri might be furious about being excluded when he learned about this meeting, but Pauline, I suspected, would be relieved.

We were early and had to wait in the anteroom. As Josée crossed the room to examine several framed caricatures of lawyers and judges, I admired her dress. It was dark blue, in deference to Antoine, but the fabric had a subtle sheen and it was cut in the latest fashion, with a short cape over wide sleeves. The cape was fastened at the neck with one of her Roman cameos; smaller cameos hung from her ears. Her fiery red hair was now shot with grey, but she carried off that and the other signs of aging – a few lines in her face and hands – with a nonchalance that gave her an air of youth. There was only six months' difference in our ages, but beside her I felt old and dull in my mourning dress of an appropriately restrained style.

After a few minutes, we were admitted. I was becoming all too familiar with the purposeful bustle, the rustle of papers and the scratching of pens of lawyers' offices. Derville scanned the copy of the will I had brought with me and asked a series of penetrating questions.

I answered them as honestly as I could. Yes, I had met Cécile; yes, I brought her to our home when my husband was ill. Yes, my husband and mother-in-law had admitted to me, verbally, that she was his daughter, although I did not believe it was written in any legal document. In his will, Antoine had referred to her simply as his ward. His sister and her family had accepted the girl as a blood relation and she was a visitor to their home. Amongst Françoise Simonier's acquaintance, too, Cécile was spoken of as Antoine's daughter – here I repeated my conversation with the neighbor, Madame Mauvre. Yes, Antoine had wanted us to adopt her or at least take her in after her mother's death, but I had put my foot down. There were limits, after all. Antoine had known how I felt, yet he had made her his heir and, to add insult to injury, had made me one of the executors of his estate, with the responsibility of seeing that our marital assets were handed over to her. It was humiliating! My eyes filled with tears.

Josée handed me a handkerchief and patted my arm sympathetically. Maître Derville looked on impassively.

"Courage, Madame. No tears! Let those memories fuel your anger instead. You will need it."

I wiped my eyes and faced him calmly again. "That's better," he said. Uncharacteristically, he hesitated. "In addition to challenging the rights of Mademoiselle Simonier, there is another tactic we can pursue in breaking the will. Forgive me for asking this, Madame Gros – but – was your husband of sound mind at the end of his life?"

My stomach lurched. It was inevitable that this question should come up. Certainly, he had been disturbed. Privately I admitted that he could have taken his own life; publicly I had invested much effort in denying it. To appear to reverse myself now merely to gain hold of his estate would put me in a most unflattering light. I could not do that. As I was mulling over how to respond, Josée spoke up.

"Maître Derville, I knew Monsieur Gros for almost twenty years, so perhaps I can shed light on this subject so painful for Madame Gros. After decades of magnificent contributions to the artistic legacy of France, he found himself maligned and ignored by the current administration. Of course this upset a man of his sensibilities, and not even the support of a loving wife could entirely counter the effects of this unjust treatment. It contributed to his bodily infirmity, the aneurysm that killed him, but it would not have affected his writing of the will." She spoke calmly and clearly, with every appearance of candor.

"Nobly said, Mademoiselle Sarazin de Belmont. You defend your friends well." He too spoke calmly, but one eyebrow was quirked skeptically. I realized that he had known the answer to his question all along and wondered if asking it had been a test. Would he now decline to take my case? He glanced down at the papers on his desk and appeared to come to a decision. When he looked up again, the ironical expression was gone.

"Very well. I will inform Monsieur Sorel that we are bringing suit. This will exempt you from being an executor on behalf of the girl; one of the other executors will no doubt be appointed to protect her interests. I know them both as men amenable to negotiation" – he said the word with an almost sinister relish, as if he could only with difficulty refrain from licking his lips – "and if you would return to my office in two weeks' time, I believe I will have good news for you."

The day after my meeting with the lawyer, Monsieur Sorel and his assistants came to our home to carry out the *inventaire après décès*, the inventory of the possessions of the deceased that is required by law. They had done so upon the death of Maman Madeleine, so that I was familiar with the process. What had been a matter of routine, however, now became a nerve-racking ordeal. Each item, by virtue of appearing on the notary's list, could be snatched from me as part of Cécile's inheritance. Together with one of Derville's clerks, I made sure to accompany the men as they made their round from the furnishings of the front room to the copper pots in the kitchen, the linen press, clothes cupboards, and contents of the bedrooms, writing them down and assigning values. I took care that each object belonging to me personally was noted as such. I stayed with them even while they inventoried Maman Madeleine's room, the one room whose contents, I reflected, Cécile was more than welcome to take. My head was pounding by the time they left and my face felt set in a permanent scowl of disapproval.

I let Derville's clerk attend the inventory of Antoine's studios in Paris and Versailles. Monsieur Sorel had asked Antoine's student Paul Delaroche, now a highly regarded history painter, to give his advice and expertise regarding their contents and value, and I knew I could trust him.

Sorel sent me a copy of the inventory after it was registered with the city. I would inherit an estate worth in excess of five hundred thousand francs. Or Cécile would. I shivered despite the July heat. I had not yet heard from Derville.

The lawyer greeted Josée and me with a smile of triumph on our return visit.

"I have excellent news for you, Madame Gros. Although it is customary to leave one's estate to one's children, with a life interest in it for one's widow, an exception is made in the case of a child that is the result of an adulterous relationship. This, Mademoiselle Cécile Simonier most certainly was. The law is clear that an *enfant adultérain* may not inherit to the detriment of any legitimate heirs. We thus have excellent grounds to break the terms of the will."

My body relaxed for the first time since the reading of the will. I exhaled the long breath I seemed to have been holding for weeks. Josée squeezed my hand.

"One of the first inquiries I made was to see the girl's birth certificate. It states that her father is 'unknown.' I believe this was done so that the child would not bear the stigma of being known as the product of an adulterous union, as she would had your husband been named as the father.

"Moreover, my research has revealed that your husband has already settled a sum of money on Mademoiselle Simonier for her care now and a dowry later. It is quite customary in these circumstances. If you wish, we can attempt to recover this money as well."

"No. She brought him joy when few things did. Let her keep that – it was Antoine's gift to her." I felt magnanimous in my victory. "She may keep any money he settled upon her prior to his death," I said in a steady voice. "I wish only to inherit my due as his widow."

Settling an estate or a lawsuit is never a quick and easy process, but within a very few months I was declared indisputably Antoine's sole legitimate heir and took possession of the bulk of the estate. Returning home – mine and no one else's – from Maître Derville's office after signing the papers, I immediately packed up everything in Maman Madeleine's room – her clothes, furniture, personal effects, and jewelry – and sent the whole lot to Marie Amalric. I could have ordered the

330

maids to do this, but it was a good outlet for the bitter energy that had possessed me ever since the reading of the will. For good measure I added any gifts I had received from my mother-in-law that I had never used or been fond of. I was tempted to send them to the Cécile with a note – "Perhaps you would like these mementoes of your grandmother; she was so happy for her son when you were born" – but thought the better of putting this in writing. It gave me deep satisfaction to finally exorcise the old lady's presence. I gave orders to the maids to scrub the walls and floor thoroughly and air the room out. I had the walls repainted and opened the shutters to let daylight flood the room. I had decided to move my studio here, the room with the best light.

Josée and I went to the art supply shop to which Denon had taken me over thirty years before, to get new easels, canvases, paints and other supplies. Fashions in dress had changed, but the eager voices and purposeful energy of the young men and women who thronged it – some of whom I recognized as Antoine's students – were very much the same as on that first visit. When I closed my eyes, I was overcome with a wave of déjà-vu. I was simultaneously fourteen years old and forty-six, starting my career and re-starting it after all too much in between, with all too little to show for it. Then, Denon had sung the praises of a young painter named Gros, and now I was his widow.

Fortunately, Josée was there to touch my arm and bring me back to the present with a cheerful word before my memories could lead me into melancholy. I paid for my purchases, gave directions for their delivery, and we left.

I saw Pauline regularly in the months that followed but Henri only rarely. His habits of dissipation were beginning to tell upon him. Even as an adult, he remained the perennial spoiled younger brother, not bad, but not good either. He died two years later, in 1837, without ever fulfilling whatever promise he may have had.

He was buried in the Gros-Dufresne family vault at Père-Lachaise, in the chamber next to Antoine's. He had finally achieved his ambition of being recognized side-by-side with his brother-in-law the prominent artist.

As it turned out, he had more in common with Antoine than we had realized. When Pauline and I went to his rooms after the funeral, we were startled to find a strange woman who seemed very much at home there, sorting through his things.

"You must be Baudouin's sisters," she said to us calmly.

"Baudouin?" we exclaimed.

"I know you called him Henri, but he liked me to call him Baudouin. It was not so ordinary and thus better suited to him as an artist, he said."

That sounded like Henri. "And who are *you*?" we asked the woman.

"Liliane," she replied, extending her hand to be shaken as a man would. Her accent was provincial, overlaid with Parisian working-class, but her hands were smooth. "I was his" – she hesitated slightly – "companion these last five years."

Our astonishment said more clearly than words that he had never mentioned her. She shrugged philosophically. "We met at the Palais-Royal," she offered by way of explanation.

Pauline and I shared another startled glance. Had Henri been supported by a prostitute?

Once again, she read us accurately. "That is where we *met*," she said firmly. "Baudouin insisted I leave the trade after I was badly beaten by another client. He found me work as an artists' model, and he never took a sou of those earnings either. He took good care of me and the children."

"The children?" we echoed. There was no sign of them in the room.

"Madeleine is four," she replied calmly. "Marie-Adelaide is two. We don't live here. Baudouin didn't have much patience with babies."

"Madeleine was—"

"His – your – mother's name. I know. Baudouin missed her very much, even after all these years." Her eyes filled. "Just as I will miss him." Her tough façade dissolved as tears rolled down her cheeks and she began to sob.

Pauline went to her and put her arms around her, murmuring words of comfort. I busied myself filling the kettle and lighting the stove so that we could boil water, then went out to purchase tea and pastries. (Henri had stocked only stronger drink.) There was much to discuss.

Henri a father, yet he had never mentioned it to us! Had he thought we would reject Liliane and their daughters out of hand? True, ordinarily I might have done, but there was something forthright about Liliane that I liked nonetheless. I think Pauline felt the same. Had she been of our class, we could have been friends.

Later that day, we went with her to the room where she lived with the girls. There was no doubt about their paternity. Madeleine looked much as our mother must have done when she was a little girl. Marie-Adelaide – named for Louis-Philippe's queen – looked like Henri, especially when displaying her two-year-old's temper.

Our brother had never been very prudent with his money, but we were relieved to discover, in the days that followed, that while he had spent the 50,000 francs of capital our father had left him, Maman's money that had been left to him upon her death was intact. It did not provide a large income by our standards, but Liliane was pleased. It was arranged that Henri's daughters should inherit it in trust and that their mother would have full access to the income.

They did not stay in our lives for long, however. The following year Liliane's mother died, and she and the girls went to live with her widowed father on his farm in the Basses-Pyrénées. We have had only the barest news of them from the notary who administers Henri's estate.

After this, my life fell into a routine of painting in my studio, going to daily Mass and visiting Pauline and Josée. It was a soothing, undemanding life. I needed peace after all I had been through. The twin betrayals of Antoine's suicide and the terms of his will had scarred me, leaving me with lasting suspicion and distrust. I did not seek new friendships, and I certainly had no thoughts of remarrying.

My life constricted rather than expanded in my newfound freedom. It came about so gradually that I did not realize how pinched and soured I had become until the celebrations for the return of Napoleon's remains drove me from Paris to Toulouse, from my routine to new activities, from suspicion to a wider acquaintance and a little girl who is teaching me to love again.

Now, at last, I rejoin the living.

Chapter 15

Toulouse, 1840

It is 31 December 1840, the close of the old year, and a fitting date for the conclusion of my memoir. I am writing in my room in the home of Madame Lapierre, sitting at my desk by the window with its view of the tower of the church of Saint-Sernin. The pale winter sunshine lights the room and a cheerful fire burns in the grate. The ring of voices outside is clear and distinct in the sharp air. There is a child's laughter in the house – Jeanne, my landlady's daughter and my friend.

I fell in love with the church of Saint-Sernin last summer, when the sunlight coming in the clear windows gave a golden sheen to its walls and arches, articulating the purity and simplicity of the architecture. I have visited many times since. My heart lifts just to be there. I rejoice at the presence of the relics of the saints. In Paris the Revolution did away with relics, but here they are venerated as they have always been. Even the Baroque figure of St Sernin at the main altar, incongruous in style with the rest of the church, seems the fitting expression of an uplifted soul.

At services on 1 November, the Day of All Souls, my attention was drawn to a mother and daughter I had seen several times before, a young blonde woman in widow's black and a little girl of seven or eight with hair the dark brown mine used to be and grey eyes set in a solemn face. Her winter coat was too small and I guessed that the mother was trying to make it do for one more year. She was impressed by the mystery and majesty of the Mass and clearly yearned for the day when she would be able to join her mother in taking Communion. But there was such sadness there! The mother's face was neither so rapt nor so sad. She felt her loss, but she was occupied in coping with it, supporting and making a home for the two of them. The little girl's grief was purer. Reliving my own losses as I had been, my heart went out to her as we exchanged the kiss of peace at the end of Mass.

Afterward, I asked the priest about them. Jean Lapierre had been killed only a few months before in an explosion at La Poudrerie, the gunpowder factory on one of the islands of the Garonne. Even in times of peace, it seems, the materiel of war goes on killing men. He had made a good living for his family. They had been generous to the church, Père Grégoire said approvingly, but not a thrifty couple, and what little savings they had was coming to an end. The lodger his widow, Marianne, had taken in to help pay the mortgage had proven unreliable…

"Is she looking for another?" I cut into his doleful litany of the Lapierre family's misfortunes. The eagerness in my voice surprised me – I had spoken on impulse. He gave me her address in one of the nearby streets.

The house, one of several in the row, was proud to stand among its neighbors but showed slight signs of neglect, its step not quite so white as the others in the street, its knocker and doorknob unpolished. She should scold her housemaid, I thought, and then realized that this pointed to an inexperienced mistress trying to do these humble tasks herself.

Marianne Lapierre answered my knock. She had changed from her Sunday church dress and wore an apron; I could smell food cooking. Her expression of mild annoyance at being interrupted gave way to a smile of recognition. "You sat next to us at Mass." She spoke the local dialect, but I was surprised to find I understood her with only a little difficulty. Evidently I had absorbed more than I realized during my weeks here. I responded in French, speaking slowly and distinctly as I had learned to do, and was relieved that she understood me. I explained my errand, saying that the priest had recommended her to me. I apologized for coming while she was busy and offered to return at another time, but she assured me their dinner could wait, and eagerly invited me inside.

"Who is it, Maman?" The little girl, too, had changed her frock and was drying her hands on her apron. She gave me a look that was half friendly, half wary, unsure what this new circumstance would bring into their lives. I longed to bring the carefree look of childhood back into her face.

Together, the mother and daughter showed me their home. It was clean but furnished with the bare necessities, all frills and ornaments having been sold. In the winter they lived mostly in the warm kitchen at the back, even bedding down there at night. The empty front room was used for drying laundry when Madame Lapierre returned from one of the wash boats on the Garonne. Upstairs, the mother and daughter had moved into the smaller front bedroom and rented out the larger one in the back. Without a steady lodger it was a real struggle for her to keep up the mortgage payments, she told me, but she was determined to hold on to the house for as long as she could. To be a widow in lodgings, with no property or means to her name, was something she dreaded more and more as that day seemed to be getting closer.

The back bedroom overlooked a yard and stables but Saint-Sernin rising above the humble scene lent nobility to the view. It would gladden my heart to be so near the church and hear the summons of its bells. The room itself was clean, the planks of the bare floor scrubbed to whiteness. There was a hearthrug in front of the fireplace, but no smell of a recent fire. The walls were painted Mediterranean blue – her favorite color, Marianne explained, because it matched her eyes – with white trim at the window. The bed had a thick straw mattress, and the armoire, table and chairs were simple but solidly made.

"It's perfect," I told them. "I know I will be very happy here." Marianne and Jeanne gave me relieved smiles. I paid a month's rent in advance with louis d'or. Jeanne's eyes grew wide at the sight of the gold coins. She later told me that, "Papa used to have coins like that on payday, but since he died we only have silver and copper ones."

I spent the next two days happily shopping, packing, and arranging for the rental of a feather mattress and a wide *bergère* armchair and footstool. Marianne was helping her uncle at his market day stall when I moved in, so it was Jeanne who helped me unpack my trunk. She is seven years old, about to turn eight, she says with an air of self-importance, holding up her fingers to be sure I understand. She paid my few possessions flattering interest, holding my fur muff to her cheek with a dreamy expression that I longed to paint. Later, when I wasn't looking, I heard her whisper words of love to it as though it were the kitten she longed to have. My paints and brushes and pencils and steel pens, my expensive sketching and writing paper, my drawings and manuscript tied up with red ribbon, were fascinating to her. I take living with artists and writers for granted, but to her I was a strange new creature. She made me think of Denon in Egypt, eager to comprehend the wonders around him.

I was glad of her curiosity, for it helped us to overcome our mutual shyness. When I took her out for hot chocolate afterward to thank her for her help, we were smiling at each other like old friends. We paused on the way home to buy biscuits from a woman who carried her wares in a tower-shaped tin box on her back.

Jeanne likes pretty things, like bright ribbons for her hair. Sugared almonds and chocolate dragees in pastel colors, crystal violets and rose petals delight her as much to look at as to eat. I began to keep bowls of them in my room, and eating my own share, I have started to gain a little weight and to look less pinched.

I do not have many things here, compared to my apartment full of a lifetime's possessions in Paris. But I do not miss them. More and more, I think of them as dead objects from a dead life. It is the new clothes I have bought in Toulouse, the new sketches I have made, and above all the growing pile of manuscript pages of my memoir that are the living things, the things that matter.

The thought of going home to rooms shut up with all their unpleasant memories oppresses me. I wonder if it would be possible to avoid returning altogether: to hire an agent to pack up the studio and my personal things, sell the apartment and its contents at auction. At the very least, should I decide to return, I will clean out the rooms of everything shabby or evocative of bad memories, and redecorate.

Jeanne, Marianne and I spent a happy Christmas together. I treated all of us to new dresses, letting Jeanne pick out the fabrics – soft red wool for me, green for her, and blue for Marianne, to match her eyes.

What fun we had, Jeanne and I! We had the shop deliver the parcels to the dressmaker, then went home to get her mother and bring her with us. Jeanne refused to tell her where we were taking her. "It's a surprise, Maman," she said firmly, pulling her along. Marianne did not want to come at first – too much to do, too tired, and dinner not yet begun – it was with half-stifled annoyance that she finally gave in and came with us. She melted completely when she felt the fabric – lighter, softer and warmer than any dress she'd had before. Then she looked frightened and protested that she couldn't accept such a gift. I didn't argue, just kissed her cheeks and said firmly, "*Joyeux Noël.*" She was stunned for a moment, then startled me by kissing my cheek in return and saying, mimicking my tone, "*Merci beaucoup!*" Then Jeanne insisted on kissing both of us in the same way. Christmas came early, there in the dressmaker's shop, with ease and warmth flowing among us. The moment did not last long – the seamstress and her assistant needed to take our measurements, and then we went on to consider styles and details – and Marianne to remind the dressmaker to fashion little Jeanne's dress so that it could be let out and lengthened as she grew. But the warmth and the softness of the moment stay with me, as pleasant and caressing as the fabric itself.

The following week, after collecting our purchases, we went to the milliner and the shoemaker. The milliner pleased me immensely when she called Marianne and Jeanne "your daughter and granddaughter." When we had made one last stop to buy coats and parasols to complete our outfits, we went to a café to celebrate. Patrons looked up as we entered, three ladies in pretty dresses, laughing among ourselves.

My memoirs are finished, the good and bad of my past contained in these pages. Now I look forward to new adventures. Josée responded to my Christmas letter with an invitation to join her in Rome this winter. At long last I will fulfill my dream of seeing that city's wonders. I hope to meet the Holy Father with a heart cleared of bitterness and filled with joy.

After experiencing Italy I will return to Paris to sell the apartment on the rue des Saints-Pères. I will leave behind all things with unhappy memories and return to Toulouse. Perhaps, in twenty years' time, I can write another memoir entitled "Happiness."

Chapter 16

Rome, 1841

Carnival. Everyone tells me I must be in Rome in time for Carnival.

To prepare for the journey, I read eagerly Stendhal's *Promenades in Rome*. He was there fifteen years ago, but what is that in the Eternal City – the blink of an eye. I trust the Coliseum is still there, and Saint Peter's, and the masterpieces of Raphael and Bernini. The fountains still spout water, and the Tiber flows through. The ghosts of my past wandered there – Antoine, Géricault, and Denon – will I feel their presence as I too walk these streets?

I cannot make Stendhal's recommended coach trip from Paris, of course – and I do not wish to experience the Simplon Pass in the dead of winter – so I devise an alternate route. I will go by coach from Toulouse to Marseilles, thence to Civitavecchia via steamer, and from there to Rome again by coach. My banker gives me a letter of credit to cover my living expenses. Josée, now that the return of Napoleon's remains is over, is delighted at the twin prospects of a reunion and of spending the winter in a warmer climate than Paris, and promises to make all haste to meet me there. She writes to the Conte del Borgo to rent rooms for us in his palazzo. (She stayed there before and the rooms have north light that makes them ideal for painting.) I pack my trunk, bid a tearful farewell to Jeanne and Marianne, and set out on a cold January morning. On this journey, however, I am not running away from my memories but toward a new adventure and whatever the future might bring.

The Mediterranean is my first experience of the sea and voyage by steamship. I am not sick for a moment and stay on deck as long as I can, reveling in the blue above and below. Docking in Civitavecchia, I find that the Italian phrase book I studied *en route* has been of benefit (though sometimes my shyly proffered phrases elicit an enthusiastic torrent of words I understand not at all). I exchange my francs for a handful of *scudi*, *paoli*, and *baiocchi* and board the coach for Rome. Light is failing as we arrive, and the palazzo, with its grimy exterior and overgrown courtyard, has a forbidding air but the Conte's housekeeper is expecting me. Suddenly worn out from my days of travel, I make an early night of it, smiling to myself as I drift off to sleep. *I'm in Rome ... Rome ... Rome ...*

Waking up in Rome, in this foreign city, I have a sense of renewal, almost a rebirth. I have no history here, only a future. I am no longer the grimly disappointed woman who arrived in Toulouse four months ago. Writing this memoir has caused me to remember the young, hopeful woman and artist I once was. Here, away from the routines of home, I have a chance to recapture her. A chance, too, to revive my artistic ambitions with fresh subject matter and the inspiration of the masters of the Renaissance and Baroque. My hands long for drawing materials, for paints and brushes.

The delicious smells of coffee and bread still warm from the bakery draw me from my bedroom. A young woman serves them at a table in the sitting room, and between my phrase book and pantomime, we manage to communicate. She is the old housekeeper's daughter, Gloria. After breakfast, I unpack my trunk, pin up the pencil portraits of Jeanne and Marianne, and explore the flat, two bedrooms and a sitting room that will serve as our studio. The rooms are light and clean, I am relieved to see, not at all like the building's exterior. The setting and furniture are grand but have grown shabby, the remnants of the splendor of the Baroque. It is comfortable but not as intimidating as one would think of living in a palace. My bedroom has a desk and chair by the window for writing and sketching. There are a wardrobe and bed, a washstand behind a screen, and a faded carpet on the floor. I have finished the ream of paper purchased in Toulouse (the memoir stays wrapped in my trunk) but the writing habit is upon me. After I visit the bank to deposit my letter of credit, I will get more paper and ink.

I exit the palazzo – the courtyard is not so forbidding in the daylight – and follow a tangle of streets to the Via del Corso, the principal thoroughfare of fashionable Rome, where the Carnival will take place in two weeks' time. Numerous shops are selling masks and costumes; there is a sense of anticipation in the air. I find whimsical feathered hair ornaments for Josée and me and give myself up to the delights of browsing and wandering slowly. Carriages pass to and fro; city men and women in fashionable dress mingle with brightly clad *contadini* and *contadine* from the countryside; couples are strolling, sometimes arm in arm, all intent upon enjoying themselves. This must be the habit of *dolce far niente* that Josée has recommended to me, the sweetness of doing nothing. After taking care of my business at the bank, I find a shop that sells both stationery and art supplies and purchase writing paper, a sketchbook and drawing materials.

I sit down at the window of a café, order coffee and pastries and continue to observe the crowd. On impulse, I take out the sketchbook and begin to draw the scene before me. After an hour of happy absorption, I make my way home for the dinner that Gloria has promised. I spend the afternoon sketching the view from my window, a roof-scape dominated by the dome of Saint Peter's Cathedral in the distance, and surrender myself to the dream and reality of at last being in Rome.

The next day, I go to Saint Peter's for morning Mass, to give a hearty prayer of thanks. After the service I stand in the midst of all the grandeur, the lush art of marble, bronze, gold, paint on canvases and on the dome, the dramatic use of light, and let it sink into my senses. I wander here and there, sometimes alone in front of a work, sometimes on the fringe of a crowd, hearing snatches of conversation in multiple languages and accents. I find Raphael's *Transfiguration* and stand rapt before it, taking in the calm of the Savior and the prophets above, the chaos of the crowd below, pointing and gesticulating – much as the crowd of admirers of art is doing all around me. I feel a laugh welling up inside, wondering whether Raphael anticipated this would happen and was poking gentle fun at his admirers. Michelangelo's *Pietà* moves me greatly, encapsulating the poetry of mourning, the living and the dead so beautiful and at peace. It tugs at my heart, remembering all the loved ones whose loss I have written about, a gentle catharsis and an affirmation of beauty.

But it is Francesco Mochi's *Saint Veronica* that most catches my attention – the antithesis of the calm Mary – windblown, with strong emotions, her veil that retained the imprint of Christ's face when she gave it to him to wipe his sweat away during his walk to his death and her whole being indignant at the injustice, her mouth open in a scream of pain, her drapery evidence of her tempest of emotions. If Raphael's *Transfiguration* gently mocks the crowd, Mochi's *Veronica* exhorts them to pay attention, to fully comprehend the horror of what she has seen. I thrill to the emotional power of her, feel a kinship to her after all the intense emotions I have faced and chronicled in my memoir. I gaze up at the saint with sympathy as the indifferent crowd jostles beneath her. Occasionally someone with a guidebook will stand beside her and glance briefly at the sculpture as though mentally checking it off his list before moving on to the next monument recommended in the book. I stand before it for some minutes more before I tear myself away.

Outside in the winter sunlight, I am amazed to discover I have spent two hours in the cathedral after Mass without being aware of the time. I am suddenly a little faint with hunger and hire a calouche, a Roman fiacre, to take me home. I know there will be biscuits, cheese and fruit there, and a flask of good wine.

I spend the next few days wandering about, pausing to sketch when something of interest catches my eye – a flower growing out of an ancient Roman fragment, a Baroque fountain sculpture, a group of children playing – getting lost at will, but finding my way again by using the Dome of Saint Peter's as a guide. Returning to the Corso, I purchase bouquets of flowers for our rooms to have them in readiness for Josée's arrival.

Finally, she arrives. I have a brief sense of dislocation upon seeing her, having written of her as part of the past recalled. Now that she is before me in the present, I recover to give her a fierce hug. She draws back in pleased surprise, giving me a long appraising look, noting my new dress that is no longer widow's black, my less severe hairstyle, and a more relaxed air than when we parted. She smiles approval of what she sees and reaches out to caress the curve of my cheek as if wanting to reassure herself this is indeed the same friend who lived a life of pinched disapproval in Paris. I laugh out loud at her amazement.

"What a beautiful dress – that deep red suits you!"

I twirl like the Merry Augustine of old.

The Conte's housekeeper, who has known Josée for years, brings tea and cakes and promises a delicious supper of favorite items. After she departs, I help Josée unpack, while she regales me with gossip of Paris and the art world. I hear about Bonaparte's interment and the ceremonies surrounding it, and what a good price her paintings will fetch when she completes them. (It is the promise of that income that enables her to borrow the money for an impromptu trip to Rome, the fulfillment of our long-held wish to be here together.) I feel at once part of it and at a remove. But it matters to Josée and Josée matters to me, so I listen and make the appropriate responses, gradually relaxing into our accustomed companionship.

The next day, Josée lays out an itinerary of places to visit as well as plans to get in touch with her many friends and contacts in the artist community of Rome. I will enjoy meeting them, she says. I hesitate, remembering the gathering at Horace Vernet's studio, where I was recognized principally as the widow of the man who painted *Jaffa*, but she reassures me. We are far away from the fame of Gros and his paintings of a long-dead emperor. I will be judged only on the merits of my own work.

My own work. I long for brushes and canvas. Josée takes me to a shop where many artists buy their supplies. She meets old friends there. An English painter, James and his French studio mate, François, ask if we will join them in sketching at the Vatican *Stanze* tomorrow, and Josée accepts on our behalf. I am surprised at the ease of acquaintance, after so many years of being solitary with only my sister and my one friend for company.

The Papal rooms decorated by Raphael and his pupils are already crowded with easels when we arrive. A crowd of attentive pupils sits before *The School of Athens*, copying groups and individual figures. We wander through the rooms to find a place where four can sit together, finally settling in front of the *Expulsion of Heliodoros*. My eye goes immediately to the angelic horseman, the beauty and energy of both rider and beast. I think of Antoine's *Murat at Aboukir* and Géricault's *Charging Chasseur*, paintings I loved by men I once loved – copying this figure is a tribute to both them and their work. I lose myself in my task to the extent that when Josée compliments me on my drawing, I am surprised – I had forgotten she was there.

Waiting for my companions to finish, I glance around the room at the others, paying particular attention to one young man who appears to be in his late twenties, the same age Antoine was during his visit to Rome. I tiptoe behind him to find he too has been copying the horseman, but in oils. Standing there, I have the odd feeling of watching the young Antoine I never knew, as he snatched time from his art-gathering duties to paint and to study. My heart warms at the thought, surprising me by the new compassion I feel for him. Just then the young man turns and catches sight of me, and the illusion of Gros is gone, but we share a smile. I give an appreciative nod to his painting and he a small bow of thanks. My spirits give a little skip. If I were twenty years younger, I might flirt with him, but I am all too conscious of my age and dignity. (I want to be a new woman, but not to the extent of making a fool of myself.) With another smile, I make my way back to my companions, who are packing away their things.

We have our midday meal at a trattoria that is evidently a favorite of the artists, for all around I hear conversations about art: what new colors to try and where to purchase the best ones, recommendations for which collection to visit next, and debates over the merits of this artist or that.

François is clearly smitten with the beautiful Italian girl who serves the meals, while James is a little in love with Josée. We discuss the expeditions we will make to the Campagna and Hadrian's Villa when it is warmer. François and James share a studio on the Pincian Hill with its magnificent vista of Rome; they do a brisk business in views of Rome and its surroundings for the many English and French visitors who wish to take home souvenir paintings.

James asks which is my favorite Roman monument – or, since I am newly arrived, which one I would wish to see first. I am taken aback by the question. My associations with Ancient Rome were not those of a youth spent reading the classics – I had not – but of David and his harangues on the superiority of the subject matter, and of the cold sterility of Antoine's late style. But I did not want to be governed any longer by these unpleasant memories of my past.

"I don't know," I reply instead. "What do you recommend?"

Thus it is that I find myself standing in the Coliseum that afternoon. It is unusually cold for January and there seems to be the sparkle of ice crystals in the air despite the brilliant sunshine. I draw in my breath at the sheer immensity of the space, dwarfing the visitors who come to admire the monument or kiss the Cross set up at its center, where the Christian martyrs perished. With all its open arches, the Coliseum is a structure made for warm weather, and we shiver in the wind that whistles through it and through us as we stand there, but I cannot be other than impressed by the size and ambition of the place, imagining that the wind is the noise of the crowd cheering on the skill of the combatants and the doom of the loser. The ancient past is alive in that moment but then the wind dies down and I become conscious of conversations in French, English, German and Italian all about me, as well as some languages I cannot identify.

"You see?" Josée says, gesturing to the seats, aware of my experience which must have paralleled her own.

A little breathless, I nod. The Rome of old does indeed come alive here.

I return to the shop on the Corso again for more sketchbooks, then paints and canvas. The shop also rents easels, and I arrange for two to be delivered for Josée and me. I begin by painting the roof-scape from my window and work up other sketches to put on canvas.

François and James invite us to a party at their studio, where the conversation is similar to that in the restaurant – art and artists, evaluating the merits of the masters of the past and the more ordinary folk of the present. Josée introduces me to the others as simply, "My friend Augustine Dufresne, painter from Paris." Even the students from the nearby French Academy at the Villa Medici don't associate me with Antoine or *Jaffa*. Everyone accepts me as an artist in my own right. It enhances my sense of coming into my own, helps me recover the self-confidence of my youthful years in Madame Benoist's studio.

When others ask me what I paint, for a moment I am at a loss for a reply. I have done landscape and still life and genre, the lesser categories of the hierarchy of art – I have learned not to announce too much ambition or threaten those who think of themselves as creating high art – a habit left over from years of marriage, of moving among the great men of the art world. But while that is what I have been accustomed to paint, I am in search of something new, of the artist I could become. I amend my reply. "I have done landscapes and still life, but now I am in search of new subject matter."

Everyone applauds. It is the reason so many of the others have come as well – that spirit of adventure. "What about preparing something for the Salon?" someone asks. Josée and I share a smile, remembering when she brought that up in Marie's studio so long ago.

We enter into the spirit of Carnival, renting an open carriage and costumes, tossing bouquets and sugarplums with abandon and returning home dusted with sugar as though we ourselves were a species of confectionery. My sides ache with laughing, a good ache. Having lunch afterward, replete with happiness, my mind turns to how to use Carnival to good artistic effect.

I spend the rest of that day and the following one filling a sketchbook with memories of what I saw, sometimes a larger subject like the line of carriages, imagining how it might look from a balcony's vantage point. Others are details, such as the slightly battered posy I retained, now in a glass of water on my desk.

During the last two days of Carnival, the Corsa dei Barberi is run, the race of the wild Berber horses that so excited Géricault. Having written about his planned painting in my memoir – before that, I had not thought of it for years – I was curious to experience the race for myself. The first day, we stand near the Piazza del Popolo for the start of the race. The fiery, spirited horses wear ornamented bridles and ribbons, and the grooms can barely hold them back. A cannon booms and they are let loose. The crowd roars. Their hooves drum. My heart beats loud in my ears to the rhythm. I am sure Josée, too, must be able to hear it. The race does not last long, perhaps three minutes, but in those minutes I have lived, felt fully and truly alive.

The next day, we are fortunate enough to be able to view the race from a friend's balcony high above the Corso where we can see both the beginning and the end of the course. There is not the same excitement as the nearness of seeing the horses brought in, but it is still thrilling to see their manes and tails streaming as they gallop toward the wall of carpets that marks the finish line. Afterwards, I say to Josée, "I can see why Théo was so taken with this scene and wanted to paint it!" The old nickname rolls off my tongue before I can stop myself.

"Théo – it's the first time in years I've heard you mention Géricault. He was always such a bitter topic for you, even when he died you hadn't forgiven him yet."

"I was thinking over that old business not long ago."

I have not yet told Josée of my memoir. I have lived alone with it for so long that I am reluctant to bring it to light, as though it would disintegrate and crumble away to nothing when exposed to open air, like the friable remains from ancient tombs that Denon had once described. But Josée is my oldest friend, and so many of the things I wrote about are ones to which she too was a witness. The book is in some ways a memorial of her life, the part of it we shared, as well. I can trust her.

When we turn our steps toward our palazzo, I link my arm through hers. "When we get home, I'll show you what I've been working on these past months."

"A sketchbook?" Her face is alight with interest.

"In a way," I reply, thinking, *Yes, a sketch of my life.* That night I present it to her, my precious ream of manuscript, with my heart again thudding in my chest, but intent upon taking the risk of sharing it. Risk, too, is part of this new phase of life I have determined upon.

"I wrote my life," I tell her, "and the more I exposed my bitterness, brought it out to air, the more it evaporated. The paper was listening and gave a sympathetic hearing. I don't need to insist on feeling bitter anymore."

Josée reads it through in two evening sittings, and I can tell from the play of emotions across her face that she is moved deeply by it. When she finishes, she puts it tenderly in its brown paper wrapping and hands it back to me as if placing it in solemn trust.

"When we return to Paris, you must see about getting this published. It speaks for so many women artists of our generation – for so many *women* of our generation."

The Lenten season is quieter than the time of anticipation preceding Carnival, a time of recovery from indulgences and of quiet reflection. I give up the customary foods – meat, pastries, chocolate and bonbons of all kinds – as an outward sign of grace. I have already given up the most important things – bitterness, bad memories, self-doubts. I do not give up painting or writing but make them thank-offerings from the bottom of my heart. My soul grows lighter each day as Easter approaches.

Spring comes early in Rome. The gardens blossom with daffodils and crocus and fruit trees begin to bud. Fruit vendors sit at the edge of fountains that keep their wares cool. Josée and I join the crowds strolling along the Pincio, the hill that overlooks the Piazza del Popolo, greeting other artists from France in the grounds of the Villa Medici. We make frequent visits to the Borghese Gardens and venture out into the Campagna and Hadrian's Villa to look at more remains of Ancient Rome. It is in drawing these with care and precision that I feel close to Denon, who lavished the same care on the monuments of Ancient Egypt.

For us it is an intensely productive time in sketchbooks and on canvas. We go out every day it is fine and paint in our studio when the weather is inclement. Each Sunday we attend Mass in a different church and stay to view the paintings and sculptures found there. Other artists are doing the same and we engage in lively discussions with them. I do not hold back my opinions, which are listened to with respect. Sometimes a group of us gather by appointment and go to a trattoria afterward, where I am happy to pay for those who cannot afford it. Quietly I give them each a few *scudi* to help tide them over, and I refuse all offers of repayment. My happiness overflows into a generosity of spirit I did not know I possessed. I draw and paint with an abandon that astonishes even the productive Josée.

Ever eager to find buyers for her paintings, Josée makes the acquaintance, through James, of a group of English tourists and invites them to our apartment. She urges me to set out my work as well, and to my delight I sell two scenes of the Carnival and one of the Coliseum. It is the first money I have ever earned as a painter in the thirty-seven years I have been practicing my art. After they leave, I throw my arms around Josée as we congratulate each other. Our visitors in turn recommend us to others, and each time I make a sale. I keep these coins in a little casket I bought on the Corso, and for Easter, I treat myself to a necklace and earrings of micro mosaic scenes of Rome.

On Easter Sunday, we stand within the great Colonnade of Saint Peter's to receive the benediction of Gregory XVI and then attend Mass in the cathedral. We walk around the grand church afterward, for no matter how many times we visit, there is always something new to discover that we have not noted before. As always, I stop to greet *Saint Veronica*, now an old friend, to reassure her that at least one person in the crowd is paying attention and making note.

Arm in arm, we walk out into the sunshine.

Epilogue

Paris, 1842

Sadly, my friend's stay in Rome did not end as well as it began. She began to feel ill after Easter with an ailment that defied all the skill of the Roman doctors to diagnose it. We left Rome in June to spend the summer in Switzerland, hoping that a doctor at one of their famous spas could diagnose and cure whatever ailed her. They could not, but we made good use of our time filling our sketchbooks. The illness dampened but did not entirely erase the good spirits she had enjoyed during her Roman sojourn. "I cannot afford to spend any more of my life being bitter," she said to me. "I cannot help feeling that it is the bitterness that took root and is causing me this trouble."

Finally, we returned to Paris, with its renowned medical schools, in the hope that one of their doctors could treat my friend. Numerous treatments were prescribed, but none of them helped. Her sister and I did all we could to make her comfortable but I was forced to watch my dear friend waste away. She died on 5 January 1842.

Before then, however, she entrusted her memoir to my care and spoke of her pleasure in knowing that it, like her paintings, would bear witness to her time on earth. Thus I have brought it to publication, revealing the whole of her, good and bad, the real person.

She was buried in the Gros-Dufresne family vault at Père Lachaise Cemetery. It was the Gros family who chose her epitaph, ironically linking her name to the painting she had so disliked to be reminded of:

Augustine Dufresne
Veuve d'Antoine-Jean Gros
Peintre de Jaffa

[Augustine Dufresne
Widow of Antoine-Jean Gros
Painter of Jaffa]

Louise-Joséphine Sarazin de Belmont

Historical note

Augustine Dufresne (1789-1842) was a real person. Most of the factual information known about her is gleaned from the biographies of her husband, the painter Antoine-Jean Gros (1771-1835). Their marriage was, by all accounts, not a happy one. None of Gros's biographers – with the exception of Jean-Baptiste Delestre,[1] who wrote during her lifetime – had anything good to say about her or about the marriage. J. Tripier-Lefranc was particularly vituperative about her, characterizing her as shrewish and excessively pious; but at the same time he is one of our best sources for documents, including in his work the texts of the 1809 marriage contract and her will, written in Rome in the spring of 1841.[2]

I first became acquainted with Augustine during 1985 to 1999, when I researched and wrote about Antoine-Jean Gros and his paintings for Napoleon. After living with Monsieur Gros myself for fourteen years, I knew that he was not the easiest person to consistently like and admire,

---

[1] Jean-Baptiste Delestre, <u>Gros, sa vie et ses ouvrages</u>. Paris, first edition, 1845; second edition, 1867.

[2] J. Tripier-Lefranc, <u>Histoire de la Vie et de la Mort du Baron Gros</u>. Paris: Jules Martin, 1880.

and I developed a sympathetic fellow feeling for his wife, the more so as she had to put up with twenty-two years of his adoring mother into the bargain. Augustine must have been a hopeful young woman once. What had led her to marry a man twice her age? Had the marriage been unhappy from the beginning? Or had it started with the best of intentions but soured in the course of time? What role had Antoine played in the failure of the marriage that his biographers weren't telling? As my interests turned from art history to writing fiction, I wanted to explore these questions. I also thought Augustine would make a good subject for telling the story of this intensely masculine era from a woman's point of view. And, having dealt for so long with Napoleon's mythmaking, I wanted to tell the other side of the story. Thus I came to write about, and in the voice of, Augustine Dufresne and make her a Bourbon sympathizer.

Her family members are real, with the exception of Grandmère Augustine, a fictional character based on my own Grandma Augusta, who didn't approve of me much either. Augustine's father, François-Simon Dufresne, was a friend of Dominique Vivant-Denon, who later arranged her marriage to Gros. The romance with Charles Legrand is imaginary but, like many other women of the era, she could well have had a soldier boyfriend who was killed. Augustine's brother Baudouin-Henri in fact died in 1831, a few months before Gros's mother, but I have placed his death several years later in the novel. Their mother died in 1829, but I have placed her death two years earlier to underscore the emotional impact of the discovery of Gros's lovechild.

All the artists mentioned in the novel existed, as did the paintings and decorative arts named and/or described in detail – Antoine-Jean Gros, *Bonaparte in the Pest House at Jaffa* (Paris, Musée du Louvre), *The Battle of Aboukir* (Versailles), *Portrait of Empress Joséphine* (Nice, Musée Masséna), *Posthumous Portrait of Charles Legrand* (Los Angeles County Museum of Art), *François I and Charles V at Saint-Denis* (Paris, Musée du Louvre), *Louis XVIII Leaving the Tuileries, the Night of 19-20 March 1815* (Versailles), *Embarkation of the Duchesse d'Angoulême at Pauillac* (Bordeaux, Musée des Beaux-Arts), and *Hercules and Diomedes* (Toulouse, Musée des Augustins); Théodore Géricault, *Charging Chasseur*, *Wounded Cuirassier leaving the Field of Battle* and *The Raft of the Medusa* (all Paris, Musée du Louvre), *Head of a Drowned Man* (St. Louis, Missouri, St. Louis Art Museum), and *Portrait of a Black Man* (Los Angeles, California, J. Paul

Getty Museum); Eugène Delacroix, *Dante's Boat* (Paris, Musée du Louvre); and Louise-Joséphine Sarazin de Belmont, *View of Gros's Tomb at Père-Lachaise* (Toulouse, Musée des Augustins). The *tazza* that Denon describes in the storerooms of the Louvre is generic rather than specific; but the clock that Jacques Amalric gives to Augustine as a wedding gift is the description of one in Kansas City, Missouri, The Nelson-Atkins Museum of Art; the seventeenth-century Florentine cabinet with pietra dura panels of Orpheus and the beasts mounted in ebony that Napoleon commandeers for Marie-Louise's jewels is the description of one in Detroit, Michigan, Detroit Institute of Arts; the chandelier described in the Amalric home in 1815 is based on one of a slightly later date in Los Angeles, California, J. Paul Getty Museum.

Nothing is known about Augustine's artistic training, so I have invented it. I have never seen one of her paintings and am not sure whether or where any of them survive. Thus I based the description of her 1814 Salon entry, *Coquilles peints sur vélin* [Scallop shells painted on vellum] on a marvelous still life of shells and corals by Anne Vallayer-Coster (Paris, Musée du Louvre).

Augustine and Louise Joséphine Sarazin de Belmont were close friends, and the latter is sometimes described as her companion.[3] Through her husband she would surely have known Géricault, who was only a year or two younger than she, and Madame Larrey and Madame Benoist. Madame Benoist did encourage other women artists, but the description of her studio and its rose scents is entirely imaginary. I had Augustine accompany Gros to Brussels to confront Jacques-Louis David so she could say to his unappreciative teacher what *I* have long wished to say to him. (In fairness to David, however, I should note that he in fact kept his painting abilities to the end of his life.)

We do not know whether Augustine ever met Napoleon and Joséphine, but one can't write a novel about the era without their presence. The ministers of the Imperial household complained that Denon held back treasures they wished to place in the palaces of France, so I made the Louvre storerooms the setting for her meeting with the Emperor. Similarly, the scene in which she participates in the painting of Joséphine's 1809 portrait in the Indian shawl dress is imagined, although the painting is real.

---

[3] When Augustine died, she published a memorial pamphlet, "Notice sur Mme Augustine Dufresne, veuve d'Antoine-Jean Gros, le peintre de Jaffa, née à Paris le 10 octobre 1789, ravie à sa famille et à ses amis le 5 janvier 1842" (Paris: H. Fournier, 1842).

The Gros marriage did not produce any children, but Gros fathered a daughter, Françoise-Cécile, with his mistress Françoise Simonier. Augustine was not happy about this. As described in the novel, he left the bulk of his estate to the child and made his wife one of the executors of his will. Understandably, Augustine was not happy about that either.

I borrowed the character of Maître Derville, the lawyer, from Fabrice Luchini's marvelous portrayal of this Balzac character in the 1994 film *Le Colonel Chabert*.

All Toulouse characters are fictional. The description of the city circa 1840 is as accurate as I could make it. Gros's family came from Toulouse and Augustine gave several of his paintings to the Musée des Augustins, but we do not know that she ever visited that city. I chose it as the setting for the writing of my book because it is a place I love and doing so gave me a convenient excuse to revisit and research it and extol its beauties. I hope I have done it justice.

Acknowledgements

Writing this novel and bringing it to publication has been a long process, and many people have given me help and encouragement along the way. My thanks go first and foremost to my editor at Accent Press, Jay Dixon, who saw the potential in my story and helped me to polish it into publication-worthy form. I have benefited greatly from the advice of those who read the manuscript all or in part in its earlier stages: Judith and Ron Akehurst, Charissa Bremer-David, Peter Briggs, Susanne Dunlop, Barbara Furbush, Cathy Gaines, Karen Glow, Joy Hartnett, Barb Head, Joyce Holmen, Ian Kennedy, Mary Sebastian, Marilyn Stokstad, Susan Tipton, and the members of Brian Shawver's fiction class at The Writers Place, Kansas City, Missouri. Joyce Gilhooley provided hospitality in Paris during the initial research; the staff of the Musée du Vieux Toulouse assisted with research for the sections set in that city; and Amelia Nelson assisted with research for the chapter set in Rome. The members of the Border Crimes Chapter of Sisters in Crime have cheered me through revisions and the publication process.

Profound thanks are also due the Amazon.com Breakthrough Novel Contest of 2008, which selected this book as a semifinalist under its working title *The Artist's Widow*. This gave me the encouragement to continue to pursue publication in the years since then.

Biography

American museum educator, grant writer, and lecturer. Ann Marti Friedman has published numerous articles on art and artists in various academic journals. This is her first novel and is based on extensive research. It was a semi-finalist on the 2008 Amazon.com Breakthrough Novel Contest, though has been substantially re-written since then. She is currently working on a murder mystery set amongst the artists of 1670's Paris.

www.annmartifriedman.com

Proudly published by Accent Press

www.accentpress.co.uk